CW00607306

# Someone To Watch Over Me

# Someone To Watch Over Me

*Jacqueline Jacques*

PIATKUS

To my mother

Copyright © 1997 by Jacqueline Jacques

First published in Great Britain in 1997 by
Judy Piatkus (Publishers) Ltd of
5 Windmill Street, London W1P 1HF

**The moral right of the author
has been asserted**

*A catalogue record for this book is available
from the British Library*

ISBN 0-7499-0405-4

Set in 11/12pt Times by
Creative Print and Design, Harmondsworth, Middlesex
Printed and bound in Great Britain by
Biddles Ltd, Guildford & Kings Lynn

# Chapter One

Nice girls didn't. And Lucy Potter wouldn't. Not until she was safely wed.

Just as well she hadn't, as it turned out. Just as blooming well.

'Filth!' she flung at him from the upstairs window, together with his khaki great-coat and various items of soldierly kit. He staggered down the path, socks sticking to the frost, braces dangling, trying to button his flies.

'You b. . .' But though a few choice b-words came to mind she had to make do with 'Beast! You dirty, rotten s. . . so-and-so, Roy!' Frustration spoilt her aim as one marching boot, then the other, sailed past his head.

'But Luce. . .' he pleaded, ducking and dodging, 'I love you!'

Of course he did. She was a catch. Sweet and twenty. Well . . . on the face of it, sweet; at first blush. But he should have thought of that.

'*Love*!' she heard some harridan shriek. 'Call that *love*? Going with prossies, soon as my back's turned? A fine wedding present you'd've given *me*, Saturday night! You're vile, Roy Sykes, a lousy, stinking piece of sh—!'

She screeched to a halt. In 1942, nice girls didn't resort to gutter language, not even when their future was gurgling down the drain. Nor did they shout their business from the rooftops. Up and down the terraces, there were aspidistras twitching with earwiggers, and circles of hot breath fogging cold windows. The neighbours'd all be loving this.

Grinding her pretty teeth on the vilest of words, the ones

1

she would never forgive him for putting there, she channelled her fury instead into throwing things. His forage cap flew over the front hedge, like a bird, and landed beside the milkman's horse. Blinkered against the chaos of war, the mare shied between the shafts, dolloping dung in the road, before moving off.

Ever alert, Old Man Harris, double-digging for runner beans and Victory two front-gardens down, grabbed his bucket and hurried out to shovel it up, just as Roy's shaving tackle made a soft landing.

'Brings the rhubarb on a treat,' the old boy observed. 'Marvellous stuff.'

Across the street, Aggie Moffat's scrubbing brush had slowed to a soapy standstill. She didn't miss a trick, that one. Look at her, sitting back on her heels, ears a-flap under her knotted turban. Well, that was all she was getting.

Lucy slammed down the window with a bang, knocking out a couple of the cardboard panes and, with a tight face, watched Aggie get to her feet, straightening her bony knees like the old cow she was. Then they both focused on the soldier putting on his boots and, with bowed head, clumping out of their lives.

Still staring, long after the sound of his boots had died away, hardly breathing, mind and body numbed by what she had done, a part of her became aware of Aggie wiping her hands on her pinny, darting indoors and hurrying out again with her shopping bag. The click of the gate made her blink. A cog shifted.

So Aggie was off to the shops, and news of the bust-up at number 41 would be all over Walthamstow by dinner-time.

Lucy's groan came from somewhere deep.

'Why?' she ranted, as the shreds of his photo flew about her like confetti and the cup and saucer smashed against the wall.

'Why?' she stormed, stamping in savage dance upon her new hat from C&A's.

'Why, Roy . . . *why*?'

And, receiving no answer, she punched the pillow in lieu of the man, punched it and fell on it and wept into it.

Her mother's voice drifted in, from the end of the street, through the panes where the cardboard had been. A draught moved the curtain and somewhere a door slammed. Ma was yelling at the kids on the bomb site. It was an eerie, echoing wasteland up there, now that the terraces had been reduced to rubble.

'What d'you think you're up to, 'Arry Jenkins? You clear off, you 'ear! Pickin' over poor people's misfortune like a bleedin' vulture. And you, Patsy Bell, get down off there. Your poor mum's got enough to worry about without you breakin' your blinkin' neck! Don't you cheek me, you little monkey, 'less you want to feel the flat of my 'and!'

At last, Lucy heard her battling through her own front door, shedding shopping bags right and left. Things spilled out, higgledy piggle, across the lino.

'Luce?' she wheezed. 'Luce!' Advancing down the narrow passage, opening doors. 'Luc-ee! You up there?'

Lucy didn't answer, didn't move, knowing her mother would find her.

The heavy tread creaked the stairs and moved across the landing. She was mumbling to her ghosts, telling them about the rush and bother, in between gasps for breath. At last her face, pink with cold and concern and effort, peered round the bedroom door.

'Oh, Luce. . .'

Aggie Moffat had caught up with her in the greengrocer's, she explained. '"Nora," she says, "*Nora*!" top of 'er voice, so's the whole queue gets an earful, "You best get off 'ome, gel," she says. "Your Lucy's in a right old two an' eight".'

Well, of course she'd come straight home when she'd heard the news.

'Lucky I'd already done the butcher's. He'd kep' a nice bit of liver by for me, under the counter. There was a big queue when I come out . . .' and in the same breath '. . . oh, look at you, Luce, what a state to get yourself in. He ain't worth it, whatever he's done.'

Lucy realised she was still in her dressing gown, unwashed, uncombed. She must look a sight: pale and blotchy. She sat up, with her chin dug mournfully into her knees.

'Ma!' she wailed, a child again.

'Come on downstairs, duck, and you can tell me all about it while I make a nice cup of tea.'

The trousers had been looped by their braces over the hook on her brothers' bedroom door. Roy was putting up at theirs until the wedding, since Jack and Charlie weren't due home until the day itself, and the room was going begging. It made sense.

He'd gone back to sleep. The cup and saucer, last of the bone china set, containing cold tea now, was as she had left it half an hour before, on the bedside table. Poor love, he must be tired after all that travelling. Careful not to jingle the pockets, she had gathered the rough material to her, breathing in the Roy-smell, the cigarette smoke, the sweat, the maleness, and then she turned towards the bed, where he lay, a slight sheen of sweat sticking tendrils of bright, blond hair to his forehead. Her fingers itched to smooth them away, but she reached instead for his jacket, hanging on the back of the chair. As she folded it over her arm, she watched his gold-fringed eyelids, softly closed, moving to the rhythm of a dream and asking to be kissed. But she had to get a move on if she was going to drop the uniform into the cleaners on her way to work. Leave it any later and it wouldn't be back in time for the big day. Quietly, reluctantly, she had pulled the door to.

Downstairs she piled keys and coins and bus tickets, the complicated penknife Nora had given him, his crumpled handkerchief, all onto the wooden draining board. In the jacket pocket she found his wallet, with his identity card, his leave pass, pay packet, a bill for five pounds eighteen shillings from Fish Bros, the Jewellers, stamped *PAID* for a wedding ring (her heart skipped), her last letter, setting out the wedding arrangements, photos, one of them together, arm-in-arm on the prom at Southend, six of herself in multiple miniature, a Poly-photo strip of 'spot the difference' poses. They'd had them taken at Selfridges the day they got engaged. Not bad, she supposed. Too much forehead, though, made her face look long. The fringe was an improvement. And her nose could do with being a bit narrower, shorter, or something. And, of course, her mouth was way too big, flashing all those teeth . . . But her eyes were nice. Big, green eyes. He was always going on about her eyes.

What was this, tucked into the back of his wallet? A dog-eared Out-patients card. He'd kept very quiet about it, if he was suffering. Not like her brothers; they let everyone know. What hospital was it? She flipped it over . . .

. . . and flung it from her like some foul, smelly thing.

She found herself at the sink, washing her hands under the full blast of the tap. Soaping and scrubbing with the coarse red soap. And again . . . and rinsing them pink and wet and cold and *clean*. Water sprinkled from her shaking finger-ends onto the stone floor and the smell of soap, vaguely antiseptic, penetrated, at last, to the root of her nausea.

Roy was attending a VD Clinic.

The disease of the rusting notices, nailed to the doors of the lavs in the High Street, advising sufferers to attend St Thomas's for treatment.

VD.

So obscene, you didn't even whisper its real name, and you spread sheets of Bronco on the wooden seats against the germs, which gave you running sores and scabs and itched and were ever so catching and sent you mad, in the end. Or blind. Something like that.

*And Roy had it*! There was no mistake: he'd kept four appointments already. And there was only one way he could have caught it. Only one way, for a man, that much she knew. Not off the lavvy seats. He'd been going with dirty tarts. And she could not marry him now.

As Lucy told the tale, she watched her mother pour the tea. Hot and strong, and sweetened with a spoonful or two of condensed milk, it brought you up sharp. Put things into perspective. In the Potter household there was always tea simmering on the hob, a great brown enamel pot of the stuff. Rationing or no, there was always tea. Ma regarded it as her right, one of the perks of early-morning charring up at the hospital, along with STs and Lifebuoy and government-issue lavvy paper. Some houses smell of cigarettes, or cats, or boiled cabbage, some of lavender polish. Their house

5

smelled of tea. Except on Mondays when Ma lit the brick copper in the scullery for the weekly wash. Then the place smelled of Sunlight soap, but so did everyone else's.

As she sipped the thick brew, Lucy's head came up, like a thirsty pot-plant, whose veins swell with watering.

'Why, Ma? Why'd he do that to me?'

She watched bitter replies flitting across her mother's face before she, in turn, asked, 'Why does any man do it, duck?' And Lucy knew her mother was as mystified as she. If any of the men they knew had cheated on their women they'd hidden it well. In the Potter family you made your bed and you bloody lay in it, if you had any backbone at all. They weren't saints, 'course they weren't; the family cupboard rattled, same as anyone else's. There was her dad's Auntie Vi, who'd been a lazy slut and driven poor Uncle Harry to drink, but he'd not taken up with any floosie, not ever, not as far as anyone knew. Her own grandad had 'played the gee-gees' and finished up broke, but he had stayed true to Grandma Potter, despite her nagging, to the bitter end, much good it did either of them. No, what Roy had done was as far beyond Ma's experience as it was beyond her daughter's. It was something you only read about in the Sunday papers.

'He tried to make out it was my fault!' Lucy's voice was gritty, despite the tea. She massaged the ache in her throat. 'He said not doing it was driving him up the wall. He had to go with the . . . those other women to get relief.'

Her mother spluttered into her cup. '*Relief*!' she shrieked. 'I'll give him relief, dirty tripehound! Chop the bugger off, I will, let him show his face round here again. If it don't *drop* off of its own, nasty thing!'

Lucy found rogue muscles pulling at the corners of her mouth, putting a twinkle in her eye.

Ma squeezed her hand. 'That's more like it, duck. Oh Luce, you're well out of that and no mistake. Just thank your lucky stars you found out in time.'

Oh, she did! When she *thought* . . .! A few more days and they'd've been on their honeymoon. In a double bed, in the best room, in the boarding house at Clacton. Suppose she hadn't found out till then? What on earth would she have done? Divorced him? Unless . . . unless he hadn't told her.

6

Would he? Or would he have soldiered on, regardless?

Her smile faded.

Just showed you, didn't it? She hadn't really known him at all.

Ma was patting her hand, talking about how she could forget him; how she was only young and there was plenty more fish in the sea . . . and Lucy's mouth began to droop again. There weren't. Not like Roy.

Roy had been the prize catch, the biggest and best in *her* pond. On Saturday he would have put that ring on her finger and she'd have lived happy ever after in the Lake District, in a big house, with a car, one day, when Roy learned to drive, and their own door-making factory. Face it, Ma, she thought, where are you going to net another fish like that? Not in cheek-by-jowl East London. No, now she was stuck with it, with the munitions factory, with nutty Nora and her ghosts. The lot.

For a long time she slumped, propping up her gloom with cupped hands, legs tucked under the chair, vaguely aware of the woman clattering in the scullery, putting shopping away, peeling potatoes and boiling up the peel to mix with bran for the chickens. Then she could hear her out in the yard, crying, 'Coop, coop, coop!' which the chickens had learned meant 'Come and get it!'

At some point another cup of tea was placed before her by hands that smelled faintly of onions, warm hands that stroked the ache from her forehead, through her hair and away, through her hair and away.

She heard Ma rooting in the coal cupboard, watched her shovel lumps onto the dying fire, and when, at last, the bright flames caught, they glittered in her eyes.

Lucy straightened and yawned, her narrow shoulders pressing the back of the chair.

'I suppose we'll have to cancel everything, won't we? The church and the flowers and the cake and everything?'

Ma shrugged. 'The cake'll keep for Christmas, wrap it in greaseproof. The icing's only cardboard, after all's said and done.'

'What about Clacton?'

Clacton had been *Ma's* treat, saved out of the egg money.

The hens had been laying well all summer and, instead of putting the eggs in buckets of isinglass for winter, she had sold them to neighbours and friends. The dried stuff from America didn't hold a candle to a soft-boiled, melt-in-the-mouth, crumbly new-laid egg, and people had been glad to pay over the odds, specially as it had been in a good cause.

She frowned. 'Don't suppose we'll get our money back, not on the train fare nor the guesthouse.' She tutted. 'Bloomin' Roy. Bloomin' nuisance. I never liked him.'

This was news.

Her mother caught the disbelief in her eyes.

'No, honest, Luce, I been ever so worried since the day you fetched 'im 'ome. I knew he weren't right for you, him being well-to-do and that. Not that I got nothing against real class, but he was jumped-up. I 'ate that, as you know . . .'

Didn't she just? Being jumped-up was the eighth deadly sin, the worst of the lot. Commit this one, pick up the aitches that your mother dropped, or correct an 'ain't' or a 'you was', and you'd get a back-hander, followed by icy silence or, if you managed to duck and make it up the stairs in time, you'd get the insults slung against the bedroom door . . .

'Don't you come the old acid with me, girl. Think you got everyone fooled, don't you, Miss Goody-goody, butter wouldn't melt . . .? But you ain't. Oh no. Know what the kids next-door call you? Eh? Swank-pot! That's bloody nice, innit? And what you got to swank about, I'd like to know. Eh? Who the hell d'you think you are?'

Or

'Who else talks to their mother like that, eh? Go on, who else? Don't know what I ever done to deserve you. A right little madam, that's what you're turning out to be!'

Or

'What possessed me, sending you to that bloody snobby school, I don't know! Teaching kids to be lah-di-dah and uppity, looking down their noses at decent people. Coming between a mother and daughter!'

And so on . . .

As if that were the only thing between them. There were also six wonderful, do-no-wrong boys, not to mention an army of ghosts.

''Course,' Ma was saying, 'with his looks he could twist everyone round his little finger. Only had to smile, didn't he? But his eyes was too close together. And all that grease on his hair! Wouldn't trust him no further'n I could throw him.'

'You might've said . . .'

'What – and get me teeth pushed down me throat for me trouble! No, duck, you made it pretty clear you thought the sun shone out of his backside. Didn't you tell me he made you go weak at the knees? Well, I thought, if he makes you happy . . .' She sighed.

'But it was your place to tell me, Ma! Your responsibility. God, I could've caught some horrible disease off him . . .'

'I wasn't to know that now, was I?' She plucked at the table cover, her rough skin catching in the soft fibres of the chenille. She said, almost embarrassed, 'I didn't want to lose you, duck.'

Lucy studied her mother's face. They never spoke of love, the bond they sometimes admitted to sharing being that of gender: two females in a family of men. Now all the men were gone. Was there something else? Was love the reason her mother wanted her? She reached across to rub her mother's arm, in case. The skin wrinkled against the pressure, like setting jam. Ma smiled grimly.

They both stared at the fire. It was a gloomy room. The French windows backed onto a narrow yard, flanked by the kitchen and next door's fence. Rain had been threatening for days.

A coal shifted, and Ma brightened as inspiration came.

'How about *we* take the room for the weekend, Luce – you and me? Might as well, save it going to waste.'

'Oh, I don't know. Is that a good idea?'

''Course! Got to buck you up a bit, ain't we? And Gawd knows I could do with a day or two off from this lot.' It was unclear whether the jerk of her head meant the bombardment of London by the Germans or more pressing domestic demands. She sorted out the practicalities.

'Mrs Next-door'll see to the chickens. She owes me, times I've looked out for her cat.' She paused. 'Oh blimey, there's the flowers, ain't there? All them bleeding chrysanths Roy wanted round the church . . . and the bloomin' bouquet!' She sucked air through her teeth. 'Tell you what, if they can't get rid of them round the shop, I'll ask Matron. They'll be glad of 'em up the hospital. Sweeten her up when I ask her for Sunday off.'

Lucy let herself be swept along by her mother's bustle. They said she was the same at work, bossing the other cleaners, making things tidy.

'Mary won't mind working a double shift; she'll be glad of the money.'

She ticked that item off her mental list.

''Ave to put the boys off, of course. They won't want to waste their leave. What d'you reckon a telegram costs? Or you can phone. Tell 'em to put the presents by for when the right man comes along, eh? He will, you mark my words. One of these fine days.'

Lucy's smile had vinegar in it.

'Oh, come on, girl, look on the bright side! It'll do us both a world of good, you'll see. We'll get dolled up, shall we? Got to have some excuse to wear me new frock. Couple of smart smellers we'll be. And you can wear your pretty hat from C & A.'

'Oh!' The hat! The damned hat!

'Lucy?' Nora's voice was heavy with suspicion and Lucy could only hang her head in shame. A naughty child.

'*Where* is it?' The older woman heaved herself out of the chair.

Lucy whispered. 'Upstairs. In the bin. And Ma ...' hanging for a sheep as well as a lamb, 'there's a cup ...'

She listened to her mother mount the stairs and, with stricken heart, traced the laboured progress across the bedroom floor over her head; she thought she heard a sharp intake of breath, before the explosion.

'Oh my Gawd! *Look* what you've done! Two bleedin' guineas that cost, covered in tea-leaves! And look at this! Oh, Luce!'

She came down, carrying the wallpaper-covered 'bin', that had once sloshed with whitewash and now chinked sadly.

'I was a bit upset.'

'Me best cup and saucer, Lucy! Smashed to smithereens!' She picked out the hat and Lucy bit her lip as her mother

10

poked and prodded the sorry object for some semblance of shape.

'I lost me rag with it, somehow.'

'You and your rag. Bloomin' spitfire, you are. Do real damage one day, you don't get an 'old of yourself.' Her expression softened. 'Oh well, it's only money.' She flicked the veil with a blunt finger. 'Ow, it's gone all floppy!' Her eyebrows were jiggling and suggesting quite another image. 'And look at its poor feather! Bent! Ain't no bleeding use to nobody, now,' she said, flinging it onto the fire. When the damp straw fizzled a feeble protest they tittered. When it hissed on the hot coals they snorted. And when it gave a sad sort of whistle and a smell of scorching feathers they cackled and crowed and cried with laughter.

'Good riddance to bad rubbish,' said Ma, sniffing and dabbing at her eyes with her hanky. She looked up. 'And *you* can laugh . . .!'

Who?

She wasn't looking at Lucy but smiling and nodding over at the armchair where shadows flickered and reflected firelight leapt on the cushions.

Nora was seeing things again. One of her 'old dears'.

'Oh, Ma.' Her heart sank. Why, whenever her emotions were stirred, did Ma take refuge in the dead? As though they were a bolt-hole in which to hide from the living, or a safety-valve to release some ferment of her brain.

'It's your Gran,' she said now, smiling happily.

Gran?

No, please no. That would be too obscene.

'You're not making out you can see Granny Farthing now?' Lucy said.

Her mother sobered quickly, sensing trouble. 'She only come to tell us not to worry,' she insisted, 'nothing dreadful. "Don't worry," she says, "everything'll come out in the wash".'

'No, Ma.' She couldn't take this, not on top of everything else. She twisted her hands to stop them shaking. 'Don't, Ma, please.'

But Ma wasn't listening. She was staring hard at the chair,

absorbed in her madness. 'Well shot of him, yes, I told her,' she was saying. 'You said he was a bad lot, didn't you, right at the start.'

Lucy pushed away from the table, knocking her chair lopsided against the sideboard. Her nails dug into her palms, her face tightened. 'Don't go dragging Granny Farthing into it! She's not one of your rotten ghosts. You can't have her too!'

'But look, she's—'

'Oh, stop it, Ma! It's wrong; it's . . . terrible!'

'No, Luce. You should see 'er, gel. Bright as a button, she looks.'

She turned to the chair again, to explain. 'Lucy don't believe in the Other Side, Mum. We had that barney, couple of years back, remember? Over Uncle Harry that time. Put the wind up her good and proper.'

Now her head was on one side, a thrush's cocked to hear the worm turning.

Lucy was seething, breathing hard. Granny Farthing was not to be tampered with . . .

And the words bubbled up, like marsh gas, from somewhere deep and stagnant. 'It's not funny any more, Ma – it's horrible! Gran's not a ghost, no more than any of the others. She's dead, poor old thing. Gone. She's never coming back. So don't meddle with her. Don't!'

'Lucy, girl . . .'

'No!' She waved her hands to fend off Ma's protest. 'You don't know what you're doing, Ma! You're bloody barmy. Certifiable!'

And stuffing her fingers in her ears against her mother's speechlessness, she ran upstairs to the bathroom and slammed the door.

# Chapter Two

Nora stood in the scullery, swilling the cups and listening to the rumble and bang of the hot water in the pipes.

She shouted up. 'Mind you don't overfill that bath, Lucy! Five inches, you 'ear? You turn them taps off this minute!'

'All *right*! Keep your flipping hair on! I heard you the first time!'

That sounded more like the old Lucy.

A hot soak would do her good, poor kid. She'd had a right day of it one way and another!

''Course, you know who she takes after . . .' Nora pitched her voice for another's hearing. 'Two peas in a pod, you and her. Cor, light the blue touch paper and watch out! Thing is with her, you never know what's going to set her off. Just when you think you're getting on all right for a change, having a bit of a giggle, she goes for you! Heaven alone knows what set her off this time. I mean, she takes it all in her stride, of a rule, me and me ghosts. Oh, she thinks I'm off me rocker but we can have a laugh about it. Then she goes and bites me bloomin' head off.'

There was no reply.

'Mum? I say she's got a temper on her, our Luce. Reminds me of you.' But when Nora looked round the door, the armchair was empty. 'Tch!' she clicked in disgust. 'Talk to your blooming self!'

There was a bit of her gran in Lucy's looks, too. The same pointy chin and sensitive mouth. The same 'good' bones and curly hair.

Nora's was poker-straight. She tucked a lifeless wisp back

13

into the hairnet. Didn't look nothing unless you crimped it with tongs heated on the gas. Had to be careful though. Get them too hot and there'd be a sizzle and a pong and there was your hair all frizzed up to nothing. Did a lot for your looks, that did!

She put the casserole and a rice pudding in the oven on a low gas, dried the cups and hung them on the dresser, poured bleach down the drain, mopped up the slime where the draining board was rotting, and hung the cloth over the tap. All done. She turned out the light and stepped up into the living room.

As a girl, she'd been a looker, too. Quite a catch. Bit on the plump side, but nobody minded in them days.

She eased her back as she stood to admire the sepia photograph of her younger self, hanging to one side of the mantelpiece. She glanced at the red-grained cheeks of the woman in the mirror, at the eyes, staring back like a startled bird's, at the greying hair trapped in the net. She poked at it from habit, without interest. Wouldn't hardly think it was the same woman. Had she really been that creamy-skinned girl with the dimples? Her Fred had thought the world of her then. And she of him. Proper love-match, that'd been.

His photograph, on the other side of the fireplace, came under scrutiny now. Proper old-fashioned he looked with his dark, feathery moustache and stiff collar. She had his colouring, did Luce. And his eyes. Big, clever eyes. That was her problem, her cleverness. Always thought she knew better than everyone else.

'Cause *she* knew for a fact there was no such thing as ghosts!

'They've done scientific tests, Ma,' she would say. 'They've proved the whole thing is a load of bunk. Fraudsters playing on poor bereaved people's emotions, just to get money out of them.'

Well, that was it, then, wasn't it? No more to be said. And *she*, Nora, was 'certifiable' for thinking otherwise!

She stabbed the fire with the poker and watched the sparks fly up the chimney.

It wasn't a thing you could prove or disprove. Lord knows she'd tried. She'd told them exactly what Uncle Harry was wearing, down to his lace-up boots and his neckerchief and watch and chain. She'd told them how he was leaning against the mantelpiece stuffing his pipe with baccy. She'd told them what he was saying, word for word, but it made not a blind bit of difference. They still thought she was making it all up.

If only! Gawd, with an imagination like that she'd have made her fortune long ago.

Lucy had imagination, like her dad. She used to get top marks in her lessons. But she couldn't see what was in front of her nose. Same as him.

Pity she never took after Fred in other ways. Been more easygoing. It would save all these upsets.

'But it must be hard when you've got an education,' she said to the ghost of Granny Farthing, who had now returned, bringing her knitting with her, and a bag of peardrops, to keep her daughter company by the fire. 'They teach you not to take things on trust, don't they? Question, question! Lucy wants to know the ins and outs of a pig's arse!'

'Language, Nora,' said her mother.

She'd been surprised, herself, coming to live in her new husband's home and finding it already occupied with aunts and uncles, long-gone grandparents, great-grandparents and greater still, older-than-ancient family and friends. It looked like 41 Bampton Street was home to them all.

'Pushy lot, them Potters,' said the ghost. 'Young couple starting out don't want the likes of them poking their noses in.'

'Ssh,' said Nora, her eyes darting.

'It's hard enough getting to know each other without having your missus pestered by a lot of silly old hasbeens.'

'Mu-um . . . they'll hear you.'

The old woman shrugged. 'S'only the living don't 'ave to speak ill of the dead, girl!'

Fred had certainly been puzzled, never having noticed anything untoward, though he had lived in the house all his life.

When she told him, on that first morning, that she could see his Auntie Vi, sitting on the stairs, waiting for the tally man to call, he had humoured her, thinking that the wild night of wedded bliss had gone to her head. When she began talking to the old dear, he expressed concern. She told him she had never seen ghosts before. It must all be to do with her married state, her 'eyes being open', that sort of thing . . .

'I ain't complaining, duck, don't get me wrong,' he'd said fondly, kissing her plump white shoulder, her neck, her cheek. 'No one could wish for a better wife. Long as you don't expect me to say "How do?" to thin air.'

And when it was confirmed that she was expecting their first, he was happy to believe that the 'flights of fancy' were, indeed, all part of her condition.

'Chap's got to expect something of the sort,' he said. 'Some ladies get an 'ankering to eat coal, or bloaters, they do say. And you have your feet planted so firm on the ground the rest of the time, Nora.'

'Cause she was thrifty, wasn't she? Always had been. Take care of the pennies and the pounds'd take care of themselves. Every Saturday night she sorted his pay into tobacco tins marked 'Rent' and 'Coal', 'Gas' and 'Insurance', 'Food', 'Furniture', 'Clothes' and 'Rainy Day'. Anything left, and there wasn't much in them early days, she gave him back. After all, a man who worked six days a week making safes for banks and stately homes was entitled to a drink or two with his mates. And anything cropped up unexpected, you robbed Peter to pay Paul.

She had it all organised.

Every morning she got up early to cook his bacon and eggs, and get cracking on the day's jobs, different depending what day of the week it was. Monday was Washday, of course, then came Baking Day, Doing-Downstairs day, which meant scrubbing and polishing the floors, taking up the mats and bashing them with the beater. In them days she'd have to blacklead the stove, whiten the front step and polish the brass as well as all the furniture. Then came Doing-Upstairs day, which meant cleaning all the windows and turning out the cupboards. They didn't have a bath to scour, not then, which was a blessing. Ironing day was when she had to starch the collars, sew on loose buttons, strengthen hooks and eyes and put a stitch in falling hems, while she was about it. Then came Market day, which spoke for itself, and

16

Sunday. Only when her ankles swelled up did she stop to put her feet up for five minutes; Sunday was never a day of rest, not for a woman, not even when a baby was due. In between times she had her chickens to see to, she grew lettuces and runner beans, cleaned the grates and laid the fires, dusted, shopped, put by a few preserves, cooked the meals and kept them both supplied with cups of tea. In the evenings, when the supper was cleared away and washed up, she sat in the chair across from Fred's, did the serious mending and knitted for the baby.

So when the talking to his dead relations didn't pass, as expected, Fred was anxious that she might have been overdoing things. But she said she felt fit as a flea.

'A good man, your Fred,' said her mother, a boiled sweet clicking on her teeth. 'Pass slipped stitch over . . . A good husband and a good dad.'

'Oh, he was. So long as his tea was on the table when he come in, he let us get on with it. Carried on like it was me mates come round for a chinwag. "I can see you're busy," he'd say. "I'll take the kids up the Rec, kick a ball around for 'alf hour." And I'd go, "Why don't you stop in, Fred? Your Dad's come to see you".'

'You see to 'im, Nora,' he'd say. "Give 'im me best".' She leaned back, smiling, into her memories. And then she sighed.

'We used to have a laugh, me and Fred, specially after he'd gone over, but I ain't seen 'im in a while – must be a month or more.'

'He's all right, Nora. Just keeping out of your way for a bit.'

'Yeah, you said. I don't get it, though, in more ways than one!'

'I told you, Nora, you gotta save your strength. You ain't a young woman, no more.'

'And this was his idea, this rest cure?'

'No, it come as a shock to him. He's your husband, girl. He don't see you wrinkled and old and running to fat. Not like me.'

Nora winced. 'You was never one to mince your words, was you, Mum?'

17

'We don't want you popping off before your time, do we?
No, be honest, he was quite cut up, poor sod. Thought it was
all his fault, your very close veins and your indigestion.
'Cause he died young, left you to it, like.'

Nora grunted. There'd been times when she'd blamed him,
too.

'What's it all in aid of, then, Mum?'

The old woman sniffed. 'War effort, I gather. But they
don't tell you much. Only know I had to get down here and
give an eye to the both of you.'

He had died when Lucy was two.

There'd been a lot of blind eyes that day at the safe-
makers. Nobody at Harding & Willow, it turned out, had seen
him cut himself. Well, they wouldn't, would they? Nothing to
do with them if a curling shard of chiselled steel cuts a
workman's hand. Shouldn't've tried to carry on with a wound
like that. Well, of course, he might not've had a job to come
back to, but that was down to him. Teach him to be more
careful. And everyone knew you could get lead-poisoning off
them heavy doors. He should've known. That septicaemia
would set in. That he'd die. That was his lookout.

So it finished up that Nora got no compensation, no
pension and, if it hadn't been for the insurance, nothing but
young Arthur's paper round between her large family and the
workhouse. As it was she had to take in washing to make
ends meet.

'Not the rosy future I 'ad in mind when I married him!' she
remarked.

Her mother was casting off. 'No, you had it hard (three,
four . . .) – still, we managed between us (seven, eight . . .).'

'Not the best way to bring up a family, though.'

'Beggars have no say in it, gel.'

'Never had a lot of time for the kids.'

'You kept a roof over their heads and shoes on their feet.
You got nothing to reproach yourself for.'

'But Lucy, poor little scrap, I never 'ardly saw her. All
them years when you 'ad her for me, I was too busy.'

'She was all right. She got to the Central, didn't she?'

'But then she always had 'er 'ead in some book or other.

Honest, Mum, I don't feel I know the girl, not really.'

'No, you don't, not yet. Still, things'll get better. Not straight away, but it'll be all right. Mark my words.'

She took the wool between her long, yellow teeth and gnawed it through, before spreading the piece of knitting over her lap. 'What d'you think – that look fourteen inches to you?'

Nora fetched her tape measure. She dared to ask her mother why, when there was no weather to speak of 'over there', she felt the need of extra woollies.

'Oh, it ain't for me, duck, it's for your dad. Be a nice surprise for Christmas.'

# Chapter Three

The walls, painted forest green, were wet and cold as a cave. Lucy pulled the hot water over her shoulders, but felt her bones chill with loneliness.

She sighed as she began soaping her arms. Now she had no one.

Her friends from school had already begun the long climb up and out of Walthamstow; they were either married or had joined up.

The factory girls, give them their due, had included her in their trips to the pictures and to dances but after she had met Roy, last season, at the Football Club do, she had had to turn down their invitations. He hadn't liked the idea of her going out, possibly meeting other men while he was away. So she had stayed home in the evenings, or gone out with Ma and, if she were really honest, she had been glad of the excuse.

Because they weren't her sort. When they played their games with the men at work, cheeked the supervisors, when they gave the boys on the dance floor a cheap and cheerful come-on, it was all rather alarming. She would bite her lips and blink at their boldness and because she couldn't bring herself to do the same they thought she was uppity. A swank. She knew it. She hadn't needed her mother to tell her.

Or that Roy wasn't right for her. Deep down, she had known.

Sometimes she had found herself looking at him hard, trying to find the man she knew, the man who kissed her tenderly, in the petulant little boy who sulked when he lost at cards, or in the pompous prig who brayed others down.

Popular songs or politics, films or battle campaigns, it didn't seem to matter what turn the conversation took, he had to be right. He had to win. Have the last loud word. Always. Then, almost sensing her disapproval, he would turn to her with his smile, bewitching her into forgetfulness.

God, that smile.

The hand, soaping her breast, slowed, slid and cupped the heaviness, found the nipple that hardened at the touch of slippery circling fingers.

That smile. His eyes full of secrets she could not understand. Suggesting things she could not imagine, making her blush. His mouth, curving slowly, explicitly, playfully . . . tiny muscles twitching with terrible thoughts.

She closed her eyes, relishing a pleasure so akin to pain it made her wince. And somehow her fingers were drawn down there, to the nub of 'thou-shalt-not' and began a comfort that merely aggravated the need, the desire, the demand of the thing.

Her thighs pressed tighter. Her breath came faster . . .

Oh please, she yearned.

The water rippled quietly.

A sudden aching surge made her draw up her legs. And the water, noisy in their wake, brought her to her senses. What was she doing?

Quickly, she went back to washing, legs, belly, trying to ignore the pain that would not go away.

Oh no. She would not be seduced by the smile of a cheat and a liar.

She soaped her face, and slid under the water. It filled her ears, stretched skin over her bones. She shook her head, loose-necked, feeling her hair swirl with the current she had made. When she surfaced, she had made up her mind.

No regrets, no sentiment. She would put him out of her mind. Forget him. And sooner rather than later.

All right, so now she had no one. All the better. She was free to please herself. Do what she liked, go where she liked. She could join up if she wanted. No one to keep her here.

Only Ma, mother of boys, so unsure of her daughter's love she was afraid to express misgivings about Lucy's choice of husband.

Only Ma, so ignorant of Lucy's hopes and fears she saw her longing for a better life as betrayal and 'swank'.

Only Ma, so insensitive to her daughter's feelings she had turned Granny Farthing into a ghost.

Granny Farthing who had brought her up. Granny Farthing who had taken her in, loved her, when her mother had had no time or money.

She had taken Jack as well, while the other five kids were at school, on her daily shopping trips to the High Street, looking for bargains and cheap cuts, filling the pockets of their memories with riches . . . the colour and clamour of the street market, the cries of the vendors:

'A-apples-a-pound-pe-aars!'

'Ripe tomate-ers!'

A bolt of lovely material thumping unrolled for display, the clatter of dishes magically tossed and caught and never broken:

''*Ere's* one, '*ere's* two, '*ere's* three! An' I don't want half-a-crown . . . not even a florin. 'Ere y'are, lady, one and a tanner the lot.'

The clunk of weights and scales, the chink of money.

Stalls of shoes, the smell of leather. Dainty heels and pointy toes for grown-up ladies, new button-boots for other little girls. Not her. Hers hurt her ankles and squeezed her toes, especially after a barefoot summer, but better them than cast-offs with cardboard in the bottom, that had already 'done-for' three pairs of growing feet by the time they reached her.

Stalls of hats that the smart young women, from the 'posh' end of town, pulled down over their pencilled eyebrows, pouting their cupid's-bow lips at the mirror. Lucy had to tilt her chin to see them under the brim of her own brown straw 'shape' that pressed her fringe flat into her eyes.

Racks of waistless dresses, that the ladies held up to their shoulders and round at their hips, frowning doubtfully. There were wrap-round coats with bits of fur on the collar. Even for children. But not for the likes of Lucy Potter. She fingered the big brass buttons on her dad's old Guards' jacket, cut down to fit. Though it was bright red, though the buttons had kings' crowns on them, she knew it wasn't what proper children wore.

The biggest crowd was round the second-hand stall, a battleground where men and women would squabble like dogs at a piece of meat, over smelly trousers and shirts and motheaten skirts. Granny made her wait beside the next stall, selling parrot-food and cats' meat, so she wouldn't get trampled.

Here she would stand, a grubby little ragged girl with big green eyes, listening, entranced, to the gramophone across the way, playing catchy dance music, charlestons and tangos, black-bottoms and one-steps. She would jig up and down, watching the people 'squashing-flies' and kicking out their legs on the cobbles, until the gramophone wound down.

Granny had her regular stops and her big shopping bag would gradually fill with a penn'orth of pot herbs and a couple of marrow-bones (free: she said they were for the dog) to be boiled up and made into soup, or scrag-end of mutton, potatoes, pearl barley, bread, bacon, pudding rice, topped off with a ha'p'orth of broken biscuits, a pound of cooking tomatoes, a few pieces of spoiled fruit (free), and darning wool.

Flowers, ribbons, make-up were things other people bought. But Lucy was at liberty to feel them, breathe in the scents, admire the shapes and colours, store them away in her memory.

In the forest-green bathroom of a different era, she could wander again through the market, examine the meat and wet fish, smell oil lamps and paraffin heaters, sarsparilla and cough candy, though Gran preferred pear-drops and might buy two ounces if she was flush. She could see the chickens in crates, the puppies in cages, eels squirming as the man in the boater chopped off their heads and their middles and their tails. Chop, chop, chop. She could look up and see Marsh Street church-spire leaning, leaning about . . . to . . . fall! And the stall with the dead rabbits and the man turning one inside out and asking Granny if she wanted to make a fur coat. And the big weighing machine outside the swimming baths, where posh children swung and you breathed in the shrieks and splashes and chlorine while the fat man piled shiny brass weights on the balance.

The beggars. The little man without legs, sitting on the

kerb, singing Irish songs. The blind one that played the violin, with 'Wife and six children at home' written on a card beside his hat. The zither-man outside Woolworth's where Granny always, always bought them something: a tiny pink dolly to sit in her hand, or a book, or a whistle, or a windmill, or a ball that made Ma's face go tight and red when they got home.

'Oh, not more toot, Mum!' she would snap. (In those early days of her widowhood she had a short fuse.) 'Making a rod for your own back. You can't afford to waste money on rubbish for the kids.'

'It's my money – I'll spend it how I like. And what does it cost to make a child happy? Only a farthing or two.'

Lucy reached over the side of the bath for the jug of shampoo. And yelped as she poured the suds over her head. It was stone cold! The water had been hand-hot when she had added the powder, as per the packet's directions. However long had she been lying here?

Gingerly, she rubbed her hair into a lather and soap dribbles stung her eyes.

She filled and re-filled the saucepan with a mixture of hot and cold from the taps and sloshed it over and over her head.

Though she didn't remember the naming of Granny Farthing, she did remember the rainy days when you couldn't move in Ma's house for wet sheets and shirts draped over lines and furniture to dry, when her Granny took them round the block to her house.

They would sprawl on the floor, sorting through greasy old records to play on the gramophone. Funny ones, like *Mrs Buggins's Christmas Party*. Fast, clever ones, *The Flight of the Bumble Bee* or Chopin's *Nocturnes*. Lucy and Jack would take it in turns to wind the handle and Granny Farthing would screw up her whole face to see the needle onto the right groove. And they would try to sing *Two Little Girls in Blue, lad* . . . and Granny would pant '*One*, two, three, *one*, two, three,' holding Jack and then Lucy under the arms and whizzing them around and up in the air when their feet got into a tangle.

Sometimes Charlie or one of the others was off school, sick, and would have to lie on the sofa while they dressed up to entertain the invalid, Granny, too, in her funny old dance dresses and feathery hats and they would wobble about in her high-heeled shoes, until the squabbles started and they would end up bashing each other with her chain-link evening bags.

When Jack started school, Granny and Lucy would go for 'treats'. 'Up West' to Gamages in Holborn, to see Father Christmas, 'over the Plains' at Chingford, where Good Queen Bess had hunted deer, ''undreds and 'undreds of year ago' and they would picnic on condensed milk sandwiches and blackberries picked in the forest, or they'd go 'down the Rising Sun' for a pedalboat ride and cream soda with an 'icy' in. Always back by half-past three to fetch the little boys from school.

When Lucy started at the Infants, Granny would be there to meet her at the gate for the walk home through the narrow terraced streets to Lloyd's Park, to feed the ducks and play on the swings. Ever after, the smell of flowering lime trees would conjure up the soft sweetness of Granny's face.

'Any trouble she'd be there like a shot,' Ma would say, waxing sentimental over her Saturday Guinness. 'Died of the gastric, poor old soul. Horrible, it was, see her fading like that. Lucy musta been about twelve. You'd passed for the Central, by then, hadn't you? Poor old Mum.' She poured herself the other half. 'Don't know what I'd've done without her.'

But Lucy could remember rows, slanging matches, she and her brothers bawling, and Ma stomping out to the scullery to mangle the sheets, growling as though she were turning the handle of some mediaeval instrument of torture, and Granny Farthing would slam the front door so hard the knocker knocked and the letterbox clattered.

''Course, we didn't always see eye to eye, specially over *them* – you know, the ghosts. She didn't 'old with them when they was alive, leave alone when they was dead. No such thing, she always said.'

'Putting it mildly!' one of the boys might snort, referring to the times when the old woman would scream, 'You ain't right in the 'ead, Nora! Sitting there, jawing away to yourself. You look bleedin' ridiculous, gel! They cetch you they'll lock you up and throw away the key. And they'll 'ave my blessing! You ain't fit to 'ave charge of my old cat, let alone a bunch of kids, poor little mites . . .'

Which was why Granny Farthing would have been the last person to sit beside their fire and haunt them.

It was all rubbish. She made it up as she went along. If you listened to Ma, nowhere was safe. Ghosts were everywhere, spying on you. Even in the bath!

Lucy shivered. Scum had formed a silent seal on the surface. With an effort of will, she pulled the plug and rose from the water. The towel was rough, too thin, too small and let in the draught. A quick dusting of talc to help the clothes go on. Too quick. She banged the tin down on the wash-stand and a cloud of powder puffed into the cold steam.

She and her brothers had never seen so much as a wisp of ectoplasm but when you've grown up with a mother who chats to empty chairs and blank walls you simply accept it. Like early-morning charring at the hospital, fish and chips and a bath Friday night, a bit of a flutter and a Guinness of a Saturday, and Sunday roast after church, it was just her way. She did no harm. In fact, you could go a long way to find a better mother. Even Lucy had to admit that since she had got the job at the hospital, since the boys started bringing home wages, since Granny had 'passed over' and left her the insurance, and her few sticks of furniture, Ma had had more time for her kids, patching their quarrels, their clothes, and lately, their hearts. She was a good 'plain' cook, a terrible cheat at cards, an incurable gossip and, though they didn't always see eye to eye, in need, she was a friend. She was practically perfect. Just ever so slightly cracked.

'Eccentric,' Lucy said, with the benefit of Central School education.

'Round the bleedin' bend,' said Charlie, less succinctly.

And because they loved her, they put up with her. But they didn't encourage her. Not any more.

'*Goldilocks* – I'm getting *Goldilocks*. Does the word Goldilocks mean anything to you, dear?' The voice quavered and head and hands shook feebly. Ma, in her trance, had come across Great Auntie Maud, who had been a penny short

26

of a shilling most of her life.

'Someone you know named Goldilocks, Luce?' prompted her mother, helpfully, in her own robust tones. 'Or it could be the storybook, I suppose.'

'You tell me,' said Lucy, with one eye on the clock. Her mother had caught her between assignments: a critique of the use of imagery in Milton's *Paradise Lost* and the more pressing matter of what to wear for her date at the pictures.

'Well, dear,' Auntie M doddered on, her frailty again pervading Ma's plump person, 'you must be on the lookout for Goldilocks . . .'

Who's coming to sleep in *my* bed? thought Lucy wistfully.

'I see dark shadows looming . . .'

'A great big one, a middle-sized one and an itsy-bitsy baby one!' suggested Lucy.

Her mother twitched, sensing a certain scepticism.

There were more messages from the Other Side, mostly stern warnings about staying out late and the pitfalls of dance-halls, drink and talking to tall, dark strangers – the very things, in fact, that a growing girl might find halfway pleasant and that a widowed mother might find hard to veto without authoritative backing.

She could understand her mother's need for spiritual support but understanding all did not mean that she forgave all.

'Chance'd be a fine thing,' she protested. 'No one else's big brothers meet them off the bus. No one else has to be in by ten o'clock. I've enough on my plate, Ma, without *that* lot putting in their two penn'orth.' She jerked her head towards the cracks in the walls where she assumed Ma's ghosts had their lodging. 'Heaven must be a pretty boring place, if they can find time to worry about me and Frank Sadler in the one and sixes. *You* talk to them, eh? I'm going to iron me frock.'

You couldn't ignore Uncle Harry, though. Poor Uncle Harry, dead and gone these thirty years, driven to an early grave by Auntie Vi and her slatternly ways, and his own liking for strong liquor. Ma had known him when he was alive and she had a soft spot for him but Lucy hated his visits.

27

'Ma, I've got a pile of homework to do!'

Her brothers were quick with their excuses, too.

'Sorry, Ma, it's Friday. Have to help Bert collect the milk money.'

'Must clean me football boots.'

'. . . promised Stan I'd go round . . .'

But Ma would have none of it.

'Sit down at that blinkin' table – *now*!' And when they were all in their places, shuffling their feet, she soothed, '*Poor* old Uncle 'Arry. He don't ask much, just for people to pay him some mind . . .'

'Better be bloody important,' muttered Mick, thinking his mates would already be 'getting them in' at the Lord Raglan. His big fingers, locked with Lucy's, were painful. Charlie took hold of her other hand in a loose, damp grasp.

When their mother was sure she had their attention she closed her eyes. Her neck stiffened and her voice dropped an octave. She seemed to be stroking a moustache as her eyes narrowed for second sight.

'I got a message for Charlie. Now then, son, what it is, I'm getting big mountains, Chas. Or cliffs. So you're, like, climbing up. Keep 'old of that rope, Chas. Hold on, lad. Nearly there. Made it, son, well done.

'You there, are you, Mick? One for you, mate. Reckon you're gonna be travelling over water before long. Over the sea. To the sun. Sounds good, don't it? But it ain't no picnic. You best be careful, old son . . .'

More often, though, dear old Uncle Harry was drunk. The medium would loll back in her chair, splay out feet in worn carpet slippers and snore.

And then there wasn't much else to be had from him, apart from a chorus or two of *A little of what you fancy* . . . after a few bars of which, the boys would sneak off, and Lucy would carry on with her essay.

There had been one unforgettable occasion, though, during the Blitz, when Harry had snored himself awake, smacking his lips and, slowly, the puzzled look on his face had changed to one of horror.

'Oh Lord, watch out! Get down! They've seen us!' His eyes were wild and staring. 'Oh Ma!' He shrank inside himself and put his hands up to his ears, cuddling into the chair like a child. Ma's breath rasped in her throat and Harry's voice wailed, 'Oh God help us!'

Lucy was mesmerised. Not only by the eye-rolling and shuddering that had taken hold of Ma, but by a third voice that had somehow crept into the mix that was Harry and Nora. A voice she recognised.

'She's gonna fall off her chair if she ain't careful,' said Jack, still at home, waiting for his 'call-up'.

'Should we give her a shake, do you think?' Lucy whispered. 'Wake her up?'

At this point Ma slumped, her mouth gaping open, her arms hanging limp.

'Oh crikey!' said Jack. 'I dunno, Luce ... could be dangerous. Best leave it a minute, eh?'

Then the body in the chair groaned as a form of consciousness returned.

'Oh God.' Patting its chest and breathing deeply, then, 'That was close.' A pause, then, 'Oh Lord! It's going to— Oh Jesus! He's in there. He'll be roasted alive! No-o-o!' he cried. 'Oh, please, someone ... *Fire!*' The voice, the multi-voice, was cracking into its component parts. 'Don't just sit there, you stupid —! Oh, for Christ's sake, you bugger, get out! *Fire! Fire!*'

Eventually Harry's cries became whimpers and he dropped off into a deep sleep from which Ma awoke. Her broad face was pinker than ever and beaded with sweat. 'Phew!' she said, fanning herself with the *Daily Mirror*. 'It's so hot! Open a window, Luce, for God's sake! And pour us a cup of Rosie Lee.'

But Lucy couldn't move.

The voice rang in her head. Was it possible that her mother had a real sixth sense that enabled her somehow to divine the future? Perhaps it was a warning ...

Without waiting for the siren, they had taken up their gas-masks and hurricane lamp, secured the house and scuttled down into the Anderson shelter. Where they lay open-eyed in the cold and dark, starting up at train whistles and lovesick tomcats. Not until the early hours was there a real air-raid warning. The three of them huddled together on one camp

29

bed, with blankets wrapped tightly round them, against the subterranean damp.

'You sure about this?' asked Ma.

'No,' said Jack, 'but it's not often Lucy gets the wind-up.'

'Something's going to happen, Ma, I know it.'

'These Army blankets Perce give us ain't got no warmth in 'em,' said Ma.

'Feels like a blinkin' winding sheet,' quipped Jack, shivering with cold.

'Give over, Jack,' said Lucy.

Her own shivering turned to quaking when the warplanes at last rumbled over their heads, rippling the lamp's reflection in the pools that had seeped up through the floor. The steady crackle of ack-ack and the whine of falling bombs, each with the name 'Lucy Potter' on it, were the last sounds she expected to hear. The explosions, nearer and nearer still, made the ground shake and their teeth chatter, while debris pinged and rattled on the corrugated roof.

The next one – it would be the next one!

She relived every second of Harry's ghostly terror and was stiff with it when the All-clear eventually sounded. But why was she alive to hear it?

Perhaps they were buried under the ruins of their home? Was that how it would be? Slow and frantic suffocation?

When they pushed against the door it swung open easily. Hardly daring to breathe, they emerged from their tomb into a garden that was still planted with quiet rows of cabbages and parsnips. The house was unharmed. Burning buildings lit up the sky, but in another street. Fire engines and ambulances were clanging madly, but in another street.

That was when Lucy decided that enough was enough.

'No, I'm telling you, Ma, that's the last time you get me round that bloody table. I don't want no more to do with your damn ghosts, not Uncle Harry or Auntie Maud, or any of them! Look at me, I'm still shaking! I really thought my end had come, Ma. No thanks to you I didn't die of a bleedin' heart attack! You play silly buggers if you like, but leave me out.'

'I don't understand it. He was spot on with Mick and Charlie.'

'*You* were, you mean!'

Her brother shook his head rapidly, his frown telling her not to be cruel. But Lucy had wet her drawers in fear and had to get her own back.

'Come off it, Ma! D'ya think I was born yesterday? *You* knew Chas was trying for the marines *and* that Mick's unit would go abroad. It's just a loud of old flannel. You put the words into Harry's mouth, didn't you? *Didn't* you? A cheap trick, that's all it is! You should be on the bleedin' stage!'

She watched Ma's face crumple, heard her beg, 'What are you saying, Luce? You think I made it up? Lucy! I wouldn't frighten you like that . . .'

'Oh, *wouldn't* you? You'd do anything to make out you was something special!'

'No, Luce, I wouldn't . . .' She shook her head and her eyes filled with tears. 'It ain't like that, duck, I can't help it, I swear . . .'

Lucy had never seen her mother cry. Even at funerals. Especially at funerals. 'Be seeing you,' was the usual message on her floral tributes. So her tears were fascinating. Like a snake's flickering tongue to a rabbit. Driving the fight out of her.

'No, don't s'pose you can, at that,' she sighed. 'It's just – well, Harry and the others, they're not . . . It's like it's *you* . . . the things they say.'

It was no good. How could she, just eighteen then, tell her mother that the ghosts were not real, that their voices were Ma's own voice, different facets of her own personality, and all in her head?

'Ma, take no notice of me, I'm in such a two-and-eight I don't know what I'm saying. Let's have a cup of tea, eh?'

Ma had cut out the seances after that. But the one-sided chitchat continued and, proved, in fact, quite entertaining.

'For God's sake, Auntie, put your teeth in, do. I can't make out a word you're saying. What? You don't like the food they serve up? Well, don't eat it then; you don't 'ave to keep body and soul together no more, do you? Laughing? No, I ain't laughing. Well, why don't you like it, then? You can't chew it? Well, put your teeth in, then, you silly cat!'

31

Lucy gave a short laugh. It was a vaudeville act, with Ma playing to the gallery.

'When was the last time you had a shave, Dad? You look like a dirty old meths drinker. What d'you mean, you forgot your razor? You 'aving me on? You mean you're supposed to pack your shaving mug and cut-throat when your end is nigh? That accounts for all the beards over there, does it? Go on, pull the other one! You're just a lazy old git, same as ever you was!'

More alarming was the laughter that wafted out on the steam and splash of bath night. Who did she think she had in there, scrubbing her back and sharing her fantasies? And who in her bedroom? Forcing her children to rap on the walls when the murmur of her voice kept them awake past midnight?

'Oi, Flirty Gertie, give it a rest!'

'Tell him to sling his hook, Ma; I got an early start in the morning!'

Was it their father? Or some fancy man? A favourite cousin, perhaps . . . Their young heads seethed with romantic notions.

'I should be so lucky!' she snorted.

These were pure spirits, she assured them, not driven by appetites of the flesh. Their relationships were on a higher plane altogether.

'A likely story,' they teased. And she had the grace to blush.

Later that evening, when the smell of liver and bacon became unbearable, and she had read *Picturegoer* from cover to cover, Lucy ran a comb through her damp hair and came downstairs to stand in the doorway.

'I suppose I wouldn't have thanked you for telling me what you thought of Roy. If you'd said you hated him it would have made me all the keener.'

Ma took off her glasses, polished the steam from the lenses with a corner of her overall, replaced them and went back to mashing potatoes.

Lucy slid to the sink and ran her finger up and down its edge.

She couldn't see her mother's face as she reached down two plates from the rack over the stove, and dolloped mounds of milky-white potato on each. Then she opened the oven door with a tea-towel and carefully drew out a small earthenware casserole. A thin brown spattering round the lid told of a rich mixture within. Onions, carrots, herbs, the liver and a few rashers of streaky peeled from their weekly ration, bubbling in a broth of cabbage water, bottled tomatoes, gravy browning, seasoned and thickened with a little flour.

Lucy took a long step to stand beside the woman at the table. She was taller, by a head, than her mother.

'Mmm, that looks good!' She licked her lips for the lie. 'And . . . and, Ma, it's nice to know Granny's still around, keeping an eye on things. It was just a bit of a shock, that's all.'

She bent to give her mother a quick peck on the cheek, straightened and shook her hair back from her face. It wasn't on, was it, joining up? What had she been thinking of? She couldn't leave this woman with no one but her ghosts, in war-torn London. Could she?

'Just a few sprouts for me, please. That'll do. That's fine.'

# Chapter Four

Clacton was a mistake. She knew it even before the train set off. No one goes to the seaside in November, apart from intrepid honeymooners. And a few hundred servicemen. Far from having the train to themselves, as they had hoped, Lucy was dismayed to see first the corridor, then their compartment, fill with heaving khaki, navy and airforce blue. Doors slammed up and down the platform and the guard blew his whistle.

'Ere, you ain't *all* off to Clacton, are you, son?' Her mother was poking a spotty young soldier who had ducked into the seat beside her.

Blushing madly, and flicking anxious glances at Lucy, sitting opposite in the window seat, he stammered that his unit was, in fact, bound for Butlin's.

'Going on your 'olidays, are you, duck?' Her mother was in her element, playing to the crowd, while the poor boy next to her squirmed with every nudge and wink. 'Got your bucket and spade?'

But he didn't get the joke. He explained with the utmost gravity that Butlin's was an Army practice c-c-c-camp these days. They were going to teach him how to fire a Bofors g-g-gun before s-s-s-sending him into action. He looked too scared to burst a paper bag but you never could tell.

Ma's jaw dropped.

'Oh, bli— we come away for a bit of peace and quiet, not bang, bang, bang all day long!' Someone gave a snort of amusement but Ma sailed on. 'Get enough of that at 'ome, don't we, Luce?'

No one laughed this time. Everyone knew what Londoners had to put up with and it wasn't funny.

A plump and sweaty Northerner, next to the spotty one, took great satisfaction in telling them that the guns didn't stop firing until four in the afternoon, most days, when the light began to fade. The last of the sun and telegraph poles glittered now on his glasses.

'Four o'clock!' squawked Ma. 'The landladies must be doing their tin-tops! Up the church, praying for a direct hit, I shouldn't wonder. Well, we'll just have to stick cotton wool in our ears, won't we? And go for our paddle up the other end of the beach. Don't want to get picked off by no stray bullets, do we?'

'Paddle? In November, Ma!'

'Tha'd 'ave a job getting down on t'beach, any road,' said the Northerner, hugging himself with glee. 'Lessen tha's brought wire-cutters along.'

'Eh?'

'There's barbed wire, lass, all around t'coast. Keepin' Jerry out!'

She had known about the barbed wire, of course, and that the beaches were heavily mined, but these things get pushed to the back of the brain when you have other matters on the boil. Newlyweds always go to the seaside, war or no war. Though when she and Roy had booked two nights at Sea-Breezes, paddling and sandcastles hadn't been all that high on their list of priorities.

Now it was a different story.

Each man had his two penn'orth to put in and was rewarded by a shriek of, 'Oh, my good Gawd!'

It did sound awful. There was barbed wire on both sides of Kings Road, they said, where Miss Filmore's guesthouse faced the sea. Army instructors had taken it over, for shooting practice. A slow-moving lorry would rumble up the road and down, on the seawall side, trailing a target, a sort of fireproof sleeve. Guns would be lined up outside the houses, in the road, and the trainees would have to try and hit the sleeve as it went past. Quite entertaining, the men agreed, specially if you were the driver! You'd see all ranks out there, from squaddies to pen-pushing Majors and Generals. No idea at all, some of them. Then there were the Yanks, smoking their cigars and throwing their weight around. All sorts . . . being licked into shape by the barked commands of the Sergeant-Majors. And there was every kind of weapon being tested: guns, rockets, you name it, making one hell of a racket.

Cotton wool would be no use at all.

'So what *is* there to do in Clacton, of a Saturday night?'

Not a lot, judging from the way her question killed the conversation stone dead. A goatish snort, quickly stifled, pulled the strings of Ma's mouth tight but Lucy knew there was no prospect of turning back. Her mother had paid her money and would get its worth, no matter what. So while the wheels jigged over the rails, and puffs of steam and smoke from the engine danced lightly past the window, inside their compartment was gloom and doom.

Then a crackle as the newspaper next to her was lowered.

'There's a concert in the Beaumont Hotel.'

'Eh?' Lucy twisted to get a good look at the joker, a long, lean airman, with hair the colour of amber, and strange speckled eyes.

'String quartet,' he went on, perfectly serious. 'Beethoven and Mozart. Should be good.'

She blinked with disbelief. 'Sounds nice,' she observed politely. 'You playing, are you?'

'Me? No, no,' he laughed. Clearly such an idea was ludicrous. 'Not my instrument.'

Ma winked at her and Lucy rolled up her eyes. Things would have to come to a pretty pass if they could find nothing better to do than sit in some seedy hotel, in their posh frocks and shoes, listening to squeaks and scrapes. Not even if their host was halfway good-looking.

'No thanks,' she said.

'No ta,' said her mother.

Unperturbed, he went back to his paper.

Her mother couldn't stay down for long. Diving into her bag for letters and snaps she proceeded to regale the pimply one (whose name was Eric, she quickly discovered), and through him the rest of the carriage, with stories of her own sons' exploits. There was her Arthur on his ship. Didn't he look lovely in his uniform? Quite a lad with the ladies, her

Arthur. And that was young Jack working on one of them big tanks. He was out in Africa, in the desert, poor little sod. Spent his time frying eggs on the bonnet of the engine, by all accounts. At least they got eggs out there! And her Charlie was in the marines. Up to all sorts, him. Secret missions and that. Very hush-hush. (Lucy's warning frown was water off a duck's back.) And there was her Siddy . . . and Perce . . . and Mick . . .

'How many boys you got, then, Nora?'

'Six,' she said proudly. 'Six boys.'

Not until she was prompted did she think to mention her daughter. But that was always the way. The six boys were the achievement.

Eric was trapped. Inside a pink porridge skin, in a conversation from which he was too polite to extricate himself, in a war that could kill him. But then so was she. Trapped. Look at her. All dressed up in her ridiculous wedding finery: new dress, new coat, new shoes, and for what? A weekend in dead and alive Clacton, with her *mother*!

Sensing her stare, the boy looked up, and she turned away to the window where bleak November fields slid by.

But her eyes didn't slide with them, didn't flicker. A squall of rain drummed on the glass and she hardly noticed.

Her blood didn't boil any more. Hurt and let-down and contempt for Roy had reduced to a thick sludge of sadness that would clog her veins for a long time. Forgetting wasn't that easy. She studied the sad ring of white skin, on the fourth finger of her left hand. She missed being engaged. Idly she wondered what he was doing right now. Was he back at the front? Was he thinking about her, thinking that in a few more hours they'd have been walking up the aisle? Her lip quivered with the remnants of self-pity and she felt for a handkerchief in her coat pocket.

'Cigarette?'

The man beside her held out a pack of Senior Service, without a smile. She shook her head, sniffing and cross. You know what you can do with your fags and your stupid string quartets, she wanted to snap. Leave me be.

He merely shrugged, took a cigarette himself and tamped it down on the pack, before fixing it to the cushion of his

37

bottom lip. When he struck a match and leaned across, first to her mother, then to Eric, with the flame guarded in his cupped hands, Lucy realised the bloke was just being polite. Generous. Not fresh at all.

She saw the flexing muscles of his jaw, saw how deepset were his eyes, in profile, noticed how the fine hair, the colour of apricot jam, tapered into a tanned and tender neck. He had nice ears, too. Different from Roy's.

Of course, any children you had by him would be ginger, for sure, she caught herself thinking, specially if your own hair had chestnut tints. And blushed at her own boldness.

It was too late to apologise: he was preoccupied with catching the last of the light himself, and their eyes didn't meet until he was shaking out the flame. She gave him what she hoped was a rueful smile but he half-closed his eyes against the sting of smoke, and looked away.

Suit yourself. With a hunch of the shoulder to freeze out an army, she returned to the window. But this time she wasn't thinking about Roy. She was rattled.

Now she realised how hard it was raining, and irritably rubbed a hole in the condensation, to see sodden black fields through the slanting trickles on the glass, trees like roots, some lagged with ivy, dark, misshapen monsters, lonely farmhouses, sad, sway-backed horses. Just the day for the seaside! (Even worse for a wedding!) Wouldn't she have been ten times better off spending the day in the armchair by the fire, keeping warm, and wallowing in what might have been, with Bing and Glenn Miller for company?

*House and Home* was sticking out of Ma's bag and Lucy plucked it out, for something to do. It wasn't her usual read, but at seven-thirty on Liverpool Street Station, with the train coming in, there hadn't been time to pick and choose. One and six, she had paid for it, and it was pocket-sized; but it wouldn't have occurred to them to cut the price as well as the paper. Still it smelled rich and glossy and the pages turned smoothly on stories of brave middle-class ladies, keeping their ham-bones for Salvage and cutting up their old fur coats to make warm winter linings for 'fuel-less days'.

There were recipes for 'fish cakes' using potatoes and anchovy essence and Christmas cakes made with grated

38

carrots and gravy browning. They probably cut them out for the 'help' to cook while they were busy knitting socks for the boys in the Officers' mess.

Lucy riffled the pages. Make do and mend, save, save, save. She wished she had saved her one and six.

She didn't fancy the love story; about some girl meeting a Yank in an underground station, during an air-raid, and falling for his looks and charm. Falling for his lies and his flattery, more like. Men were all cheats.

And the problem page . . . *'Continue to say No, my dear, and be glad that you are sending your boy to his duty with a clear and lovely vision of a girl he loves and feels is worth all that he can give and do.'*

And then she found herself reading an article about women in the services. *'We're Proud of You!'* it was called.

'Leave the fighting to the men,' Roy had said, when she had suggested leaving the munitions factory and joining up. 'We'll be married soon. You stay home, Lucy, and keep your mother company.'

At least he had thought about her mother. Her brothers hadn't given Ma a second thought. It was understood that Ma was her responsibility. She was the girl.

And now she didn't even have marriage on the horizon. But she wasn't cut out to be a twinset spinster, sitting at home every night with her mother, over a fire banked up with tea-leaves, turning worn collars, and sheets sides to middle, mending and making do. A twinge of panic made her grip the journal tighter. She was young and fizzing with energy. She didn't want to make do. She wanted . . . oh, new people, new places. She wanted a change.

What sort of life was it when a weekend trip to Clacton was a high spot? Compare that with the glamour of the WAAF and the WRNS and the ATS. They were up to all sorts, driving cars, operating radios. Some were no more than clerks or secretaries, like her, but they were out from under their mothers' skirts, seeing the world and having fun!

Lucy shivered. The war wouldn't last for ever. Win or lose, these opportunities for women were once and for all.

If only she could be sure that Ma would be all right.

She stared at the advertisement, at the tear-off slip. All she had to do was write down the branch of the services that interested her and add her name and address. There was no commitment.

'Got a pen, Ma?'

She hadn't, of course, but all around, soldiers were searching their pockets. No offers from the gent on her left, she noticed. She borrowed Eric's Platignum because she felt sorry for him, carefully removing a cat's hair that was caught in the broad nib.

Well, it was done. She had plumped for the WRNS, not because of the glamorous uniform, though the perky cap would sit well on her brown curls and the black stockings would make her legs look even slimmer. She wanted to learn a useful trade, radiography maybe, and see the world. She would tear out the slip and post it when they got to Clacton.

She returned the pen and wiped her slippery palms on her coat. She was more excited than she had been over the wedding, for goodness' sake! She flapped the magazine to cool her burning cheeks.

Dear, it was hot in here and stuffy. Air, she needed air! She stood up to open the window. Just an inch or two. She yanked at the leather strap, pulled it off the metal holding stud and the window disappeared with a thump, letting in a screaming blast of wind and rain and smuts!

'Damn,' she muttered. Damn, damn! What a fool! What had she been thinking of? In front of all these men, too.

She wrestled with the strap as the rain slapped her face and wet her front. If you pulled hard enough the strap was supposed to lift the window up again, but she couldn't deal with the window *and* the elements. It was like one of those ring-the-bell trials of strength at the fairground. She'd get it halfway and it would slip away again. Thump. Meanwhile, Ma was wailing; a real help, her eyes fastened shut by the blast, her hair tugging to get free of its hairnet, her hat threatening to come unpinned and fly away.

And then, predictably, strong hands came to her aid. Hands sprinkled with golden hairs, fingers brown with nicotine. Not the sort she would have associated immediately with sensitive musical instruments. She smelled the smoky breath close to her face, the fresh air on his skin.

40

'Here . . .' He shoved her aside, so roughly she bounced on her seat, and with one mighty heft he had raised the window and fastened it. Show off!

But the absence of weather was wonderful.

'Just how wide did you want it?'

'What?' Was that, could she detect . . . a sneer in his voice? Bloody man. 'Oh, j-just a little bit.' She cleared her throat in an attempt to salvage some of her dignity. 'That's fine . . . that's plenty.'

She hardly dared to look at the havoc she had caused. Newspapers were blown about, lighted ends of cigarettes had been knocked off in the scramble, and men were slapping ash and glowing embers from their trousers. Eric's hair was stuck wetly to his pimples. Ma was re-pinning her hat.

To complete her humiliation, her rescuer bent and picked up *House and Home* from the floor and laid it across her damp lap. It was splattered with rain, the ink smudged, the page smeared with train dirt and soldiers' scuffs.

'You can still send it,' he said.

Scathing words were on the tip of her tongue, about nosy people who read over other people's shoulders, not to mention men who pushed young women around, but when she saw his mouth beginning to twitch, she caught his humour and let herself smile back.

By the time they reached Clacton, she had learned that his name was Joe, that the slight burr was country-Essex, that he played piano in a band and, towards the end of the journey, when he knew her better, that the brief encounter with the rain and wind and smoke had left a large speck of soot on the side of her nose. She whipped out her compact and scrubbed it away with spit and hanky.

This time she did thank him.

As the train pulled into the station, he unearthed their small suitcase from a pile of kitbags in the luggage rack and their fingers brushed as she took it from him. She missed the touch of a man's warm hand.

# Chapter Five

Before setting one foot inside the guesthouse called Sea
Breezes, Ma felt it only fair to provide the landlady, Miss
Filmore, with blow-by-blow particulars of Lucy's dashed
marital hopes.

'*Ma!*' spluttered Lucy, 'For goodness sake!'

But Ma seemed to have taken to gangling Miss Filmore,
with her black ink-dot eyes, wide with interest, and her
mouth softly rounded into an 'O'. In fact, she reminded Lucy
of a wooden peg doll Granny had made for her, long ago,
with her straight up and down figure. Even the hairdo was the
same: glossy black braids wound and pinned into a telephon-
ist's 'earphones'. Lucy used to whisper secrets into those
painted earphones and she realised that she didn't mind, too
much, Miss Filmore knowing about Roy. In fact, her
mother's first impressions were generally reliable. Instance
the man himself. Love or hate or indifference at first sight,
was well-founded, on the whole. Embarrassingly so.

'I wouldn't buy nothing from '*im*,' she would tell her
daughter and any other customers, beating a hasty retreat
through a shop doorway. 'Gawd 'elp us, I'm goose-pimples
all over! That's the longest-legged rabbit I've ever seen, and
if that's beef in them sausages, I'm the Queen of Sheba.
Wouldn't touch 'em with a ten-foot barge-pole.' And the
hapless shopkeeper would gawp in dismay as the queue at his
counter dwindled to nothing, while his doorbell went ping,
ping. Ping.

'So that's why you got me instead of Roy in your best
double bed,' she concluded. 'It won't go no further, will it,

Marje?' They were on first-name terms already. The long and short of it, thought Lucy, like Dot and Carrie in the cartoon.

Marjorie's face creased into a hundred lines of goodness, sensibility, and acute distress that her discretion should ever be in doubt. She had been a teacher for most of her adult life, she told them, so she knew Roy's type.

'Easily led, I shouldn't wonder. Trying to impress his friends. Men take a long while to grow up. Some never do.'

Over a substantial lunch of lentil soup and home-made bread, the two women continued to forge their bonds. Marjorie told them how she had taken over the running of the guesthouse from her mother, three years before. She usually billeted soldiers these days, so had been charmed to think that honeymooners had chosen to stay with her . . . but never mind.

'Your mother's the lady in the wheelchair, is she?' Ma lowered her voice and her head in the direction of the fireplace.

Lucy twisted round to see. And cringed. There was no one, not even a painting or photograph, no clue at all.

'My mother's dead.' Marjorie's scalp moved visibly. If she had been a cat her ears would have pricked back. 'Didn't I say? I took over when she died but, yes, she did spend her last years in a wheelchair. How did you know?'

How *had* she known? Had she seen an abandoned wheel-chair, folded perhaps, and leaning against the wall in the front porch where Lucy had thought she had seen deckchairs? Or was there an old lady in one of the family photos displayed on the table in the lobby where they had taken off their coats and hats?

'Ma!' Lucy warned in a low voice.

'Um . . .' said Ma doubtfully, her eyes drawn to an expanse of rug to the right of the fireplace. 'I . . . I thought that must be her . . .'

'Must be her what? Oh, her place. I see . . . Well, yes, that was her place, all right, beside the fire. You're quite a detective, Nora,' the other woman smiled. 'What gave her away? Is the rug worn where the wheels stood? Scratches on the paintwork?'

Lucy regarded their hostess through narrow eyes. A

43

woman used to reading children, to anticipating their next moves, must have known perfectly well what Ma had seen, or claimed to have seen. Yet she had deliberately misunderstood. Why? Was she simply obeying the rules of East Coast hospitality and ignoring her guest's eccentricities?

Or waiting until she was sure before showing them the door or calling in the men in white coats?

Or what?

Her mother was slowly, surely, shaking her head. Oh Ma, Lucy begged silently, she's giving you a get-out!

But her mother who, so far as Lucy knew, had never so much as hinted, over shop-counters and doorsteps and garden walls, at the goings-on in the privacy of her home, seemed to have made up her mind, on a mere twenty minutes' acquaintance, to reveal all to this schoolmarm.

Don't do it, Ma! Don't show us up!

She couldn't bear it. She turned to face the window, and stared hard through the criss-crosses of bomb-defying sticky tape, as Ma described how she could see the old lady sitting beside the fire as clearly as she could see Marjorie and Lucy. Mrs Filmore was sewing, she said, in answer to the peg-doll's question, a piece of tapestry, a cushion-cover or a kneeler, perhaps. The design was of some kind of hooved creature. A horse, a white horse, no – a unicorn.

Lucy winced. Cheap, Ma! She, too, had noticed the firescreen, pushed to one side of the armchair, depicting a unicorn rearing to crop from an oak tree. What must poor Miss Filmore be thinking?

Surprisingly, she appeared to be taking Ma's 'vision' in her stride. She even asked the 'medium' if there were any messages for her. Humouring her until she had a chance to get on to the asylum, no doubt.

Ma cocked her head, thrush-like. 'Eh? Well, she says I gotta tell you to look no further.'

The peg doll nodded and murmured, 'I thought as much.'

Ma shrugged, and returned her attention to the fireplace.

'What d'you mean, duck?' Her lips twitched as at a joke that she didn't quite get. 'No, sorry, dear . . . say again? Can you just . . .?' She was smiling broadly but the gaze that she turned on Marjorie was bewildered. 'She keeps on laughing

. . . funny laugh she's got. Catching, like that *Laughing Policeman*. She all right, is she?'

'I'm sure she is.' Marjorie was smiling too, now.

'She keeps looking at me and laughing, see. She's saying, "You're the one, my dear, you're the one".'

'Yes, of course. Poor Nora, you don't understand, do you?'

Me neither, thought Lucy, feeling left out. Look at them both, nodding and smiling, like a pair of wooden pecking birds, her mother laughing even though she didn't get the joke. Perhaps *she* was the joke, and the punchline was coming next.

The dark eyes shuttered briefly.

'Since Mother's passing I've remained in contact with her, in spirit.'

Ah. So now there were two barmy old women to contend with.

'Through the church,' Marjorie hastened to add. 'I haven't any special gifts, though I know you have. We've been expecting you.'

'No,' Lucy was compelled to argue. 'It was me and Roy you were expecting.' But she might as well have shouted at the sea for the notice anyone took of her.

Marjorie explained that when old Mrs Filmore had 'passed over' into spirit, she had sought solace in the local Spiritualist Church. It had been good to know that Mother was out of pain and enjoying meeting friends and loved ones on the Other Side.

'I knew it was her, straight away,' she said. 'Soon as Mr Whittaker – wonderful old man – told me about her laugh. A peeling laugh, rich and ripe and infectious, he said. I knew it was her then and I knew just now. Thank you, Nora. Thank you so much.'

Ma made no reply.

Lucy watched her mother carefully. She was looking rather pale and stunned, her fingers plucking at the loose blotched skin of her neck, her body rocking slightly as though blown by a wind.

Marjorie went on to describe the invaluable advice that had been passed on through Mr Whittaker, about running the guesthouse and keeping the books, not to mention news of

45

her father and other relations. And then, one day, she said, she received a rather strange message. She was told to be on the lookout for an unexpected guest. Well, they had unexpected guests all the time; that was the nature of their trade.

'But when you saw Mother just now I knew you must be the one. Is she still there, by the way?'

Ma found her tongue.

'No, no, she went off to do a bit of gardening, she said.' She shifted to the edge of her chair, shook her head as if to clear it and swallowed. Lucy knew she had reached a turning point. 'So what you're saying is, there's someone up your church, this Mr Whittaker, and he *knew* I was coming here, to your house, this weekend?'

'I don't know about this weekend. He just passed on a message from Mother that I was to put out the *Welcome* mat.'

'Who is this bloke?'

'Mr Whittaker? One of the elders up there, a medium. But he's not the only one. There are a few of them, channels, just like you, through whom astral entities may reach out to the physical world. They've all been telling us to expect a new psychic, one already high on the spiritual ladder. And here you are!'

'Oh dear!' Ma licked her lips nervously and her eyes darted about as she attempted to make sense of this news. 'They knew I was coming? I can't 'ardly take it in, you know. You're sure it's me?'

Oh yes, Marjorie nodded.

Lucy's head was beginning to ache.

''Cause I ain't nobody. Luce'll tell you, I do a bit of charring up the hospital, that's all. I ain't go no sustificates, like. I ain't took no exams in sidekick.'

Marjorie explained what a psychic was and that yes, Nora was one such, and a good one, too, if her channelling of Mother was anything to go by.

'Well, I never.' And then: 'Hear that, Luce? We was meant to come 'ere. All that with Roy was just to get us to Clacton. How wonderful are the ways . . . how bleedin' wonderful. Oh, 'scuse language, Marje, I'm sure, no call for that. I'm just so . . .' she searched for the words 'well . . . I'm all of a doodah! Ain't you, Luce?' and refusing to be put off by the face Lucy was pulling, went on, 'Ghosts told 'em, you say?'

'Astral entities,' Marjorie corrected.

Ma's expression showed that she thought 'astral entities' was far too dignified a description for her troop of sad in-laws.

Lucy thought so too. What on earth were they getting themselves into? There was a rushing in her ears as though she were sinking, turning over and over in a deep, tidal undertow of superstitious tosh. This schoolmistress, this educated woman, this plausible and hence doubly dangerous person was telling her poor, simple mother that her madness had validity, even had special names.

And she could do nothing. Just sit by and watch as Nora was wooed and won. Oh so sincerely and oh so gently. Here was this blessed peg doll convincing Nora that she was God's gift to Clacton, and conjuring a look in her mother's eyes that broke your heart. A look of unutterable relief. The ugly duckling discovering she was a swan among swans. After all and at last.

Lucy turned away, hearing the voices as a murmur that had nothing to do with her. Ma was telling Marjorie about her own ghosts, Auntie Vi and company. Vaguely she realised how pleasant it must be for Ma to be able to discuss her life's work with someone who believed in her.

She looked out across the front lawn of the guesthouse, to a ten-foot barrier of glinting barbed wire. Beyond lay the deserted coast road, a no-man's land where the wind whipped up eddies of drying sand. On the far side lay the low perimeter wall, made ferocious with more rolls of wire barbs. The island prison was complete. This was the wall where once bathers dried their towels and picnickers opened their sandwiches and stood their flasks, where sea-gulls pecked at crumbs, and anglers fished at high tide. This wall now did double duty, keeping out an enemy more invasive than salt water. Far away, a strange sea was laid out, like cold and silver fish on a marble slab of sky.

You needed a trip to the coast, she thought, to see things in perspective. It was easy to forget, at the hub of your own importance, that you were only a pinprick in the scheme of

47

things. What were her problems, after all, compared with those of warring nations?

Insur-blooming-mountable.

Ma had about her now the wondering look of a child who knows, by the bulk and weight of a birthday parcel, that it must contain, can only contain, her heart's desire. She was asking, 'And these . . . these channels, they're like me, are they? They talk to them on the Other Side . . . and nobody thinks they're round the bend?'

'No, of course not. They are what the church is all about. Through the mediums we are able to receive God's healing power and learn His wisdom. Of course, they had to be trained in the power of prayer, so they could be channels for good. That's the difference, you see. You're what they call a passive channel. Your ghosts just appear, I gather, whenever the fancy takes them. You have no control over them.'

'No, more's the pity. Blooming nuisance they are, especially Maud, barmy old bat, don't know night from day. I tell you, Marje, that old woman'll be the death of me. Keeps me awake all hours, don't she, Luce?'

Lucy smiled wanly.

'I'm just getting off,' she explained, 'and there's Maud sitting on the end of me bed, wanting a chinwag. Night after night this goes on so I tells her straight, "It's all right for you, gel, but when you start work at six you need your kip." And it's not like she's got anything to tell me, Marje, nothing I ain't heard 'undred times before. She's got this bee in her bonnet about Lucy and this Goldilocks person. I says to 'er, "Goldilocks . . . Right, I'll tell her. Leave it with me, gel, I'll make sure she gets the message." Anything to rid of the woman. But I never, seeing as Lucy gets so browned off with it, don't you, gel? Anyhow, last week, there I am, in the Land of Nod, and all of a sudden I'm being tossed about like a flippin' ship at sea, the old bedsprings going nineteen to the dozen and my poor old heart along with 'em! Blimey, I think, that's me done for, Jerry's landed! But there's this silly old woman, going "Nora, are you awake? Nora?"

Well, that was it, weren't it? I lost me rag and no mistake. Told her she was a bleedin' nuisance and if she didn't sling her bleedin' hook I'd bleedin' move house. Not like me to

48

use language, as you know, Luce, but that woman's enough to make a saint swear.'

Auntie Maud had quivered a bit and then blown out like a night-light, according to Ma. Since when the doors had, coincidentally, slammed. Usually when you were deep in a book or listening to a play on the wireless.

There was a more rational explanation, of course. Theirs was an old terraced house, none of the windows fitted, there was a fireplace in every room, gaps in the floorboards and under the doors and this was the season of winds and draughts. But still Ma insisted the slamming doors were Maud's protest.

'And now I think of it, Luce, it could've been her way of saying, "Watch out for Roy." He was a proper Goldilocks if anyone was.'

Lucy shrugged. A bit of straight talking would have saved a lot of confusion. But Ma's ghosts always had to talk in riddles. They liked to keep you guessing.

Marjorie said, in deadly earnest, 'Yes, yes, I see. Most distressing. We'll have to sort that out. You can't go on taking risks.'

'Why? What's the matter?'

'Well, you see, Nora, as you are, you're vulnerable. An open door. Anybody, anything can get through. So far, you've been lucky. Your dear ones are fairly harmless. Benign. If some lower or dark entity decided to make use of you, what defence would you have?'

'Oh, Marjie . . .' Ma was rubbing her wedding ring. It was too firmly embedded in flesh now to twist, but it was still her first comfort.

'Don't be frightened, Nora. The church will be your protection. Prayer and the Word of the Spirit.'

Lucy leaned across the table, took her mother's workworn hand, and whispered urgently, 'Ma, you don't want none of this. Let's go home, eh?'

But Marjorie was smiling, shaking her head. 'Poor Lucy, it's all such mumbo jumbo, isn't it? Don't worry. They are good people at the church, people of God the Father, the Great Spirit. They will only do what's best for your mother.'

'What do you mean? What are you going to do?'

49

'Nothing at all, dear. All I'm going to suggest is that you both come with me to the meeting tonight and let Nora make up her own mind.'

And a double barricade of barbed wire was no defence at all.

# Chapter Six

'Got your penny for the collection?' Nora knew she was fussing but she couldn't help it. It was a distraction, a mother's way of easing her child through an ordeal. Or trying to.

'Collection!' Lucy hissed, with a face like thunder. 'I wouldn't give this lot the drippings off me nose!'

'Ssshh!' Nora looked around furtively and, catching curious eyes, shrugged a jaunty what-would-you-do-with-her grin, before hustling the girl through the entry.

'You don't have to come, if you don't want to,' she had assured her, with a largeness of heart that she did not feel.

'Oh, what?' Lucy had been busy at the mirror, working in lipstick with her fingertip. Nora had watched her pout and preen, fitting her looks, like a surgical glove, over those of some smouldering screen goddess whose image she projected onto the glass. Now pained disbelief registered. She swung round to check Nora's face for truth, and found her bouncing anxiously on the double-sprung mattress, her feet a good fifteen inches off the floor.

'You'd never let me hear the last of it!' she snorted, before returning to her reflection, ducking slightly to tease brown curls onto her pale forehead. Nora regarded her daughter with a fond, uncritical eye. The linen two-piece suited her, its simple lines showing off the narrowness of her shoulders and waist, her long legs. She'd have looked a treat going down the aisle.

'And I might as well come,' the girl went on, dabbing scent

51

behind her ears. 'There's sod all else to do in this dump of a Saturday night.'

Nora's 'Language, Luce . . .' was out of habit; the girl could have blasted the air blue so long as she didn't leave Nora to go to the meeting alone.

'There's that concert . . .'

'You're joking! Me slip showing, is it?' Lucy twisted to see round her shoulder-pad.

'No, you're all right,' then, 'he seemed a nice boy, that Joe.'

'Good Gawd, Mother, off with the old isn't in it! It's not like riding a bike, you know, pick yourself up and try again. I've had it with men for a good long time.'

'Mmm. Want a lend of me stockings, duck? Ain't decent, bare legs in church.'

'More decent that your smelly stockings, Ma! I'll never land that millionaire in rotten lisle stockings.'

'I thought you'd finished with men?'

'Oh well . . .' She grinned. 'Here, give us your hanky.' Nora handed the lacy square over to be sprinkled with Goya *Black Rose*. 'Give the boys a treat, eh? Right, we're ready. Now remember, don't eat or drink anything while you're there. I've heard of these places.'

'They're God-fearing people, Lucy, not bloomin' white slavers.'

'More's the pity!'

Saucy cat! She was bearing up well. It was hard to think of her as a grown woman, old enough to be married. Her baby.

At last! she had thought when they'd put the squirming bundle into her arms. A girl. Someone who'd understand. Even her mewing cry was different from the strident bawl of the boys. This one would be easy, undemanding. And so would Fred, now he'd got the daughter he'd wanted. Now she could put up the shutters . . .

She had been wrong on both counts!

The next baby had miscarried, with a little help from 'Aunty' in Islington, and not long after, the shutters had gone up finally and irrevocably on the whole caboodle when poor old Fred died.

And Lucy was never one to be babied; she wasn't one of

52

your clinging, dimply little girls, wanting kisses and cuddles. Sit her on your lap and she'd fight to get down again. She might look as though a puff of wind would blow her away but she had a will of iron and what she wanted was to try out her spindly legs, see where they took her, explore life. You needed eyes in the back of your head. It was no use locking doors or tying her leg to a chair. Proper little Houdini. The times she'd gone missing and they'd found her sitting in the muck in the corner of the chicken run, jabbering to the hens. Or wandering down the street with a bunch of flowers she'd picked Lord knows where. Or one of the neighbour's kids would come pounding on the door:

'Your Lucy's got her head stuck in the school-railings, missus.' Or: 'Your got a little girl with curly hair? You best come quick, she's over the Rec, up this tree.' Or worse.

Nora would rush out in a panic, leaving Jack and Charlie to play in the parlour with the dolls that Lucy never looked at, and there she'd be, down the street in the recreation ground dedicated to the dead of the Great War, white with shock, hanging by the hem of her little frock to a broken branch, or up to her skinny neck in the duck pond.

She'd been glad to pass her over to their gran when Fred died. Times was hard enough. You couldn't have kids running loose round coppers and boiling washing and mangles and that, could you? And they loved going round their gran's. Of course, they'd all be home for their tea and seven kids, all in one go's enough to give your head the arse-ache.

'Ma, Ma, tell 'im, he's 'ad four spuds already, gutsy pig!'
'Ugh, Ma, do I 'ave to sit next to 'im?'
'Don't bolt your food, Mick.'
'Stuffin' it down like there's no tomorrer.'
'If you ain't gonna eat that dumplin' give us it 'ere.'
'Oi! Give us it back, you. I was saving that till last!'
'Too late . . .'
'You bleeder!'
'Mick, language!'
'But, Ma!'
'Oh, stop your squawkin'. You should've ate it while you 'ad the chance.'

53

'Ma, you comin' to the match, Sat'day? They put me in centre 'alf.'

'Nah, she can't. She's 'elping out down the Scouts' Jumble.'

'Who's "she"? The cat's mother?'

'Ma! You said you would, you did, you said—'

'No, she never.'

'She did.'

'Didn't!'

'Did.'

'Quick, Ma, the baby's choking!'

'Bang 'er on the back, Sid. Oi, oi, oi! Not that 'ard! What d'you wanna do that for? You made 'er cry, now, you big lummox! I thought I told you to cut her meat up small. Oh, for God's sake, Lucy, he didn't 'urt you. 'Ave a drink, duck. Pour 'er some water, Chas, there's a good boy.'

'In the cup, Chas, you clumsy little git, not in my bloody dinner!'

'Language, Arthur!'

And so it went on. All night. Arguments, flare-ups, demands, demands, demands.

So what do you do? You get the little ones off to bed, quick as you can, and chase the rest out of your hair, into the street for a muck-around, into the front room for a game of cards or a read, anything so long as you can put your feet up for five minutes before you have to make a start on the ironing. Was it any wonder she looked for a friendly face among the spirits?

Before she knew it Lucy was at school, and then, somehow, Nora had missed her childhood. Gone in a blink. It was only lately, really, that they'd had any time for each other. Woman to woman.

The boys was offhand, that was it. Bleeding handful, boys was. She knew what she'd done. Riding along in a bus, with the boys in front and her and Luce behind. Anything interesting out the window, you lean and tell them. 'See that crane picking up the girder!' Or, 'Look, there's a boat on the river today. Wonder where it's off to.' Or you'd be sitting in the train telling them that that's where Aunt Aggie and Uncle Bert used to live and how you used to play there as a kid, and this and that, and suddenly remember little Luce on your other side who hadn't heard a dicky-bird and you couldn't be bothered to go over it all again, and in any case, you'd gone past the place. Poor old Luce. Never got a look in.

And time was getting on. Put the wind up you, it did, how little time there was. Not that she was scared of dying exactly. The Other Side sometimes looked quite inviting. No more charring. No more washing.

But she wasn't ready just yet. Not now things seemed to be looking up.

Lucy had gripped Nora's arm, painfully, all the way to the meeting house, and Nora was never sure whether the sighing and moaning she heard, as they stepped out along the sand-drifted pavement, was the sea, the wind in the barbed wire, or her daughter with the hump. This was to have been her wedding day, after all.

While Nora was being introduced to some of the leading lights, in the entry hall, she kept one wary eye on her daughter. Twenty already, and looking tall and elegant in her fitted coat and felt hat-on-the-slant, but in her present mood she was quite likely to say something rude. Thankfully, she seemed engrossed in the notice-board, consultation times for healing and clairvoyance, Land Army recruitment and a whistdrive. Maybe it wouldn't be so bad.

'This is Mr Whittaker, Nora,' said Marjorie, at her elbow.

'Mr Whittaker? Oh, oh, right!' Nora allowed herself to tune into what the old man was telling her. How their little church had never been so popular. The war, you know. So much loss and desolation. So many bereaved relatives seeking contact. Sad times, sad times . . .

When she looked again, Lucy was peeping through what seemed to be a curtain made from Army blankets, dyed dark red, and her face, when she turned back to Nora, looked as though she'd been sucking lemons.

It was nothing like the parish church, back home. St Peter's could have swallowed this little meeting-house whole, and a couple more besides. But it was warm. In St Peter's you wore two pairs of drawers and two pairs of socks against the draught, winter and summer. There was no danger of dropping off in the sermon, you was too busy shivering.

55

In the Church of the Holy Spirit the stale, almost foetid, warmth came out to meet you, embraced you as you entered, ushered you down a length of coconut matting and tucked you into your seat.

Both heat and smell could be traced to half a dozen large gasfires, arrayed round the walls like leaky Stations of the Cross. There were few other adornments unless you counted the Michaelmas daisies, languishing in too-big glass vases, with too little water, on either side of the speaker's platform, a kind of landing between two shallow flights of stairs. There was a banner painted high on the wall behind. It bore the legend, in gold and black Gothic on flaky maroon: TO THINE OWN SELF BE TRUE.

Dead brown oilcloth covered the floor, like skin, pressed and moulded to the bones of the boards beneath by years and years of shuffling feet. Here and there, holes had been worn by the attempted scuff and scrape of chairs which, you quickly found, were immobilised by a discreet joining at the hip to the next one along.

The windows, too high for Peeping Toms and sealed with black-out against enemy aircraft, made for stuffiness. It was like hot flushes all over again. She unbuttoned her coat and, with Lucy helping from one side, Marjorie from the other, dragged it off and hung it over the back of the chair. That was better. She'd felt she was suffocating.

Lucky she'd worn her posh frock. She tugged the flowery skirt over her knees, relishing its softness. Home-made, of course, but no one would ever know. It hung satisfactorily over her new stays, and the detail across the bosom, the pleats and the touch of lace, were the latest thing. Lovely bit of stuff. Off a stall down the High Street, or rather, under the stall. Black market. Had to pay over the odds but if you can't make a bit of a splash for your only daughter's wedding, when can you? (Her eyebrows rose and fell with her internal chatter.) She fretted that her hat was maybe a touch too frivolous for church. You could achieve a measure of godliness with the right sort of hat, but this little thing, a froth of bows and netting was more inclined to wickedness. All right for a wedding, but . . .

A busty woman in a complicated hand-knit, smelling of

mothballs, came along with raffle tickets.

'Tuppence each or four for sixpence, but only if you can afford it, dear. For the new roof. War damage, dear,' in reply to Nora's query, nodding her head to the far end of the building. 'They patched it up with corrugated iron but it won't do. Sounds like Fred and Ginger up there whenever it rains. Can't hear yourself think. Gonna have a go, dear? If you win you get a big basket of Victoria plums, no windfalls, or a bag of mixed veg off Dad's allotment.' She nodded at Mr Whittaker. 'He's a good grower.'

People emerged from small side rooms and curtained-off booths, blinking like bemused rabbits. Sensing Nora's curiosity, Marjorie dipped her head. Her cloche was out of the Ark, pulled down over her ears and trimmed with navy-blue felt flowers.

'Iris MacInnes and Connie Ellingham are clairvoyants,' she explained with peppermint breath. 'They give readings before and after the service. Ernie Riches and Ted Brathwaite are healers. You'll meet them, later. Ssshh, they're going to start . . .'

The service got going, surprisingly, with a rousing little ditty, introduced by the raffle-lady:

'Oh Death where is thy sting-a-ling-a-ling,
Oh grave, thy victory?
The bells of hell go ting-a-ling-a-ling
For you but not for me.'

'*Why should the devil have all the good times*?' twitted Marjorie between verses, nudging her arm. Everyone seemed to be enjoying the romp, beating time with their heads, smiling and winking as if they shared some wonderful secret. Only Lucy looked grim.

During the last chorus, Mr Whittaker levered himself out of the front row and made his way slowly up the stairs, one hand on the banister, the other clutching a worn Bible to his chest. He stood on the rostrum, rocking slightly, with his eyes closed, in prayer, presumably.

When everyone had settled down again, the main overhead lights were switched off and the hall was illuminated, solely and dimly, by a few pink-bulbed side-lights.

57

Nora thought it gave the place a cosy feel, but her daughter muttered testily, 'Nothing up my sleeves . . .'

The old man did, indeed, look theatrical, in the pink-dark glow, but he leaned on the rail as though it was a garden wall. You forgot his collar and tie, forgot you'd never seen him before in your life. He was the man-next-door; he'd seen your kids grow up; he was complimenting you on your dahlias. He was pleased to see so many old friends and extended a special welcome to any first-timers, many of whom, he knew, had only recently suffered loss.

"'*Come unto me, all ye that are heavy laden, and I will give you rest*.'" He made it sound as though he was offering you a roll-up. 'For though your dear ones have been snatched from this world in a cruel and barbaric way, they want you to know that they are now beyond hurt, and enjoying the wonderful experiences of the spirit world.'

And his voice could not have been more matter-of-fact as he described how the spirits were waiting, just beyond a prayer, with messages of comfort for the living.

"'*Ask and it shall be given you; seek and ye shall find; knock, and it shall be opened unto you*.'"

'Amen!'

Then he began to pray, and although his creaky voice projected to the back of the hall, he and God might have been discussing the poor state of his onions. For the world he sought peace, for his country, victory, for the congregation, reassurance and reunion with their loved ones, not to mention a spot of eternal bliss, if it could be spared. For himself, and those others whom God had seen fit to bless with psychic gifts, he asked for spiritual armour, 'For loins "girt about with truth", for the breastplate of righteousness . . .' slapping his chest as though hunting for his baccy pouch '. . . for feet "shod with the preparation of the gospel of peace . . .'" grunting a little with the effort of pulling on his invisible wellies. 'For the shield of Faith, the sword of the Spirit – "which is the word of God" – and for the helmet of Salvation.' This last he put on as though it were a favourite cloth cap. There was a furtive rustle as others in his gang did likewise. Nora's fingers twitched but Lucy's look of horror kept them in her lap.

'For, Great Spirit' and here he gave in to temptation and raised his skinny arms to heaven, as many a shaman had done before him, 'Thou knowest that we wrestle not against flesh and blood, but against principalities, against powers, against the rulers of darkness and spiritual wickedness. Father, Great Spirit, grant that we may be able to withstand in the evil day, and having done all, to stand.'

'Amen!'

'Now let us pray silently, friends, for our own needs.'

Into the hush that followed came rattling, as shaky hands opened a box of matches. There was a rasp and a flare split the dark. Now, through the curtained rail, you could see he was lighting a large candle on a table in front of him.

Nora winced as Lucy's tongue sucked the roof of her mouth with a loud Tch! Someone cleared their throat. A book dropped to the floor. It seemed to be getting cooler, and Nora shivered. She didn't want to spoil the stillness by faffing with her coat again. Her hands were still very hot, though. Sweating. She wiped them on her dress and the swishing of the material against her stocking tops seemed to echo through the hall.

Mr Whittaker stared into the flame, but his eyes, glittering in the deep recesses of their sockets, did not blink. His jowls, heavy with light, did not move. He waited.

Everyone waited . . .

. . . As people crept through the doors and the walls, soundlessly jostling one another, seeping through the congregation to gather at the front of the hall, eager to mount the steps of the rostrum, to commune with the families they had left behind.

A fisherman, his shoes squelching water, his voice deep as the sea:

'Annie girl, it's me. Don't 'ee fret, m'dear, I'm all right now, I am, an' that's the truth. So the buggers managed to sink the boat an' all, did they? You can claim on that, ye know. Not a lot but it'll tide y'over till us meet up again . . .'

A woman, middle-class, middle-aged, hat, gloves, smart shoes, smart vowels:

'I hope you know this is me, little love. Just to let you know that I'm fine, so not to worry. About your father, little

59

love; he is very low at the moment. What he did was for the best. See if you can't find it in your heart to forgive him, dear. Take him a present, a book or something. Cheer him up a bit . . .'

Nora frowned, worried at how little of the messages the old man actually passed on. He seemed to be tearing at it, like candy floss, and coming away with little more than the gist. He got the connection with water and the cheering-up-Father bit, but missed the love and concern. To make it seem more than it was he bulked it out with bluff. Stuff about spirit guides, Sisters of Mercy and Hopi Indians. How the departed were preparing gardens for the loved ones, from which they have picked a bouquet of red roses or a bunch of forget-me-nots. How the subject should develop their own healing powers and other psychic gifts by coming into one of the church's 'circles'. The package was then wrapped round with a tissue of auras. Greens and reds and pinks and blues. To hear him, you'd think the hall was wreathed in a smoke haze of rainbows.

'I see green around your heart, my dear, and that makes me suspect that you have a very caring nature. Do you work with children, dear?'

'Now I don't want to alarm you, my friend, but this patch of red in the area of your lower spine, it don't bode well! Do you have a back problem, my friend? Well, the spirits are telling me that you'd be wise to take care of that back. No heavy lifting. Get the missus to take out the dustbin for a change!'

He popped in a few names and places that might have had some bearing on the person's future, slapped on some signif-icant dates, and sealed the lot with 'God bless you!'

It wasn't fair, thought Nora, to muck about with someone's message like that. They'd probably gone to a lot of trouble sorting out what they were going to say in the space provided; like in a telegram. And then he goes and leaves out the important bits.

What would she say, she wondered, if she passed over? If she was bombed or run over by a bus? To the boys? To Lucy? Always supposing someone could get them to come to a meeting like this.

Be a bit cheeky to say, 'Who's certifiable now?'

60

She smiled. Poor old Luce.

'Tripe!' she was muttering under her breath. 'Mumbo jumbo!' She was folded back into her seat like a defensive deckchair, shoulders sticking up, her pretty face pale and suspicious, eyes darting about for clues, for a script or an accomplice, a Boy-Scout doing semaphore. Something. She must think old Whittaker, or some labourer in the field, had really done their homework. How else was he able to get it right so often?

'I'm getting the name Gilbert.'

'Yes, oh, yes!'

'And a child now in spirit. A little girl, with long hair.'

'Maureen!'

It was all so simple, really.

And so exciting. A shiver spilled down the back of Nora's neck, making her scrunch up her shoulders to catch it.

She felt Marjorie's eyes on her and flashed her a happy smile.

Marjorie was nice. They were all nice. Ordinary and nice. That was it, really: she was comfortable here. She fitted in, without pain, like a bunion into an old slipper. Not a freak, not here.

He was making mistakes now. The poor old stick was past it. His second sight was dim and his hearing off. She found herself correcting or prompting him, under her breath, until a sharp dig in the ribs made her stop.

'I see a family likeness. Your father, is it? Same piercing eyes as you. And he's wearing a uniform. Was he in the services?'

'No,' came the disappointed reply, 'he never wore uniform.'

Lucy snorted mirthlessly.

No, thought Nora, the father didn't, but the grandfather did. Guard, First World War. That was the grandfather Mr Whittaker could see. The poor bloke kept telling him but the old man didn't catch it; too busy wittering on about May or June being a time for celebrations.

'Is there a Joan or a Jane here tonight?' he dithered.

'Only about six of each,' hissed Lucy.

He fastened on one. 'Well, dear, George says he's finished

his bath . . . or that could be path, yes, he's finished laying it and the garden is perfect now. He can't wait for you to see it. He sends you a big bunch of lilies.'

'Lilies?'

'Arum lilies, his favourite.'

'Not arum lilies. They reminded him of funerals.'

'Ah . . . No, of course, my mistake, they're tiger lilies, aren't they? Tiger lilies, of course.'

'Is your husband in spirit?' he asked a silver-haired old dear.

'That's a pretty safe bet,' mumbled Lucy.

'He's here now. A smartly dressed man. Always very smart, in suit and collar and tie.'

The little old lady was looking puzzled.

'Whenever he went out he liked to look smart.'

The old girl was shaking her head.

'Probably a brickie!' chortled Lucy.

'He's waiting for you to join him. Oh, not yet . . . no, no,' he added hastily. 'You have a long while to go. Hrrmph!' He cleared his throat. 'He seems to be rubbing his chest. Was it chest trouble that took him? Heart or lungs?'

'Usually is,' muttered the sceptic.

The raffle-lady had been hovering at the foot of the stairs for a few minutes. He had seen her but hadn't chosen to take the hint.

'He had a bit of a temper, your old man. A bit hasty – no? Ah, I see, that was his trouble, he's saying, he tended to bottle up his feelings. Not a very demonstrative man, at all. Didn't throw his arms around you as much as you might have wished.'

The old lady was looking more and more confused.

In desperation Whittaker said, 'Well, there's a strong love-link, now, my dear. He cares very much for you. God bless you. Now, who's next?'

The raffle-lady bounded up the stairs, grey perm bristling and, grabbing one of her father's wasted old arms, hauled him away.

They had another hymn and the notices and the collection. A couple of ladies ducked out to put the kettle on, and then it was someone else's turn on the rostrum. A younger man in soldier's uniform. His face was familiar.

Lucy cocked her head. 'It's Eric!' she whispered, 'from the train. The spotty one.'

'Who? Good Gawd, it is an' all. Eric. Well, I never.'

'I wonder if Joe is here, too?' Lucy craned her neck and was clearly disappointed not to catch sight of a ginger head.

Nora crossed her fingers for Eric but she needn't have bothered. True, he took a long time to compose himself, eyes closed, but when he opened them, when he began to speak, he was very different from the shrinking violet they had met earlier. Without blushing or stammering, he held the fort for a good ten minutes, relaying two or three messages, word for word and no trimmings.

Nora clapped wildly as he came down the stairs. That wasn't quite the thing to do, apparently.

This time it was Marjorie who nudged her.

'Go on, go on,' she urged. 'Your turn!'

And so Nora, hot and flustered, squeezed past her daughter, ignoring her horrified looks and picked her way through the spectral throng (''Scuse me, duck, can I just . . .? Ta, love. Oh, beg pardon, I'm sure.'), down the aisle to the front of the hall.

You couldn't move in the tea-room afterwards, with people clamouring to shake her hand, thank her, congratulate her – kiss her, even. Others had their diaries out to book her for meetings and readings. Could she come to Walton? They'd love her in Felixstowe, and she'd go down a bomb in Colchester.

She told them that she wasn't a proper clairvoyant, that Marjorie had said she had to be trained, and that.

'Nonsense. You're a natural, my dear. A remarkably clear eye.'

'Spot on,' Marjorie concurred, with a glow.

Nora blushed even deeper. She told them regretfully, 'I'm only up 'ere till tomorrer, then I'm off 'ome.'

But that didn't seem to put them off; they'd come down to London or, better still, pay her expenses to come back to Clacton. Perhaps a tour could be organised. Or they could put her on the circuit . . .

63

'Ooh, I don't know. Matron's a bit funny about us taking time off.'

'We'll make it worth your while, Nora.'

'How d'you mean?' she wanted to know, and her jaw dropped at their generous offers. But she made no promises. She'd have to talk it over with her daughter, she said firmly.

Lucy, of course, was nowhere to be seen, not even when Nora craned on tiptoe, not even when Marjorie stood on a chair. Someone said they'd seen her leaving the hall during Nora's clairvoyancy. Off to stretch her legs, Nora guessed. She still liked a wander. Growing up hadn't changed her.

She drained her cup and went off to find her girl. Again. While Marjorie and Doris, the raffle-lady, tried to divert the crowd by getting Mr Whittaker to pick tickets out of his trilby hat, for a basket of fruit, a bag of mixed veg and a pair of knitted mittens, popped in at the last minute.

# Chapter Seven

It was black-out dark when eventually she found Lucy, a shadowy figure on a shadowy wall outside a brooding hulk which was the guesthouse. She was staring into the muddled distance where sea mirrored night.

'Look, Ma.' Her voice squeezed through her lips. 'Look at the smithereens floating on the water.'

'Eh?' Nora's bloom of happiness gave way to a chill of foreboding. It was always a bad sign when Lucy tried to be clever.

'Smithereens,' her daughter said. 'The half-moon's other half fell into the sea, and was blown to smithereens by mines.'

The wind tugged at her hair and her skin gleamed cold. Nora squinted at her. What was she supposed to say to such whimsy? 'Oh!' or 'Fancy!' or 'Never mind, duck?' It was hard to tell in the dark. She sounded browned off. Bitter, even.

'Thanks for coming tonight, Luce.'

The girl muttered something that became the angry roar of a wave being thrown out onto the beach.

'What?'

'I said you didn't need me,' she said flatly. 'I could've gone to the concert.' The sea changed its mind, and sucked back what it had lost.

'You never wanted to go to no concert! Beethoven was boring, you said. Anyway, I did need you.'

'Oh, no. You didn't need anybody. You knew exactly what they wanted and you gave it to them. They loved you.' She paused, whispered, 'I didn't,' and this time Nora heard her. She had known, of course.

She said nothing.

'I hated every minute, watching you . . . *perform*!' Her snarl was as sharp, as cruel as the barbs on the wire, also glinting with the moon's 'smithereens', that rolled on, on and on, down both sides of the road, beyond the limits of night-vision.

The churning ocean filled the silence as Nora continued to wait. She was used to the pain of children.

'What you were doing to those people, Ma, manipulating them, trading on their grief . . . that was so cruel. How could you? How *could* you!'

Nora could only shake her head in wonder.

She hadn't thought of it like that at all. Trading on their grief? She wouldn't. She wasn't like that. Not cruel. No. How could Lucy even think . . .? She had failed, then. Her success tonight was nothing. With her daughter she had failed.

Funny how things had turned out. Instead of it being Lucy's big day it was all hers. It was she, Nora, who had crossed the threshold. Come into her own. And when they were pleased with her, when they told her she was a very good channel indeed, her happiness made her almost want to cry.

Really, she had known as soon as she mounted that rostrum. As soon as she had told the young wife of that soldier how anxious he was about having to leave her up the spout; as soon as she had let him speak through her:

'I know about the baby, Sal, and I'm real proud. She's going to have the best mum in the world. Call her Susan, will you? After me mum. Tell her about me, won't you? Tell her I love you both and we'll all meet up again one fine day. And you mustn't worry, Sal, you're gonna meet Bill, a smashing bloke, and if you've any sense you'll marry him, 'cos he'll be a good dad to the kiddy and love you just like I do. Thinking of you . . .'

She had heard the sharp intake of long-held breath, seen the intensity on people's faces as they sat forward in their chairs, heard their grunts of approval and satisfaction.

Then there was the little boy in the striped pyjamas, taken

66

early in the Blitz. Poor little mite. This was the first time his mother had heard from him.

'It's smashing here for kids, Mum. There's swimming and the water's really warm. Me and my friend, Tommy, we've got a smashing raft! We're going to sail round the world . . . well, round this place, anyway. His mum's here, too, and she's looking after me. She makes smashing rice pudding. She says you're not to worry . . .'

'Smashing . . .' sobbed his mother.

There was Harold who wanted to tell his mate, Nobby, that the pain in his leg had stopped and he was running around like a spring chicken. There was David who'd been shot down on a bombing raid over Cologne, reassuring his parents that his eyes were fine now and he was working on a sculpture of his grandmother, with whom he had been reunited.

Dozens of them. She'd been well away. It was as if she had suddenly discovered she could sing or turn somersaults. She couldn't stop. And no one had wanted her to. In the end, she had sort of come to and there was Doris, tapping her on the arm, saying, 'Well done, Nora. Bravo!'

To the congregation Doris had said, 'Worth waiting for, wasn't she?' And as they applauded and stamped their feet and whistled, she remembered that they had been expecting her.

They had all been so kind. Eric and Stan and Mildred and Doris and Myrtle. So many kind people.

Eric said, 'You're a d-d-dark horse, N-Nora. I never thought, on the t-t-train, never imagined . . . And this is your first t-t-t-time, they t-tell me. That can't be right?' When she assured him that it was, he said, 'That's incredible. G-g-gosh. D-d-don't know what you do now but I strongly s-s-suggest that you give it up s-s-s-s' . . . He tried again '. . . Immediately and become a c-c-c-clairvoyant. You have a wonderful gift.'

It *was* wonderful. No matter what Lucy said, it was bloomin' marvellous!

They were poles apart. Lucy didn't, couldn't, *wouldn't* understand and it was no earthly use arguing. She did anyway.

'Luce, you got it all wrong, duck.' But the girl was already bristling. Nora got in first. 'No, *you* listen for once!' she said. 'So bleeding quick to give me an ear-bashing, *you* listen. You're a fine one to talk about cruel. Think you're so bleeding clever, know it all, calling me names. What was that last one? "Mental", weren't it? Something choice ... Oh, I know: "certifiable"! If that ain't bleeding cruel, I don't know what is.

'Just because you don't get it ... Just because you can't see no further than the end of your nose, flipping Doubting Thomas. I ain't cruel, Luce, and I ain't round the bend, neither. I speak as I find, and them at the church are happy to take my word for it. *And* they tell me I'm doing a bloody good job.'

'Well, they're sadly mistaken, aren't they?'

'Why should they be wrong and Lucy Potter right?'

'Because there's no such thing as the Other Side and,' she sneered, 'astral entities. It's all a load of hooey!'

'If that's what you believe then I'm sorry for you. It's your loss, is all I can say.'

Lucy swung her head away and the wind whipped her hair across her face, masking her defiance.

Nora leaned round, trying to catch her eye. Her coat flapped and she had to hold her hat on. 'What can I do to convince you that it's a good thing I'm doing? If only you could see with my eyes, just for a minute. A second. D'you know, there was a time, when you was a baby, I could've sworn you could. Old Auntie Vi would go "cootchie, cootchie" at you and you'd kick your little legs up and laugh ... And I swear, as a toddler, you tried to walk through the wall after one of them. Got a nasty bump on your head. I thought, thank God, at long last I got someone to share it with. 'Cos it was bloody lonely sometimes – more of a curse than a gift, I tell you. But it was just wishful thinking.' She paused, but the denial didn't come. 'Still, I got more than enough people to share it with now, more than enough. And they can't all be mad, or cruel!'

The girl gave a disdainful snort.

'Getting in an 'uff ain't going to 'elp, gel. Won't change nothing. Why'n't you try and be 'appy for me, eh? Stead of all this.'

68

Lucy turned to face her, clawing hair out of her mouth, eyes sparkling with misery.

'Would you be happy for *me* if I got into witchcraft and devil-worship?'

'It ain't the same thing at all.'

'Oh, *ain't* it?' she mimicked cruelly and, with a toss of her head, flounced down the path, as a tall, flapping darkness strode into the street. It was Marjorie, back from the meeting-house, who clucked in alarm to see them standing out in the cold, and bundled them into the warm.

'You should have knocked,' she said. 'Someone would have let you in.'

It was the black-out, of course. No one could tell from the street that inside, the house was light and warm, that there were people sitting in the lounge, reading, listening to the wireless, waiting for supper.

Up in their room, mother and daughter only just had time to glare at each other in the mirror, when the gong sounded.

'That was quick!' Nora commented, meeting her friend in the hall, aware of Lucy sulking at her back.

Marjorie confessed she had prepared it all beforehand: a cold platter of seafood: soused herrings, cockles, shrimps and winkles, fresh off the boat that morning, she said, served up with bread and marge, watercress and beetroot. All she'd had to do when she came in from 'Meeting' was whip the covers off the dishes and put the urn on.

'And it's all right, is it?' Nora whispered. 'Leaving this lot on their own?' Her chin pointed to other guests on their way to the dining room. You'd hardly credit it. Back home, you'd be asking for trouble, leaving strangers in the house while you popped out for an hour or two; you'd come back and find they'd cleaned you out.

'Oh yes. Tom and Edna keep an eye on things.' She introduced them to a spindly, white-haired couple at a table near the fire. 'They're my permanent residents,' she said fondly. 'They have the room next to yours. Tom and Edna are Londoners, too.'

'Maida Vale.' Edna's clipped accents explained everything.

69

'Over the other side.' Nora nodded. A different species, these two; not to be compared . . .

'We decided to see out the war from a safer distance.'

'Evacuated, did you? Don't blame you. Wish I could get away. Gives you the ike, bleedin' Jerry whacking away at you, night after night, never knowin' if you're gonna wake up dead!'

'Why can't you get away, Nora?'

'Ooh no! There's me job and me chickens and everything. And Lucy.'

The dining room was filling up. In between fetching water-jugs from the hatch in the wall, Marjorie told them about the other guests.

There was the War Official with business at the barracks. He was going back to Whitehall in the morning. He ignored Nora altogether and grunted through a mouthful of bread and marge at Lucy. She frowned at his fatherly wink and got on with the more important business of pouring water. Nora pulled a face when he wasn't looking but Lucy's remained deadpan. Buster Keaton wasn't in it. She wasn't giving an inch.

Nora sighed, recalling the ding-dongs she used to have with her own mother. Sometimes they wouldn't speak for days.

At the next table was Connie, the young wife of one of the Butlin's camp gunnery instructors. She had a three-month-old baby son upstairs. She said she'd rather tag along with her husband than be sent off somewhere on her own. He'd had four different postings since they'd been married. The baby had been born at the second one, in Lancashire. Phil, her hubby was called. He'd be popping in later, if he could get away.

'And that's Audrey Bibbings over there,' Marjorie said, indicating a large, youngish woman in tweeds. 'Our Aud's with the War Ag. She's up here every weekend seeing to the girls, Thursday night till Saturday.'

Nora looked around, half-expecting to see little girls with Our Aud's Creamola cheeks and tea-cosy perm. Seeing none she had to ask, 'War Ag?'

'War Agriculture Committee. She looks after the Land

70

Army girls.' Marjorie's teacher-voice then sailed over the clatter of the meal to the back of the room. 'Takes you for ever, doesn't it, Aud? Traipsing round all the farms, week in, week out? She has her little car, of course,' she confided, 'otherwise it'd be impossible.' She sang out again, 'Every farm between here and Colchester, isn't it, Aud?'

'The whole blasted peninsula!' Audrey put on a mantle of lead, so heavy it made her eyes and jaw and shoulders sag. 'God, what a job! Listening to all their moans, sorting out their problems.' Her words didn't tally with the smile in her voice. She obviously loved her job.

'Watches over them like a mother hen, don't you, Audrey?'

'Someone has to.'

Marje lowered her voice, her eyes, her lean bottom onto a chair at their table. Nora thought she was going to hear something saucy and leaned closer. 'Takes them their wages, too,' Marjorie whispered. 'Keep it under your hat, though. Don't want her to get waylaid, do we? Not that there's much to take. They don't get a lot, poor things.'

Not to let her disappointment show, Nora said, 'Still, it's an 'ealthy life, innit? Out in the fresh air, making the hay?'

'It's a hard blasted life,' came Audrey's stern retort. (Ears like a bleedin' bat, thought Nora.) 'Some of those farmers are real tartars. They want a man's work out of girls no stronger than, um, your daughter there.' There was a note of enquiry hanging in the air, along with the smell of fish and vinegar.

Lucy looked up from tickling a winkle from its shell with a pin, caught Audrey's eye. And smiled. A big, bold, friendly smile.

'Lucy,' she introduced herself. 'Lucy Potter. This is my mother, Nora. We're here for the weekend.'

'Lovely!' said Aud.

Nora regarded her child suspiciously. She's cheered up all of a sudden, she thought. What's brought this on?

And when she turned to Marjorie, drawling compliments about the meal, Nora felt such a stab of anxiety, she had to change her mind about the forkful of cockles she had raised to her lips. Cockles on a nervous stomach can play you up for days. She selected bread and butter instead.

71

'Isn't it, Ma?' Lucy was saying.

'Eh?'

'Smashing supper, isn't it? I don't know how you do it, Marjorie, all on your own.'

Marjorie was also up to something. Absently pinching the head off one of Nora's shrimps, she explained that, in fact, she had help during the week. A woman came in to do the cleaning, she said (removing the legs), and another to lend a hand with cooking the evening meals; it was only at weekends she had to fend for herself. And she popped the rest of the creature into her prim mouth, and crunched it audibly, skin, tail and all.

Licking her fingers, she rose to answer the call of duty, and did another circuit of the tables, collecting dirty plates and doling out individual jelly trifles but the look of bemusement never left her face.

So it came as no surprise when, leaning over their table, five minutes later, she said, 'Nora, dear, if you've a minute after supper, I've a proposition I'd like to put to you.'

# Chapter Eight

She had been in bed for ages but sleep was the last thing on her mind. She lay stiff and awake on the pulpy mattress, despite the hushing of the sea-swell. Her brain fizzed with strategies, bubbled with images.

There was the one where she turned over in bed, remarking sleepily: '*Oh, by the way, Ma, I'm leaving tomorrow . . .*'

The idea bloomed, like soap blown through an 'O' of finger and thumb, floating on her mind, the figures distorting, revolving, separating.

She tried again. Ma was undressing, unrolling her stockings, her broad back to Lucy so the girl didn't have to see her face. Breathe gently, this was a delicate one. '*Ma, I've been thinking . . . we've not been seeing eye to eye lately. Wouldn't it be best all round . . .?*'

Round and round it went in her mind, shiny, attractive . . .

The skin of the next idea quivered and grew, and there she was reflected in the dressing-table mirror, cold-cream on her face, turning to Ma as she entered the room, and making a statement: '*Ma, I've decided, enough is enough – I'm going!*'

It swung away, heavily rolling and turning.

What about weeping into her pillow, more or less distraught? '*I can't stand any more, Ma! I'm taking the first train home in the morning to pack my things . . .*' quickly formed and as quickly released. Too dramatic.

She inhaled and prepared to be gentle, smiling indulgently as Ma jumped into bed in her fluffy pink bed-socks: '*Think I'll leave you to get on with this ghost thing on your own, Ma. I'll only be in the way . . .*' This image was a pretty thing and

73

she toyed with it as a possibility.

It was when she ran her mind's eye over the gamut of Ma's likely reactions that the bubbles burst. She wouldn't take it kindly, being left on her own, however it was put to her. She'd be dreadfully hurt. Whether she wept or begged or raged or went into one of her stony silences, how was Lucy going to deal with that?

Play it by ear.

Because it had to be done tonight, somehow, and where was Ma?

Three times she had pattered across the landing lino, to peer over the banisters for her, the second time narrowly missing Carruthers of the War Office, on his way from the lavatory. Carruthers. It had to be something like that. Or Blenkinsop. Or Fortesque-Smythe. Something upper-crusty, something laughable. You had to laugh. He was too slimy to be taken seriously. He'd told her to call him Cecil, but she couldn't. He was the sort you kept at spitting distance, right from the start. Wouldn't he have thought he'd died and gone to heaven to have found her hanging around in her new pyjamas?

She'd waited a good twenty minutes after hearing his door click shut before venturing out again. And Ma was still down there jawing to Marjorie.

In a funny way she felt jealous of the peg doll, privy to confidences that Ma could not now share with her. A wedge was sliding between mother and daughter. Subtle and thin but painful, nevertheless – although it could be useful.

What Ma was doing, of course, was giving Lucy time to drop off so that she could slip into her side of the bed without getting into another row. Counting on sleep blurring and blunting Lucy's anger. But Lucy needed her to think the wedge was sharp and keen. She needed a hook to hang her leaving on. She couldn't risk sleep.

As the War Ag woman had pointed out, Lucy was not her mother's keeper.

'You have to make your own life, dear. Your own life and your own mistakes, and let your mother make hers.'

Nora wasn't old or frail, she said, not dependent in any

way. There was no need at all for Lucy to feel responsible. If her mother wanted to be a medium, if she got herself mixed up in this barmy spiritualist cult of Marjorie's, that was up to her, surely? It wasn't as if she was doing any harm.

'Oh, but she is!' Lucy protested, and quickly glanced around in case anyone else in the lounge had overheard her outburst. The other guests seemed to be listening to ITMA or reading; all except Carruthers, who was making a big thing of pretending to write up his report, frowning when anyone laughed or spoke. If he'd wanted quiet, thought Lucy, why hadn't he stayed in his room? She knew why. He leered at her now, and raised a sweaty hand. 'He-ello-oo . . .' She swivelled her eyes away. Creep.

Lowering her voice, she fixed her gaze on the draughts board that lay between them on the table. 'You didn't *see* them, Audrey! They were crying, some of them – beside themselves!'

'Oh, poor things!' Audrey's fat cheeks lengthened in concern.

'No, no, they weren't sad.' It was important that this pleasant woman understood. 'They were happy, imagining they were really in touch with dead people. It was awful.'

'*Shall I do you now, sir?*' The catchphrase caught them unawares and they waited for the laughter around them to fade.

'Why was it awful, dear?'

'Because it was *lies*.'

'But you say it made them happy? Cheered them up?'

'Oh, yes.'

'So where's your problem?'

Surely that was obvious? 'It gives them false hopes, doesn't it?'

Audrey's eyes had beamed behind her spectacles, little blue crescent moons. 'False hopes?' she chuckled, huffing five of Lucy's pieces in one go. 'Oh dear, Lucy, life is still very black and white for you, isn't it? Your move.'

Lucy was disappointed. This was not the meeting of minds she had looked for when she had confided in Audrey Bibbings. Instead she was being patted on the head. Laughed at. She wasn't a child; she was twenty. Old enough to see

75

now that Audrey wasn't a source of wisdom, after all. Moodily she took the most obvious of Audrey's pieces.

'King, please,' demanded the other woman, triumphantly huffing home and rapping her draught on Lucy's side of the board. 'My dear girl, they'll never know there's no Other Side if you don't tell them. And aren't false hopes better than no hopes at all?'

'No,' said Lucy firmly, thinking, even as she said it, that it did sound a little harsh. Maybe even a bit immature and silly. But Audrey was beginning to sound like that snooty woman who answered the problems in *House and Home*.

'Oh, my dear . . . does it matter? Really? Does it matter if these people believe in something that makes them happy, if it helps them to get over their grief and loneliness?'

Lucy frowned in order to hide a smile. Oh, my dear, how awfully, awfully . . .

'No, Audrey,' she was able to say, at last. 'They ought to grieve properly and then get on with their lives. It's like believing in Father Christmas. It's not the adult thing to do.'

'Hmm. Have you had someone close to you die, Lucy?'

'My gran. My dad,' said Lucy, with a small sense of triumph. That do you? But she didn't say it aloud.

'Ah,' said Audrey.

Perhaps, she had suggested some minutes later, after winning the game, as she settled her large, unfettered behind into the sofa – Perhaps, she said, sipping her cocoa thoughtfully . . . Perhaps Lucy was just too close to this business of her mother's. She rested her cup on her saucer and contemplated the fragrant liquid. Perhaps it was time, she said at last, sliding Lucy a sideways glint, time for her to let go . . . She paused then, and bit her lip, obviously thinking better of completing the sentence. But Lucy knew: *Time for her to let go of her mother's apron strings* was what she had left unsaid. *Time for her to stop being a Mummy's girl*, was what she meant.

'It might be an idea,' she said finally, 'for you to get right away, leave your Ma to do things on her own.'

*If only.*

'I don't see why you don't trust her,' she went on. 'She seems to me like a very capable woman.'

76

Lucy gave a deprecating little laugh which the fat woman caught neatly and threw back.

'Oh, come on, Lucy, let her have her ghosts to play with!'

'They'll lock her up!'

'Strangely, my dear, they don't lock you up for talking to ghosts. They have to give you the benefit of the doubt, the facts in the matter being rather on the thin side. You can talk to ghosts or God or your old pet parrot, if you want, and they can't do a thing about it.'

'No, but they can have a good laugh at your expense.'

'Aha!' Her eyes opened round, full-moon, and her double-chin swelled into her neck. 'Or your daughter's, eh?'

Lucy had blinked. Was that what it was all about?

Had she been asleep? She stretched a foot into her mother's side of the bed and found it still cold and smooth, virginal. God, whatever time was it? Come on, Ma. You must have said it all by now. Some of us want an early start in the morning. Sighing, she threw back the covers again and stepped down onto the rag-rug. Turned to flick the blankets back to keep the warmth in and, on a sudden whim, no more, turned again towards the window.

One last look at the moon on the sea, the wispy clouds passing in front of the bright half-face, thousands of miles distant. She drew back the heavy black-out curtain and saw Roy standing there on the garden path.

The bugger!

He tipped up his head and she drew back quickly, letting the curtain drop as she sank against the wall, her skin pricking with sweat, her blood pounding in her ears. Take it easy, she told herself firmly. Breathe, breathe. Deeply. Oh God. What did he think he was doing? He knew it was all over. There wasn't a chance in hell of them picking up the pieces. He wasn't going to be a nuisance, was he?

Perhaps it wasn't him at all. Could be someone wanting a room for the night. On a late pass, missed the curfew or something. Perhaps it was that Joe back from his concert. Perhaps the uniform had been grey-blue, not khaki. It was hard to tell in the dark. She thought she heard the crunch of gravel as she lifted the curtain again.

77

He'd gone.

*Ma was shaking her, too roughly.*

Don't.

'*Lucy, Lucy . . .*'

She didn't want to surface. She was so deep, so far down, it was so hard.

'*Lucy, wake up, duck!*'

She didn't want to leave it unopened, that door down there. The last door. The last of Roy's doors. Across the meadow, down the steps, looming dark-black-wood, locked tight against the wailing, the bitter wailing. She reached back, back and down . . .

'Luce, you *gotta* wake up, gel! It's an air-raid. Quick!'

'Oh blimey!'

Wide awake now, she leapt out of bed, found her own coat and bundled Ma into hers. Then grabbing up their shoes and handbags, she pushed her mother through the door, and thudded behind her, pell-mell down the stairs to the siren's wailing. And even as she ran she thanked God.

It had only been a dream, of course. Roy hadn't been there at all. All part of a silly dream.

The wailing stopped as they reached the last few stairs and was immediately taken up by a fractious baby. Marjorie was gripping the newel post and hopping up and down in her dressing gown, her long black plaits turning it into a war-dance.

'Down there!' she urged, waggling a pale finger towards a trap doorway, which lay, an open mouth in the floor, howling with the voice of the child. Her eyes, meanwhile, continued to rake the stairs.

'Where are Tom and Edna? Oh Lord, you might have given them a knock.'

Give her a couple of eagle feathers and she'd be Whatsisname? Sitting Bull. Lucy giggled aloud; her sense of relief about the dream was making her quite light-headed, emergency or no. But it was true. Look at the woman, grabbing the tom-toms off the table hall (well, the dinner-gong, then), and banging away for all she was worth.

'Wake up, wake up, you deaf old—'

78

'Marje, Marje!' Ma was yelling over the din. 'They're on their way. He 'ad the door open as we come past. Look, 'ere they are.'

'Oh, quick, quick, you two,' as the old couple plied their long limbs between the stairs, like stick insects. They had taken blankets off their beds and slung them over their stooped shoulders.

'So sorry, so sorry,' Edna twittered, in her pearls-and-cashmere voice, as Marjorie closed the cellar door on the faint hum of war engines.

'She would go back for her teeth,' her husband explained testily.

'Oh, *Tom*!'

Lucy was not surprised to feel an eloquent elbow nudging her as they waited for the others to take their seats on rolls of old carpet and packing cases. Her mother had not taken to 'Maida bloomin' Vale' at all.

'Tomorrow they move to the ground floor,' vowed Marjorie, shepherding the stragglers away from the cellar steps into the vast subterranean chamber, 'if we still have a ground floor,' she muttered.

'The Jerries won't waste their bombs on Clacton, will they?' Lucy asked, rubbing her arms against the cold.

'They won't *want* to,' someone said.

'Probably leave us alone altogether if it wasn't for Phil and his lot at Butlin's.' Connie paused to light a cigarette. 'They have to have a pop at the enemy, I suppose, being coastal defence, but I keep telling him, all it does is give their position away – and ours.'

Lucy's incredulity at the crass remark must have shown on her face, for Audrey gave her a large wink as she made room for mother and daughter on a dusty chaise-longue, shoving up to cover, generously, a place where horse-hair stuffing burst from the torn upholstery.

'We've had bombs, strafing, planes coming down, the lot.' Marjorie appeared almost to preen at the attention the enemy paid them.

'Sounds like 'ome,' Ma remarked, looking immensely smug about it, Lucy couldn't help thinking. Was this a competition? About who had suffered more?

'Nothing *like* as bad.' Now the other Londoners, the elderly refugees, were joining in, and suggesting, by sorrowful shakings of their white heads that Marjorie was a bit of a fusser, that they'd have been perfectly safe in their room. Warmer, too.

A chill draught, sharp with the fossil smell of coal, drifted through from a doorless and dark second chamber at their back.

'It's freezing down here,' Edna was complaining, from beneath a mound of blanket. 'We'll all die of pneumonia, if the Germans don't get us first.'

'Oh Gawd, look at you, all to cock and any old how. You've left your poor old legs out in the cold.' And so saying, Ma whipped away the blankets, without ceremony and ignoring Edna's squawks, rearranging them so that the exposed ankles, blue-tinged and scrawny, were tucked properly inside.

'Safest place to be, down here, cold or not,' said Marjorie.

'I should say so!' Phil, Connie's soldier husband, was jigging nervously across the stone flags, around ancient wash-stands and tallboys, absently patting the squawling bundle on his shoulder with a heavy hand. 'I know where I'd rather be . . .' though the tightness of his lips belied his words. He jerked his head upwards, at the whoomp and rat-tat-tat of anti-aircraft fire. 'Christ,' his voice was quiet, reverential, 'listen to that! We're chucking everything at 'em tonight.' His expression, as he glanced at Carruthers, seemed to contain a question. Was it about the vigour of the defence, or the inclusion of some new weapon, or rocket or a gun, whose voice he had recognised?

What a strange skill, thought Lucy. As a gunnery instructor he must know the guns as well as he knew his child. Better. He could strip them down, clean them up, knew their weight and girth and all their funny little ways, including all their teething troubles. In Carruthers's returning glare was a warning: *Keep it shut, sunshine.*

Despite having a late pass, Phil clearly felt his duty lay elsewhere, as anxious a parent in his way as Connie, who was hovering on her rickety bench, ready to snatch her baby from its father at the first sign of danger or clumsiness. As he paced beneath it, the unshaded bulb began to dance and flakes of ancient whitewash floated down. Then the light went out and Lucy's arms were clutched from each side. The sharp intake of breath was Audrey's, the electric quiver that jumped across into her own frame was Audrey's, the voice that hissed into the rumbling darkness, 'Blasted Jerries,' was Audrey's. Nora's grip was fierce. Protective.

The enemy planes had made it past the first line of defence.

Somebody switched on a torch and a couple of candles were lit. The baby stopped crying at last, fascinated by the flickering flames.

Silent thoughts reverberated against the walls of their dungeon and all along the east coast.

'So now we must wait,' said Carruthers, with a curl of his lip and a tug of his moustache, 'while they nip down to London, drop their bombs and then nip back again. Any suggestions as to how we pass the time, eh, Lucy?'

Lucy pretended not to hear, pulling her coat tight across her pink winceyette pyjama bottoms.

'Oh Nora,' said Edna imperiously, 'you can't have fixed this blanket properly. There's a draught like cold steel going up my legs. Would you . . .?'

'I'll give you cold steel,' muttered Ma, twitching the blanket, nevertheless, across the offending gap. 'What am I now, a flamin' lady's maid?'

Lucy felt a great surge of affection for her mother.

'At least Jerry won't have anything left to drop on us,' said Connie, stubbing out her cigarette, 'by the time he gets back here.' Empty-handed she reached for the baby, which began immediately to cry again.

'Don't count on it,' said Marjorie.

It was while Marjorie and Phil were attempting to light a couple of smoky Valor stoves, hampered both by helpful advice and complaints about the fumes, that Lucy told her mother, in a whisper, how sorry she was for her earlier behaviour.

'Till the next time,' said her mother, grimly.

'No, really, Ma. It's not for me to tell you how to run your life.'

'Changed your tune, aincha?' Coughing conspicuously,

81

she flapped at curling wisps of black smoke, and muttered something about babies and dirty wicks.

'Um, well, I've been doing a bit of thinking.'

'Me an' all.' As her mother's face creased into a broad and beaming smirk, the candlelight making her look positively demonic, Lucy felt someone walk over her grave.

'Oh?'

'Yeah.' She nodded decisively. 'I'm getting out of London, Luce.'

'What!'

'Stoppin' up 'ere with Marje. Oh, not for ever,' she laughed. 'Gawd, you wanna see your face! Only till I get the hang of this spiritualist lark.'

'But – but Ma . . .' as the ground slipped from under her. This wasn't how it was supposed to have gone. What had got into the woman? She hardly knew her mother. Suiting herself? Putting herself first? This was betrayal and it was all wrong.

'You'll be all right in number 41 till I get back, won't you? It makes sense, duck,' she said, though Lucy was looking at her aghast. 'They'll pay me, see, more'n I get up the hospital so I can send you the rent. Marje reckons I can do it on me head. She'll let me stop with her and I can give her an 'and with the cleaning and the cooking and that – pay for me keep, like . . .'

'But Ma, I can't.' She became aware of solid insistent pressure against her thigh and had half-turned to glare at Audrey when she realised that this was her cue.

# Chapter Nine

*Sea Breezes*
77 Kings Road
Clacton

*December 10th 1942*

Dear Lucy,

Hoping this finds you as it leaves me settling in Alrite, I mean. Thanks for your Christmas card and I wish you all the best for Christmas to.

The Move went off without an itch. Ted Next Door drove us up which was kind of him to come all this way just for the price of the petrol. Evrything was covered in Coal Dust me and all but Beggars can't be Choosers. He said he wanted to black his Nose and I said he done that evry day seeing hes a Coalman he just wanted to show off his new Lorry if you ask me. Lucky for me he got rid of that old Horse and Cart or wed still of been on the road come Christmas. He is good Company Ted his Mrs dont no how lucky she is Reglar Wages coming in and him not having to be away fighting the War.

What a job we had getting them Chickens crated up! I tell you Old Randy Rooster near finished up with Sage and Onion stuffed up his bum pardon my French. The fight he put up he must of reckoned his end had come. What a palarver Lucy fethers flying and Randy crowing and flapping his old wings for all he was worth a right old Carry on it was. I had hold of his feet but he took a lump out of my hand and I had to leave go and oh Lucy he only took off over the Back Fense didn't he! I fort we

83

had lost him that will lern me to get his Wings clipped that will. I fort they was but they cood not of been, Lucky Over the Back had all come out to see what the rackit was and there Bert threw a Sack over him. Anyhow we got him here in one peace but I still got a nasty place where he peck my arm. Marje and me made a nice little coop out the back for him and the girls. Shes give them the run of her back yard. She is expeckting new-layed Eggs for Breckfast I reckon. Only thing is what with the move and the wing-clipping we give them to be on the safe side they all got the right Hump. The Hens have stop laying and they are all pecking each others bums to Buggary. That Doris at the Church give us some little cardboard Blinkers you fix over their Beeks to stop them seeing the next ones behind to pull its Fethers out. Funny it works a Treet but they do look a sight wandering round like there Blind with there poor little bear Chicken bums wagging in the Wind. Your Gran said to knit them some bloomers stop them getting Frost bit on the Parsons nose! Her and her bright Idears!

### December 12th

I am doing Alrite at the Sidekick stuff. I no you do not like to here about it but just to let you no that I am Alrite Money-wise and keeping bizzy. Nights I am mostly up the Meeting house or they sometimes fetch us to do a turn at some other Place round the Coast and daytime I do privit readings in Marjes Front Room. Sounds posh dont it cross my palm with silver! I will have to call myself something fancy Madam Noriana what do you reckon? (No not really.) I tell you Lucy I never made such Easy Money in all my born days it is not like work at all. I ask you what do I like doing best in all the World having a good old chin wag aint that right? So this is right up my Alley and it is ever so intresting what comes out family secrits and that you wood not credit what some of them got up to before they was In Spirit. Real spicey some of it. And I get payed for all of this! When I think how I use to sweat over that hot tub braking my back lugging heavy washing about and all the time I

84

cood of bin treating us all to a life of Riley well Lucy I cood cry my eyes out.

I miss being Home and it was a shame having to shut up shop but you was quite right. It wasnt on was it you out at the factory and having all the housework and the chickens to do of an evening, not to menshun the old dears. Oh now I must tell you Lucy about them. Somehow word got round that I was pulling up Sticks and they was very Oity Toity when I was packing up well your Dads Auntie Maud was any rate. The doors was banging away 19 to the doz. Not to menshun Soot keep falling down the Chimley and putting the fire out under the copper so as I cood not wash the Curtans. I wood just get the fire lit and the water hotting up nice and woosh theres another fall of soot. Wheres it all coming from I ask myself I was at my Wits ends. I mean you can not clear out of a place and leave dirty Curtans at the windows can you? Anyway your Gran give us a tip what to do so I went down Cuthberts and bort a penneth of Gunpowder poked it in that little door in the Flu and held it shut with the Broom handle whilst I lit the Fire. You never heard such a bang Lucy. Worser an a Jerry bomb. It cleared the Chimley Alrite. Soot every blooming where. The skullery looked like the Black Hole of Calcuter with me the Choclate Coloured Coon. I was in a rite 2 and 8 eye brows and eye lashes gone and hair all sizzed up to Nothink. It is only starting to grow back now. Your Gran says a penneth was too much still it done the trick and it skared the life out of old Maud (well it skared something out of her!) I ain't seen hide nor hair of her since and no more Banging Doors nither. It was very quite them last few days. The others came to say Goodbye but she kept well out of it. I hope she is Alrite. Your Gran says she is having a Sulk.

*December 14th*
Them guns are still at it bang bang bang on the Front. It is a shame it aint Clacton for me. When Dad and I come here on Holiday that time we had Arthur and Siddy then and we had a lovely time on the Sands and the kids all

85

paddling in the Sea but thats the War for you. There aint nothing the same not in Walthamstow nither still I dont half miss Walthamstow bombs and all speshly the High Street. There aint no Shops up here werf a lite no market and no sound of trafick. It took me an age to get asleep nights when there aint no airaids it is so quite! I aint got the Best Room no more. She needs it for the Paying Guests. This room I got now is Alrite but between you me and the Gate Post it aint like having a place of your Own. All I hope is the War will hurry up and end so we can get back home to number 41 and all be together again.

I herd from Aggie Moffat last week that Rene Neville down Byron Road lost her boy John come down over Germany and she only had the 1. Well Im sorry for the woman but do you no what she said Lucy akording to Aggy she said it was a shame it wernt one of mine cos I got 5 more 6 counting you. Did you ever here enything so wicked? Like I cood spare 1. What a nasty thing to say and she was all over me down Uncles. I just went to see what I cood make on a few bits and bobs help pay for the move well if she thinks shes coming here for her holidays shes got another think coming.

Did you have Mr Churchill on the wireless the other day when they had the Victory in the Dessert? What did he say? Aint the end and it aint the begining of the end only the end of the begining. I was hoping we was a bit father along than that still it is nice to chalk one up for us aint it? I reckon thats what young Jacks bin up to dont you? Stands to reason he cood not tell us Nothink. Im worried still not hearing from him but I expeck it is a bit soon dont you? I herd from Mick and he is Alrite. I am putting his letter in with this. What do you think of the photo? Dont he look soppy in his little short Shorts and I never new he cood ride a Motor Bike. Looks like hes bin out in the Dessert and all but hes not saying nither. It was sent on from Home and hes rote Dear Ma and Lucy so he cant have had our news yet. Charlie's doing something getting poor people out of France. I see he says he will be Home for Christmas and it gives

me the Pip he has no Home to come Home to. Marje
says hes wellcome here and Mick and any of the Boys
and you come to that if they will let you off of work for
a day or 2. It wont be the same as down Home but I hope
you will come.

*December 19th*
Our Aud is expeckted tonight so I will give her this
Letter for you. She says you are well and lerning to ride
a Bike. I expeck it is a bit to far to ride a bike out here
aint it so I wont expeck you but it wood be nice.

Thank you for the Post Card to say you got there safe
and sound. Doddingworth looks nice. I will look out the
bus Time Table and I will be over to see you one of
these fine days. Take care of yourself Lucy and I hope
to see you soon.

Lots of love from Ma XXX

PS Audrey just told me you had a Visit from Roy and
you are saying I am to blame for telling him the Adress
of your Farm. Now Lucy I would not do such a thing
like that and you shood of nown. I promise you he has
not been here I have not seen him or if he has been here
no ones told me. Only ones been asking after you is that
Cecil Im shore you will be pleased to here! He is a
snake if you ask me and I wood not dream of letting on
to him where you are staying. But I wood not be
surprised Lucy if he found out somehow and put Roy on
to you. I tell you girl it was not my doing I do not like
the Boy and I was happy to think we have seen the Back
of him. Im shore I do not no what made you think I
wood do such a thing like that. I hope it was not to much
of a Shock for you and that evrything is Alrite. Rite
soon and let us no theres a good girl.

PPS Guess who I see riding up and down out here
yesterday on his Motor Bike that Joe on the train the one
with the ginger hair wanted to take us to a concert. Bit
posh if you ask me but not as bad as some. He said Eric
had told him our news. I told him your working on a

Farm to put him off but he wanted your adress but I said
Id have to ask you. Didnt think you wood want him
turning up on your doorstep I see Eric up the church he
is doing Alrite.

PPPS Audrey is waiting for me to finish this so I will
stop now.

Ma.

Hooper's Farm
Oxley Lane
Great Bisset
Nr Doddingworth
Suffolk

*February 21st 1943*

Dear Ma,
    Happy New Year to you and Marjorie and all the
chickens that survived Christmas dinner!
    Sorry to have taken so long to write. I expect Audrey
has kept you up to date. When I first came here I was so
down in the dumps I did not feel like writing to anyone.
This is an old farm, rundown buildings, with thick,
smelly mud everywhere. It smells rotten indoors as well
– damp or something. They opened the door and I
thought, Oh no! Some welcome I got, too, no cup of tea,
just Mr and Mrs Hooper looking me up and down like
they were about to give me a prod at any minute, feel
my arms and legs for muscle, inspect my teeth or
something. They said they hoped I was strong enough!
(Just to put me at my ease.) She said I was even thinner
than the last girl Audrey sent and she had been a wash-
out. I reckon they would have sent me packing, too, if
they had been allowed.
    I think they are probably as old as you, Ma, but they
look older. They had a son but they never talk about
him. He was killed at the start of the war. I am sleeping
in his bed and a horrible saggy thing it is, too. She is a
right fashion plate – wears her husband's cast-offs, I

think. Dirty old jumpers you would be ashamed to give to the rag-man, one on top of the other, all out at the elbows. She must have half-a-dozen on at a time and men's trousers that she never seems to change out of. Mind you I can't really blame her – it is so cold here I have cut the sleeves out of my old blue jumper and that one with the zig-zag pattern and I have made them into socks to wear inside my wellington boots. The body bits are now woolly vests for wearing under my green 'issue' jumper. Audrey gave me the largest size uniform for the length and I have had to take everything in. You could have got three of me in the corduroy breeches!

All very well her getting me in here without any training but I could really have done with some, Ma. A real townie, me, more green than cabbage-looking, as you would say. I do not know what I expected – a healthy outdoor life and hay-making I suppose. And who was it, when I was little, telling me cows were nice gentle creatures making milk for our tea and butter for our bread? Well, you were wrong! I am more used to them now but at first I was terrified. Great smelly things and they play you up if they think you don't know what you are doing, like they squash you against the wall or land you a kick or they swish their dirty tail in your face or their foot in the bucket and I have had a few buckets kicked over and milk everywhere. Worst of all they are forever doing number twos. You soon learn to stand clear of any cow with a cough. I was sick every day that first week what with not enough sleep (up at five!) and lousy food (mostly fry-ups and bread and *marge* (all Mrs Cow's butter goes to market!) and the smell of cow muck and milk, and my hands all sore and chapped from washing down the cowshed walls with cold water, after milking, and scrubbing out the feeding troughs (made of stone, which skin your knuckles and tear your nails, only you do not feel it *at first* because your hands are numb with cold.) Oh I was in a bad way, missing you like anything and crying into my brick-hard pillow every night. I would gladly have sat through a dozen of your 'private readings' to be out of it. I tried whining to

89

Audrey but she just wagged her finger and told me to think of England. Anyway I am all right now – tough as old toenails, me.

We had a calf born at Christmas that I am teaching to feed from a bucket. You have to hold the bucket with one hand and get the calf to suck the milk off the fingers of your other hand. They have sharp teeth, Ma, but they are lovely little things. Great big brown eyes. I am getting quite fond of the cows now I have learned to milk them properly and even Mr and Mrs Hooper seem a bit happier. I told her about Old Randy Rooster and the hens pecking each others' feathers out. She says she cured her chickens the same way only she had a few more pairs of specs to make than you – forty!

They are why I had to learn to ride that old bike Audrey told you about. It is my job to take the eggs into Doddingworth (5 miles away) in egg-boxes stacked up on the carrier behind me and tied up with string. I have fallen off a few times and breakages come out of my wages, so I have had to learn to be careful. I reckon I could ride along a tight-rope now! I make the trip twice a week on my half-days off, Tuesday and Friday, and I really look forward to it. I call in at the pub while there, for a hot bath, since the Hoopers do not seem to have heard of such a thing. I am not kidding! She gives me a pint jug of hot water after breakfast (after milking) for a sloosh down and that is it! You either wash your clothes under the cold tap in the yard or they go in for a boil with everything else *once a month*! I can see you having forty fits. So what I do is I take a change of clothes with me to town and do my laundry in the bath. Waste not want not. I wring out the clothes as best I can but there is always a puddle in the gutter where my bike stands while I am in the tea-shop having a buttered bun. Well, I have to treat myself and it is nice to meet other Land Girls in the tea-shop. They work on bigger farms than me and some of them live in hostels. They moan about it but it must be nice to have someone your own age to talk to. At the Hoopers' there's only the old cowman, George, and Derek and Stan, who live down in the village. For sowing the parsnips last week they got in some Italian prisoners of war. I get on all right with Helen and Doris and go to the pictures with them sometimes if there is anything on but mostly we roam round looking at shops, that sort of thing. Or go for a bike-ride. Sowness is not far, a little seaside place with bathing huts on wheels all rotting away! It must have been nice before the barbed wire. You can't use the beach now, of course. I went to a dance at the RAF camp there last week and that Joe was there (from the train). It was nice to see him again. They do have local dances in Brand End where Doris and Helen work, or in Doddingworth, but the men are either village idiots or married! Still a dance is a dance!

Sorry I did not get to see you over Christmas. It was an ordinary working day for us, though we did go to the Carol Service in the village and there were mince pies and hot toddies afterwards in the vicarage. Lovely, as Aud would say.

About Roy, I am sorry I blamed you. Of course you would not have sent him round but you know me, when I lose my rag I tend to lash out in all directions and ask questions after. I was not thinking straight. I had already had a go at Audrey and she told me where to get off. You were next on my list. Sorry. When I think about it, all he needed to do was to go round home, find us gone and ask around. Anyone would have told him – they all knew him. Next door would have given him our addresses no questions asked, or Aggie. It was no secret. Ted might even have driven him up, you never know, having the blackest nose out! No maybe Aggie wins on points. What a stirrer! All that about Mrs Neville. There was no need for her to tell you what she said about the boys. The poor woman was beside herself, I expect, and she did not know what she was saying. You have no cause to feel bad about it. I am sure she never meant to upset you. I was sorry to hear about John, though, he was a nice bloke. Mick will be upset. Thanks for sending on his letter and Charlie's. They sound like they are having a whale of a time – all those

91

concerts and films. It must be hell!

What about this for an idea, Ma? How about meeting me in Doddingworth on one of my afternoons off? You could get the train, change at Ipswich. I will have to drop the eggs off first and miss out on a bath that day so if I smell a bit cowy you will have to excuse me but I would love to see you. Could you manage it, do you think? Any Tuesday or Friday. (Or make it Sunday if you like but the shops will not be open and I don't know about the trains.) It would mean you starting out early. Tell me what time your train gets in and I will meet you at the station. And I'll tell you about Roy. It's too long to write here and I must go to bed, my eyes are dropping out of my head. Take care of yourself.

Lots of love, Lucy XXXXXX

# Chapter Ten

You only tell your mother the things that won't worry her.

Great Bisset was a picture-book village, with picture-book people. They lived in a world of make-believe. That is, they made things up about you and believed what they liked.

Nestling in its own little valley, it was a spider's web of a place, with an overgrown turkey oak brooding at its centre, on the village green. Circling this was a gravel lane, with wider roads, like spokes, leading north to Whittleton-on-Sea and up the coast to Lowestoft, east to Sowness, west to Doddingworth, the market town, and Diss and Thetford, as the crow flies, and if you followed the fourth road you'd come, eventually, to Ipswich.

A stranger, from London, say, might think it olde worlde and quaint, with its smells of woodsmoke, its cockerel cries, its narrow gravel lanes, just wide enough for a horse and cart, or the postman's van, to pass a pedestrian. With its strip of farmworkers' cottages lying back behind hedges and extravagant front gardens. All redbrick, stained with ancient lichen and moss, they seemed to have pushed up from the ground.

The thirsty traveller might be drawn, by the smell of hops and baccy, by the glow of the fire, to the pub, the Bull and Crown, and find a small, dark cave, and cavemen, not in animal skins but cloth caps and greasy waistcoats, playing dominoes. But if you greeted them you'd still only get grunts for answers. And the weapons that would drive you away would not be clubs and stones, but their own cold shoulders.

And as you wandered, a stranger still, you'd come to the school: two rooms, some smelly lavvies and a tiny, windy playground to swing a bat. Snotty kids would stare at you as though you were the one behind bars.

Perching prettily on the high ground was the church, St Michael's, grey stone and spired, and worth a look if you liked grey stone and spires, and were getting cold. On your way out, no warmer, you'd probably glance at the grave-stones, noting ages and names, and that, even in death, the Turners and Stones, the Tylers and Coopers and Smiths were kept at a decent distance from the family vaults of Shelly and Woodleigh.

Passing by the vicarage and crossing the Doddingworth road, your curiosity might have fought through forbidding evergreens, and discovered the stone buttresses of 'Squire's' front gate. But since 'Squire' was a cantankerous old devil with a white walrus moustache, who'd bite your head off if you rang his bell, you most likely wouldn't linger, but continue across the next road, and if it wasn't too cold to hang about, admire the fine architecture of the Georgian houses, where the doctor lived and a couple of other notables, while you waited for the bus.

Otherwise you'd carry on round to Fitzell's store, and warm yourself at Hettie Fitzell's oil-stove. You'd find a number of people, women mostly, with babies and shopping bags, all with the same idea, and the same watchful way with strangers.

The first test was physical. As you pinged open the door and negotiated your way into the dark interior, over and around sacks and canisters and casks and crates, you hadn't to be too lithe, too willowy, too pretty or smell nice. And you didn't wear trousers. Lucy failed the first test miserably. She knew they had her down as a hussy.

The second test was mental. They left the interrogation to Hettie, a bony shrew with glasses and the crêpey skin of a heavy smoker. Her hair was permed grey and dyed nicotine. So was her voice.

'Post-cards is ha'penny,' she growled.

'It's for a letter.'

'Penny then. Unless it's for overseas.'

'No, England – Clacton.'

'The training camp?'

94

'Er . . .?' (Hesitation, lose two points.)

'Goes in a special bag for the training camp.'

'No, it's to my mother, actually.'

'Come from Clacton, do you?'

'No, London.'

'*Thought* as much.' Sniff. ''Ere on your own then, are you?'

'Mmm.'

'One o' they Land Girls?'

'Yes.'

'Goin' agin nature.'

'Sorry?'

'Come a bit 'ard to a girl from Lunnon, I don't doubt. Don't 'old with it, meself, gettin' smarty young girls all dolled up in uniform for muck-spreadin' and winnowin' and that. Dirty ole job for a fast Towngirl.'

Lucy's tongue was between her teeth, being firmly bitten.

'You'm the one up at 'Oopers'?'

Lucy nodded.

'Aye. Mabel were tellin' us about ee. Poor Mabel!'

Polite raising of the eyebrows.

''Ow you gettin' on with '*im*, then?'

A snort, a definite snort of laughter from the bus queue. Lucy swung round. If they knew something . . . She caught a nudge, a titter.

'What?' she demanded.

Faces closed in, became stony.

Hettie was persistent, though. She'd do well in the SS, thought Lucy.

'Last little girl up there left in 'urry. What were 'er called?'

They all shook their heads and pulled down their mouths. They looked like cows on a bad morning.

'Some sort of skin rash, they do say. A nallergy.'

Lucy had heard about this from Audrey. Eczema. A reaction to something in the soil, she told the woman.

'Long's 'tweren't t'other sort o' nallergy, s'all right, ennit?'

Lucy only had a vague idea what the woman was suggesting but found herself blushing nevertheless. The titters had started up again.

95

She paid for her stamp and got out, having failed the second test. It seemed to have something to do with Hooper.

The bus was late.

Rather than stand exposed at the bus-stop, she wandered into the shelter of the leafless oak. There was a seat circling the great gnarled trunk in ever-decreasing iron hoops and she sat down, huddling into her collar. Even through her great-coat and dungarees, the seat struck cold. Perhaps it would warm up. Iron was a good conductor of heat, and she was still burning with humiliation. A rusty plaque commemorated the planting of the tree in *this the Glorious Jubilee Year of HM Queen Victoria*. Not that old then – fifty years? But enormous. Its bony fingers could almost furl the edges of the green. It must be a sight in summer, she thought. A cool green canopy. You could hide in it and never be seen. Like King Charles on Oak-Apple Day.

The branches quivered with the wind off the sea and as she, too, shivered, she felt the seat beneath her judder. Aye-aye. Someone was sitting on the other side. Someone heavy. Someone who sniffed and someone who rocked. It was impossible to sit there as if nothing was happening when the slats beneath your bum were jiggling about in a quite dangerous manner.

She got up and walked around, a smile ready, determined not to make any more enemies that morning. A large woman sat there with a pram. But it seemed as though the pram, low-slung and sealed against the weather, were rocking her. On closer inspection, she wasn't a woman but a girl, no more than fifteen or sixteen, perhaps, though matching stones for years. She wore a shapeless red coat and her straight string-coloured hair was clipped back from dull, inward-looking eyes with a hairslide.

'Hello.'

The girl stopped rocking. Her eyes swivelled away hard, though she continued to face Lucy. It was as though she could still see her with the whites of her eyes. Even on this cold, windy day, a strong whiff of ammonia hovered about mother and baby. Poor kids, both of them.

'Where the bus?' said the girl. Her voice was harsh, expressionless.

'You waiting, too? It can't be long now.'

'The green bus. Where the green bus goin'?' Still that same rough tone, demanding, insistent.

'Sowness, I hope. I would go by bike, but the inner tube's gone. They've got a good bike shop in Sowness.'

'Where the green bus goin' arter Sowness?'

'After? Well, I think it does the round trip through Doddingworth and then up to Brand End and Beccles, over to Whittleton and then back . . .'

The girl had begun to jiggle the handle of the pram.

'Eileen don' wanna go Whittleton . . .' looking at the ground now, at the church, up into the tree, anywhere but at Lucy '. . . not Whittleton. Don't want green bus goin' Whittleton. Her bain't goin' Whittleton on no green bus. No.' She was getting really agitated. So was the pram, its handle being jerked viciously up and down. Lucy was alarmed for the baby's sake, convinced it would come flying out at any minute. How it could continue sleeping was a wonder.

'Well, I'm sure you don't have to go to Whittleton if you don't want to.'

Clearly the girl was disturbed and had to be placated. But Lucy had said the wrong thing, entirely.

'No-o-o!' shrieked Eileen, in great distress, and lunged at her, baring her teeth as if to bite her. 'No-o-o!'

Only then did Lucy realise that the girl's wrists were attached by short leather straps to the iron arms of the seat. She couldn't get up from the seat. She must have been sitting there before Lucy arrived. Perhaps the ammonia smell wasn't from the pram. A woman shouted from one of the cottages, waving her arms at Lucy to come away.

'But the baby—'

'No-o-o!' howled the girl and kicked the pram.

'Don't,' said Lucy, her hands in front of her face, dancing in and out of range. 'You'll hurt the baby.'

But the girl twisted and landed Lucy a kick on the shin that made her yelp, then kicked the pram so violently it shot away across the grass and tipped up on end, flinging the contents out onto the barky ground. Ragged bits of blanket and a battered doll, a broken mirror, sweet wrappers, a puckered end-of-Christmas balloon, a bicycle bell.

The woman hurried across the green, to the rescue. Lucy noticed she was carrying a bamboo stick in one hand and a piece of toffee in the other.

She gestured to Lucy to get back.

'Eileen, stop it!' The girl carried on screaming and paddling her feet in tantrum.

'Eileen! I'll pay you!' A threat of some sort. 'Eileen!' She swished the stick down *whack!* across the girl's legs.

Eileen hiccupped and stopped screaming. Examined with interest the stinging red weal on her leg. And held out her hand for the toffee.

'Good grief!' said Lucy.

The woman was bundling the girl's treasures back into the pram.

''Urt you, did she? Her can't 'elp it. Don't know what her'm a-doing of.'

'It's all right,' smiled Lucy, gritting her teeth against the pain. Eileen was wearing a man's working boots.

'You'm new 'ere, bain't you? 'Ave to learn, like all the rest. Leave 'er alone. Her reckon 'tis her tree.'

'It's a bit cold out here for her, isn't it?'

'Her don't mind the cold. Long as her can see buses go by. Dead set on buses, her be.'

'But not the ones to Whitt—'

'Us don't mention the W word. Sets 'er off.'

'I noticed.'

Lucy rubbed a hole in the mist on the bus window. Eileen was in raptures. Sitting there under the tree with her pram, wiggling her fingers in front of her face and smiling through them at the bus. Her body moved backwards and forwards to the foetal rock, typical of people with brain damage.

When she turned to give her fare to the bus conductor Lucy found herself the object of knowing looks and sniggers. Whatever the third test had been, she had failed that, too.

She knew what they were thinking. About Hooper. They had good reason.

'Come you in 'ere, Towngirl,' he'd said, and she had followed, like a lamb, into the barn.

He made his way purposefully into the darkest corner, turned and beckoned, and she followed, thinking he was going to show her something – kittens, new machinery, a way of binding straw bales . . . Goodness knows what she'd been thinking?

Had she known?

Sort of.

She must have.

But it hadn't occurred to her that anyone, specially this balding old man, over fifty, smelling of milk and cowshit, with a mouthful of dead teeth, handsful of thick, sausagey fingers, could seriously think of himself as desirable. Could be that blatant, with his wife only yards away in the house.

She hadn't connected him with sex.

Talk about green.

Still not wanting to believe it she had sat down beside him when he had patted the straw. And then he was all over her, pushing her back with his slobbering kisses, undoing her coat buttons, working his hand up her jumper while she struggled and pushed against him.

'Get off!' she'd pleaded. 'Don't!' And, 'Please!'

But even 'Please' didn't work.

He'd just grinned with his slack, wet mouth, his gargoyle mouth, and moved his hand between her legs. Thank God for her jodhpurs, she had thought. He'll never get into them.

. . . But he's going to, she thought in a panic, he's going to bloody do it.

He'd got his hand into the waistband, she heard the ripping of cloth.

'Don't,' she said. 'Don't tear them.' Irrationally, she couldn't bear the thought of more sewing. She'd already spent whole evenings taking them in.

And as though she were drowning her life flashed before her.

'*No one can make you do anything you don't want to.*' Granny Farthing's admonition, from way, way back, whenever her excuse had been, 'He made me . . .'

But what could she do with this heaving old brute on top of her? Her employer. Oh God, there was that. If she didn't, would she lose her job? Her hands flew to her head . . . *think,*

*think* . . . and encountered her hat. Her floppy Land-Army hat, held on against the wind – with a hat-pin.

Granny Farthing had been spot on.

So was the hat-pin. Bull's-eye in the left buttock.

He said she had led him on.

She told him she didn't come with the job. She certainly didn't intend to be deflowered by a dirty old man, and if he ever, ever touched her again, she'd stick him where it really hurt and yell for his wife to come and see.

Next day he brought her a peace offering: apple cake from Hettie's shop.

'For my girlfriend,' he said with a smarmy smile, showing his gums. She had fed it to the pig, but now she wondered what he had told Hettie.

Was he dropping hints round the village that she *had* actually . . .?

'Poor Mabel,' they'd said. Snigger, snigger.

Poor Mabel, indeed, having to bed with a toad like Hooper. But that wasn't what they'd meant, was it?

They probably felt sorry for Hooper as well. A poor country lad stood no chance against a fast girl from London. But she deserved all she got.

# Chapter Eleven

Nora had the right hump. Black from top to toe. Slapping at her coat front, she drew back, expecting dust, and cursed as greasy dirt transferred to her glove. The floors on them trains was a disgrace. And she must have caught her stocking somehow: a great white hole of leg was exposed, mapped with veins. Very pretty. Her hat was all skew-wiff and she was dying for a wee. Blooming Jerries. Two hours late, the train was at the finish. She wouldn't blame Lucy if she'd got tired of waiting and gone home. Probably glad of the excuse.

That last letter, saying where and when to meet, had been very short and sharp. Nora hadn't needed to read between the lines to know that Lucy had been in one of her moods. She *had* taken her time replying. But it was a big thing for a woman on her own, a train journey, especially to some godforsaken Doddingworth-place no one had ever heard of, out in the sticks. And having to change at Ipswich . . . Marje had told her to be careful – anything could happen. Well, it just showed you.

She looked with longing at the battered red chocolate machine. *Out of Order*. They was all out of order. Every blooming chocolate machine on every blooming railway station in the country. Nothing worked no more. And it was perishing cold, though you couldn't blame Hitler for that, she supposed.

There was Lucy! All hunched up inside her overcoat, hands in her pockets like a man. She looked so different. Must have been the trousers.

'Well, I got 'ere at last,' Nora said to the stranger.

'Ma!' Her cheeks were rosy but cold, like her kiss. She was peering down into her face, looking for suffering. 'You all right? They put it over the tannoy. God, I thought it was *your* train being bombed.'

'Oh, I'm all right. Pity them other poor buggers, though. We pulled up behind 'em. They didn't half cop it. They was ages getting them took off to hospital. Poor devils.'

But she didn't want to think of the mangled iron and flesh again, the blood, the cries. She shook her head in a vain attempt to clear it and dabbed at her wet nose with a hanky.

'What's he wanna go and do that for, eh? Just poor people getting off to business, most of 'em. What's he wanna bomb 'em for? Bleedin' Hitler!'

Lucy put her arm round her and gave her a squeeze. Nora stiffened, not used to affection, if that was what it was.

'At least you weren't hurt. You were jolly lucky.'

'*Lucky*! Look at me. Sitting there in me best, on me way to see me only daughter and smack, there's some geezer pushes me on the floor and under the bloody seat! "Keep your 'ead down, Mum," he says. "Enemy bombers." Well, I knew that! I got ears! He didn't 'ave to go pushing people about. And I ain't his mum, never was!'

'Still, you're in one piece. Come on, we'll get you cleaned up and then we'll go and have a cup of tea, eh?'

'Ain't got a penny, 'ave you, Luce?'

A swarm of shaken, dishevelled passengers, some in tears, had taken over the Ladies lavatory while the stationmaster fussed outside over a poor old girl who had fallen off the seat and snapped her wrist when their train screeched to a halt. Someone had gone to get a taxi to take her to the hospital. A little boy was sitting on a hand-basin, whimpering, snot like a fat grey slug sliding from his nose, while his mother sponged a bump on his forehead. Some were silent, some gave vent to their shock and anger. When a mirror was free Nora scrubbed off the worst of her dirt with cold water and her hanky smeared with soap, while Lucy went off to buy her another pair of stockings. Kindness and concern. How long would that last?

Twenty minutes later they were sitting in Sally Lunn's Tea-Rooms eating baked beans on toast. Nora breathed deeply,

102

trying to relax. Trying to trust Lucy's good humour. The train journey had not been the only reason she had been reluctant to come to Doddingworth.

She had been so glad to hear from the girl (the first letter, not the second), ripping it open, running an immediate eye over it for trouble, absorbing it more slowly over a cuppa, relishing her news, smiling at her jokes, glad she was happy again, and then, as she read the last paragraph and the suggestion that they meet, becoming aware of heaviness settling in her stomach. Lucy was such a difficult child.

Whenever she thought of that banner at the meeting-house, *To thine own self be true* she felt a great wave of relief. That was all they asked, that she be herself. No pretence, no guile. But she knew her own self was nowhere near good enough for her daughter, not these days.

Lucy was ashamed of her, that was the top and bottom of it. That's why they couldn't be in the same room for more than two minutes without a row. It was like she, Nora, had something wrong with her – an ugly, psychic disability. Lucy wanted her normal. She wouldn't have said No to a touch of class, and all, but she'd have put up with all the cor blimeys in the world, if only her mother could have had that nasty extra sense amputated.

Well, she was as she was, and Lucy would just have to lump it. She stretched her knees under the table, allowing the warmth of the food and the tea-shop's wood fire to soothe away some of the chill in her bones.

'How often do I get to go on the train, eh?' she remarked, for openers. 'Trust me to pick the day Hitler was gonna show off, eh?'

'You won't come and see me again, will you?' But the voice was light, the question a joke. Nora's heart lifted a little. Perhaps it wouldn't all end in tears, this time.

'Now I know the way . . .' She reached across their table by the window and grasped Lucy's hand, her touch completing the sentence. With love, she began to stroke the knuckles with her thumb. And stopped, appalled. 'Blimey, girl, what you done to your 'ands? They're like a bleedin' navvy's!'

Lucy sighed. 'I know, but that's farmwork for you. Getting

103

sugar beet up this morning. Rotten job. Days like today they're frozen in and you have to heel them out of the ground.' She rubbed her heel, ruefully. 'Loading them on the cart your hands get wet and dirty and there's nothing to dry them on.'

'I thought you was with the cows.'

'That's only part of it. In between times there's the beet to get in, all sorts. Last week was wet and 'cos we couldn't get out, he had us white-washing the cowshed.'

Nora frowned. It sounded like hard work, though no harder, probably, than she had had to do, hauling wet washing about day after day. And Lucy seemed to be coping. Had it been one of the boys she'd have said the work was making a man of him. Whatever that meant. 'I'd ask him for some gloves if I was you,' she said, and blew on her tea to cool it.

Lucy snorted. 'Fat chance! Anyway, they wouldn't last five minutes.'

'He is . . . all right, this farmer?'

Their eyes met over the teacups.

'What d'you mean, "all right"?'

'*You* know. You hear about these country yokels . . .'

Lucy gave a short laugh. 'Randy old goats, you mean.' She sipped and swallowed and her eyes darted sideways. Why did Nora get the idea she was hiding something? 'Yeah, it must be all the breeding that goes on.'

She paused.

Nora was on red alert.

'Hooper did get a bit worked up, once, teaching me to milk the cow. You know, his hand started wandering. But you can't slap his face, not when it's the boss.'

'Oh bli, I would. Don't you stop there, Luce. We'll go and get your things and you can come back with me.'

'Ma . . . I can't keep running away.'

'Dirty old bugger. You never let him get away with it, did you?'

'What d'you take me for? I started hollering. "Mrs Hooper!" I went. "Will you come out here a minute?" He was over the other side of the cowshed in no time flat. Been as good as gold since. Audrey suggested that. Says it's a sure-

fire, tried-and-tested method. Or pick your nose, she said –
that tends to put them off.'

'Luc-*ee*!'

Lucy giggled.

'Your Gran always said an 'at-pin was a good stand-by.'

Nora had to bang her daughter on the back, as her tea went
down the wrong way. It wasn't that funny!

'Oh, I'm learning lots, Ma,' she said when she eventually
recovered. 'Even seen what the bull does to the cow. I wasn't
supposed to. They thought I was off delivering eggs but I got
a puncture. I think their faces were redder than mine.'

'So what's that then? What the bull does to the cow?'

'Ma, you *know*!'

Nora shook her head, and watched Miss Worldly-Wise
squirm, saw the colour come up in the clear skin, heard the
throat-clearing that seemed so at odds with the boyish get-up,
the military-style jumper, the cords and the boots.

'When the bull mounts the cow . . .' nodding for Nora to
get the sense of what came next but Nora was all wide-eyed
innocence.

So she pressed on, 'When he puts his, you know – his thing
– in the cow's . . .' Daring to look up, she caught the twinkle
in Nora's eyes. Too late.

'*Ma*! You rotten . . .'

Nora cackled, kicking up her legs, nudging her daughter in
her skinny ribs. Better she should learn the facts of life from
the animals, than the hard way. Lucy's face was flaming, but
she was smiling. Barriers were down, taboos lifted. Nora was
delighted, glad she had made the trip, after all.

It was time for her news, but she kept it short and sweet,
places and people, this side rather than the 'Other'. She
didn't want to 'spook' her daughter, and spoil things, not
now.

She told her about Christmas, how Arthur and Mick had
come down to Clacton and what a lovely time they'd all had.
She didn't say how they'd all been on their best behaviour,
how they'd missed out on Potter Christmas customs. The
knees up, the sing-song, the 'old dears' sitting round and
smiling, the mince pies left out and only crumbs remaining in
the morning, with sooty fingerprints on the plate, the football

105

socks hung up on the bedposts, stuffed magically tight even though there was no money around, even though they were all far too grown-up for such things. She didn't say that it hadn't been the same at all. That she'd been glad when it was all over.

'You haven't heard from Jack, have you?' asked Lucy. 'It's been ages since I had a letter from him.'

She swallowed her own anxiety to reassure the girl that their favourite was probably doing something hush-hush and couldn't get a letter out.

'He's all *right* – still in the land of the living. Take my word for it,' she said, and Lucy gave her a very funny look.

To change the subject she told her how she was making money hand over fist, enough to pay for bed and board at Marje's, to keep their London landlord sweet, and to spare. She'd sent Aggie the front-door key of number 41 and a few bob to keep an eye on the place. Aggie was all right. She'd have a bit of a sort-through, knowing her, but she wouldn't take nothing.

'And it'll be company for the old folk.'

Oops. Too late, she bit her teeth together. But Lucy simply nodded. She had a dreamy look on her face and was drawing 'Chad' in the steam on the window, the bald head with the long nose and then the brick wall.

'Luce . . .'

Startled, she rubbed it out with her fist.

'What?'

'You gonna tell me about Roy, or what?'

It was the week before Christmas. Early milking was done and the cows had been taken up to the meadow at the top of the lane.

'Just me and the dog with twenty-four cows, Ma. Say you're proud.'

Oh, she was. Very proud.

Lucy had shut the gate, made it secure.

'Aye-aye!' she'd said, realising that someone was coming up the lane from the farm. It was foggy so she couldn't see who it was but she felt sure she knew the trudge of those boots. He must have got the bus into Great Bisset and walked up. It was quite eerie, hearing the familiar step and seeing no one. Her heart was going pit-a-pat and the dog was going spare. Bella didn't like men in uniform. Too many kicks from the postman.

It was Roy, of course, the last person she wanted to see, his fair hair beaded with dew drops like a spider's web, his greatcoat hanging open, and his cap pushed back on his head with a bit of mistletoe stuck in it.

'Silly arse!' said Nora.

He looked utterly weary. Like someone on Flanders Field, Lucy said, emerging from the smoke of battle.

But her heart did not go out to him. It slumped into her boots. 'I held the bitch by the scruff of the neck,' she said, 'telling her it was all right, knowing it wasn't and wanting desperately to let her go for the throat.

'His smile curdled my breakfast, Ma, I tell you. So sweet and sickly. "They said I'd find you here," he said.

'He reckoned he'd been to the hospital and they'd given him the all-clear; whatever it was he'd had, he was cured of it. I thought, pull the other one, Roy! He acted so pleased with himself, like I'd really change my mind and marry him now! He has no idea what he's done, not at all. I told him that even if I believed him, which I didn't, the VD was neither here nor there. I couldn't marry a man who would go with women like that, who would cheat on me and tell me lies.'

'Be a fool if you did,' agreed Nora.

'He tried to make out it wasn't his fault. He'd been out on the razzle with the boys and they'd spiked his drink or something. "I was plastered," he said. "Didn't know what I was doing. All I was thinking about was you. This other woman, I can't even remember what she looked like."'

'Ain't what he told you the first time,' Nora commented sourly. 'Hadn't he been "relieving himself"?'

'Exactly,' said Lucy. 'He'd done it more than once.'

She'd told him she wasn't going to spend her life worrying was he out with the lads again? Was he drunk? Was he messing about with some tart? What sort of marriage would that have been?

'But he wouldn't give up, Ma. "I've learned my lesson, Lucy," he said. "It'll never happen again." Then he brings out

107

this little packet, Ma, a brown paper envelope, all folded up tight, like school-dinner money, and it's got *Lucy's ring* written on it. "Go on, Luce," he says. "Forgive and forget. You said you'd marry me. A promise is a promise. Real diamonds," he says, as though that would swing it. I wanted to smack his silly face.

'Then he fishes in his pocket again and it's the wedding ring this time. "I'll make it up to you," he promises. "We can still be happy. You're the only one for me." Cliché after cliché.'

Nora wasn't quite sure what that meant. She understood the next bit, though.

'I told him to stick his rings. If he didn't I'd do it for him. But he went on and on. "There's only you," he said. "This is so silly, Lucy. You love me, you know you do." And I looked at him, stood there like two penn'orth of eels, and I thought to myself, call that a man? Blooming pathetic.

'"Love you, Roy?" I said. "I don't think so."'

'No,' said Nora, sipping her second cup of tea. 'You was quite right. That weren't love, nothing like. You had a lucky escape, girl, mark my words.'

'You don't have to tell me,' said Lucy. 'So then I said I had work to do and would he please sling his hook? He started trying it on, then, wanting to kiss me under his silly bit of mistletoe, so I brought me knee up sharp, VD or no VD.'

'Ooh!' Nora sucked air through her teeth, picturing her daughter's bony knee making soft contact. 'What was that, another of Audrey's tips?'

'No, Jack gave me that one. Did me the world of good. Don't think it did much for Roy! I left him there in a heap. I was very tempted to let Bella go, but I didn't want her catching anything. Lucky for him I didn't have the farmer's shotgun, the mood I was in.'

'Lucy, don't say that. He's ain't worth swinging for.'

Lucy shrugged, her lips fastened tight.

'Anyhow,' said Nora, 'let's hope you seen the last of him, for his sake. Don't want no murders!' She made an attempt at a smile.

'Haven't though, that's the problem.'

'Eh?'

108

'Oh yeah, he don't give up easy. The next time was about a month ago. He was waiting for me in the lane when I got back off the fields. I'd had a right day of it, frozen to the marrow, nearly sliced me blooming finger off with me knife . . . It's left a scar, see.'

Nora exclaimed over the white thread worming across the girl's finger.

'Brussels sprouts,' explained Lucy. 'God, I hate brussels sprouts. When they get frozen onto the stalks like that you can't get them off. That's how come the knife slipped. It was so cold it didn't bleed, not till I got back in the warm. Anyway there he was, standing on the corner by the milk churns. I thought, Right, you asked for it. I was starving hungry, Ma, tired out and just about ready for him! I geed up the horse and we rattled down the track like a Roman chariot. Ran him off the road. But next thing, he's charging after us. Well, Ma, something just sort of snapped. I stopped the horse, dived into a sack of sprouts and pelted him with them till he turned tail and ran. I must have been screaming like a blooming banshee . . . Mrs Hooper said she heard me from the farmyard. Don't remember what I said – well, I do, just – but I won't repeat it here. Don't laugh, Ma.'

'Poor bloke,' Nora giggled. 'Frozen sprouts must've stung like billy-o.'

'Poor bloke nothing. He's the bane of my life, hanging about, spying on me. He won't take No for an answer, Ma, and I don't know what to do. I've tried everything. He knows I've met someone else.'

(Nora noticed the sliding glance in her direction, and filed it away for future reference.)

'I tell you, it's getting me down, all this. I've even seen him here, in Doddingworth.'

'Luce . . .' Nora looked about her in alarm, but the windows had steamed up again. Catching the waitress's eye, she asked for the bill.

'When I came out the pub after my bath, last Tuesday, there he was.'

The day she'd sent the note, Nora recalled. No wonder it'd been short and sharp. She'd had Roy on her mind, poor kid. The note had been a cry for help!

'I told him I was going straight back in to phone nine-nine-nine. I just wanted them to put the wind up him, Ma. But when I came out again he'd scarpered.'

Nora wasn't sure. Getting the police involved was going a bit far, to her mind, but she needn't have worried. They had taken all his particulars but said they could do nothing about him being a pest. Only if he made threats or did her actual harm. And, as far as either of them knew, Roy had never hurt a fly. Well, he might have, in the war, but that didn't count.

'So how many times you seen him, all told?'

'Four or five. But I'm sure he's been about when I haven't seen him. You get the feeling, don't you – sort of creepy? How he manages to get so much leave beats me. What am I gonna do, Ma? He knows where I work, all my comings and goings . . . And I'm so bloody sick of him.'

'Right. What you do, duck, you get on to his CO. Tell him all about it and get him to stop his bloody leave!'

'Would they?'

'Worth a try, ain't it? Find out where his unit's stationed and write to them.'

'Phoning would be quicker.'

Nora wasn't fond of phones. Disembodied voices from miles away. It wasn't natural. Still, in an emergency . . .

'Come on, gel, let's find a phone-box!'

They met a gaggle of girls coming into the tea-shop and, as Nora was introduced to Ruby and Doris, she recognised, with a pang, the accents of home. Near enough. Ruby was from Bethnal Green, real East End, Doris from over the water, Kennington. She warmed to them immediately. Helen was from Cheltenham, but never mind, said Nora, her heart was in the right place, working on the land, doing her bit for King and Country.

'So where are you from, Mrs Potter?'

'Same place as Luce.' They continued to look mystified. 'Walthamstow, duck – didn't Lucy tell you?'

'Yeah,' said Ruby, regarding Lucy with a quizzical eye. 'She did.'

Chalk and cheese, that's what she means, thought Nora.

\* \* \*

110

The girl at the Exchange was more than helpful and Lucy got through to the regimental switchboard in Lanarkshire in no time at all. Thereafter she was passed from Staff Sergeant Pillar to Warrant Officer Post but, with Nora squashed in beside her, mouthing instructions, finally had her complaint registered. They took some convincing that she was not at death's door, since Roy had made that his excuse to take compassionate leave every five minutes. Once that was sorted, things got rather brisk.

'Right then, Miss. Leave it with us, Miss.'

Roy was for the chop, all right, and good riddance to bad rubbish.

'So what I thought, Luce, while I'm here, we could go and get you something nice. A new coat or a frock to go dancing, seeing I only give you them stockings, Christmas. I've saved up me coupons.'

'Ma!' Lucy was jumping up and down like a six-year-old, 'Oh, Ma! That's the nicest . . . Oh, Ma! You sure?'

'I told you, duck, I'm quids in.'

Doddingworth shops were like none Nora had seen before. They huddled around the maze of ancient streets, frowning and pushing you off the pavement if they could. Doors, through which Lucy had to duck, opened with a subdued *ping*! and down you stepped, into a world racked with fashion. Many of the clothes bore the *Utility* label but, given the go-ahead, Lucy managed to find a few that were a little bit special. A dozen or so. In each of three shops.

'What d'you think?' she'd ask Nora.

Nora was rather alarmed at how a simple frock could change a girl into a sophisticated woman, could make her look wonderful or like a tart, but it didn't matter what she said, 'Ooh, very glam,' or 'A bit old for you, duck' – Lucy would turn this way, that way, before the mirror, stroking the frock into her figure, take it off, put it back on the rack, think about it, put it on again and then discard it.

Nora sank into her ankles and surrendered to exhaustion.

At last, at last, when she had decided on a nifty little crêpe number with a scoop neck and a skimpy skirt in a zingy shade of blue that the assistant thought made her look like

Claudette Colbert, Lucy began to play up.

'I'm not sure,' she began, biting her lip. 'It's a lovely frock, but . . .'

'But what?' Nora shifted her weight from one weary leg to the other.

'Well, it's the money that bothers me.'

'Lucy, do you want a new frock or don't you?' she asked, thinking that what she wanted was a nice sit-down. There was never no chairs in these places.

'Well, I do, I suppose.'

'Do you want this one or don't you?'

Lucy nodded.

'Then let the girl wrap it up. Don't worry about the money. My treat.'

The assistant began to wrap the dress, first lining it with tissue paper and folding it reverently along the seams, as though packing were an art form. Nora sighed, picturing the steaming cup of tea that she was going to have back in that nice little tea-shop.

'No, stop. It's no good.'

'Oh Luce, don't start. Not now, duck.'

The assistant paused. Raised a superior eyebrow. Closed and opened her eyelids with a massive effort of will, sighed, and removed the tissue paper, folding it carefully in lieu of the frock.

'It's just not right, Ma. Sorry.' Her smile *was* apologetic. 'Me not believing in ghosts, getting a frock on what you make out of those silly gullible people up at your church. It's a bit hypocritical, that's all.'

Nora had had enough.

'What, you saying my money ain't good enough for you!'

'It's not that, Ma.'

'Dirty money, is it?'

'Ma!'

'It's voluntary! They don't *have* to pay me. I don't ask 'em. I 'appen to believe in what I do. I'd do it for nothing if they'd let me!'

'I know, I know!'

'What an 'orrible little prig you are, Lucy Potter! Don't know how I come by you, and that's a fact.'

112

'Ma-a!' she wailed. 'Oh, we were having such a lovely day. Now I've gone and upset you. I didn't mean . . .'

'No, I don't suppose you did. You never do!'

'Will modom be wanting the dress?' enquired the assistant.

'No!' roared Nora.

'Oh yes, yes, all right, then,' said Lucy.

'Oh, don't put yourself out, gel. Don't dirty your hands on *my* account.'

'No, then, no! I don't want the frock. Oh, I don't know what the hell to do now!'

'Look,' said Nora, 'there's the money!' They looked. There it lay, a crisp five-pound note, pristine against the dark, polished wood, slowly uncrumpling, ticking like a time bomb. 'And take what you want out of that!' The counter shook as she slammed down her ration book and stormed out of the shop.

As she stomped down the street to the station, she imagined her daughter paying for the garment, impatient while the assistant cut the coupons out of the book and went through the wrapping procedure again. Then Lucy would strap the packet to her cycle, careful not to crush it, and cycle down the hill, hell for leather, ringing her bell and yelling to Nora to wait. And Nora would turn, grudgingly, as her daughter dismounted. They'd kiss and make up and, over a cup of tea, Lucy would tell her about this 'someone else' she'd met.

But she didn't.

There was an Ipswich train already in the station when Nora arrived, and when the guard saw her dithering onto the platform, not knowing whether to hang back or go on with it, he took the whistle from his lips and bundled her into a carriage.

A grizzling child had to give up his seat for her and while her head was in her bag, hunting for a boiled sweet to make amends, the train started to move. There may have been a flash of green on the platform, but Nora had taken off her glasses to wipe her eye, and she couldn't be sure.

# Chapter Twelve

Joe was the new man, of course. Five minutes it had taken him to weasel out the name of the farm from her mother, that time they had met in Kings Road. She had been coy about the address but had given out enough clues for him to find the rest from the telephone directory. Even so, his letter had been redirected twice, once from Great Baddow and once from Oxney Green, both somewhere near Chelmsford. There must be Hooper's Farms all over East Anglia.

The Hoopers had been intrigued. They sat at either end of the kitchen table, scarcely able to swallow their bacon and eggs for the stretch in their necks, their dour discussion about bovine diseases quite forgotten.

'Good news, is it, Towngirl?' Mr Hooper's thick fingers were actually trembling around his eggy fork. His mouth opened toothlessly and he glooped down the food, without looking at it, like a baby bird. Mrs Hooper was nodding furiously at the Land Girl, her eyebrows arched high in encouragement.

Lucy had hastily refolded the letter and put it in her pocket, muttering, 'Read it later ... Rude of me.' She was very conscious of her own burning cheeks and her employers' disappointment as she steered the conversation back to Marigold's mastitis.

'So you're saying the milk's all right, even when it's so rich? I mean, there are globules of fat floating in it.'

'S'all right. Drop o' water an' none the wiser!'

'But she's got a temperature. You sure it's all right?'

'You just milk the cows, my girl, and let me do the worrying.'

Mrs Hooper was looking pensive. Lucy knew she wouldn't rest now until she had squirrelled out the letter from wherever Lucy planned to hide it.

Not that it said all that much. Just that since completing his training session at Clacton he had rejoined his unit at Sowness which, he discovered, was not all that far from Great Bisset. Five miles at the most. No time at all on a motor-bike.

Maybe they could arrange to see each other now and again? In fact, now he came to think of it, they were holding a dance at the Air Base to celebrate Valentine's Day. Would she like to come? And, of course, she was welcome to bring any friends who might be interested? To be honest, girls were in short supply, so the more the merrier.

If she could make her own way there he'd be happy to give her a lift home. Though, since he did only have the motor-bike, her friends would need to make their own arrangements.

Helen and Doris had the whole thing organised over a doughnut and a cup of tea. Doris, small and pretty, felt sure she could persuade their warden's son, Keith, to drive them to Sowness in his baker's van. He'd been making spaniel's-eyes at her for weeks. Whether anyone travelled back to the hostel with him remained to be seen. Only if the worst came to the very worst, Doris assured them, pulling a face. Keith was a fat slug.

They would pick up Lucy on the way. The van was big enough to take five girls, one in front with the driver and four in the back. Better bring cushions as they'd be sitting on bare boards. The other girls at the hostel, and they would all want to come, would have to get the twenty past six bus and take pot-luck on the return journey. Shanks's pony wasn't unheard of.

Doris had miscalculated on two counts. When the van arrived at Hooper's the fat slug had his arm around her and a possessive gleam in his eye. Poor Doris was looking a little dishevelled already. A Minnie Mouse bow in her black hair had slipped down over one ear and her lipstick was badly smudged. But she winked bravely at Lucy as Keith got out to open the back doors. That was Doris's second mistake. You *could* get four girls in the back . . . at a squeeze. A very tight, bone-crunching squeeze. But Land Girls? In great-coats?

At least one of them had been muck-spreading that day, from the smell of it. Although the hostel provided baths, three inches of tepid water was perhaps not quite adequate. Combine the lingering pong of dung (of course, it was on their coats!) with the sweet cloying smell of cake and fresh bread, and cheap 'Devon Violets' scent, add the constant jolting over ruts in the road, in a dark and windowless vehicle and you have a recipe for nausea. By the time the van reached the main Sowness road, the girls were sick and sore and cross. Keith had to stop the van twice and, in the scramble to get to the ditch in time, Helen stabbed Ruby in the knee with a pointy heel and laddered her stocking. Joan crawled into something sticky in the back of the van, and Lucy was wondering why on earth she had come. She had spent a damp and dismal day riddling and clamping potatoes. An early night was what she needed and some of Mrs Hooper's patent horse liniment rubbed into her aching back. She must have been mad, she announced, to agree to a night out with a man she hardly knew, who couldn't even be bothered to pick her up from the farm. Who, it now occurred to her, had probably only invited her as a source of dancing partners for his mates.

Roy, she realised, had made her wary of men, distrustful of their motives.

Had any of them thought, groaned Helen, crawling back through the same sticky mess that Joan had discovered, how they were going to get up for milking when they wouldn't get to bed before two?

But when Keith opened the van doors at Sowness it took only a blast of cold, salt air and a blare of big-band dance music to revive them. Toes tapping, pins and needles forgotten, they left their Land-Army hats and great-coats in the Cloakroom, repaired their hair and lipstick, and when they had washed off the jam and caramelised sugar, the lumpy green caterpillars were transformed into giddy butter-flies. Their paid their half-crowns, and made their entrance.

This was always a difficult moment. Night-blinded, knowing there were all these voracious Walt Disney eyes, blinking in the forest dark, giving you the once-over, making judgements and low whistles.

'*Mine's the little one in blue. Don't think much of yours!*'

'Oh boy!' muttered Ruby, joining them inside the swing-doors. She had stayed behind in the Ladies to remove her ruined stockings. 'Look at all the lovely *men!*'

'Oh, thank you, God!' said Joan.

'Bye, Keith,' murmured Doris in Lucy's ear. But Keith took his responsibilities seriously. He found them a table near the band and saw them all settled in with ginger beer and lemonade before whisking Doris off for a quick-step. She mouthed, 'Help!'

So where was Joe?

In vain, Lucy scanned the room for red hair, peering at dancing couples, at shadowy figures at tables, at grey uniforms propping up the bar.

Nowhere.

What a letdown, she sighed. Couldn't she just pick 'em? She squinted as the doors swung open and a bunch of loudmouths strolled in. Would she even know him if she saw him again? Or he her? Her fingers drummed on the table. She wanted to dance.

Oh, blow him. She hadn't got her glad rags on for nothing. Well, her second-best dress, then. Home-made, green and brown and white splotches, white lace collar and a thin brown velvet bow at the throat. Prim, perhaps, but it was lovely stuff and hung beautifully, showing off her slim figure. And her legs. She turned her dark-brown wedding shoes this way and that, admiring the play of light on the silk stocking. Nora's Christmas present. And just what she'd always wanted.

She looked all right. More than all right, she looked blooming good.

And girls were in short supply, what was more, outnumbered at least three to one.

It wasn't until she arrived back at the table, flushed and breathless after a whizz around the floor with a short and flashy would-be Fred Astaire, when the band-leader was burbling an incoherent welcome into a badly adjusted microphone, that she happened to look around the brightly lit stage and saw him, sitting at the piano, filling in the pauses in the speech with trills and twiddly bits. He was looking straight at her.

She fluttered her fingers at him and grinned. He jerked up his head in greeting. Of course, she should have known that was where he'd be. He'd told her he played piano. And that was why he hadn't been able to call for her: he was one of the boys in the band! Surprising how much better that made her feel.

But he didn't expect her to sit out, twiddling her thumbs like Little Miss Wallflower, surely? She pointed at him and back to herself, held up her hands and jiggled, smiling an invitation. He shook his head sadly, indicating the piano. He pointed to her and then at the dance-floor, drew rapid circles as though whisking an egg and smiled hugely. *Have a good time*, he seemed to be saying.

So she did. Waltz, tango, fox-trot, jitterbug, with faceless partners, knowing that he was watching her. She thanked her lucky stars for her brothers, for Mick and Charlie and Jack, who had each, in their turn, tried out the latest steps on her. She had been thrown up in the air in the parlour, thrown between legs in the scullery, she had waltzed through the bedrooms and even tangoed on the table. Charlie had taught her not to lead. Mick had shown her complicated little toe-tapping bits in the quick-step. When girlfriends let them down, they had even taken her to Football Club dances, and she had watched what the other girls did, twitching their skirts, tossing their heads. Now she could do it, too.

They gave Joe a solo spot while everyone else in the band sloped off for a drink. In a mumble which nobody could catch he told them what he was playing, which turned out to be *Stormy Weather*. A miserable thing, a song she had always hated. At least the first few bars were. After that she was lost, and thoroughly depressed. Whatever tune there had been was scribbled over. Awful oobley-doobley stuff. You couldn't dance to it. Everyone just stood around trying to find a rhythm to tap. She flushed with embarrassment, wishing she hadn't pointed him out with such pride to her friends. But, at the end, a lot of people clapped, and not just out of

118

politeness. They whistled, too. And stamped.

Could they really have liked it?

Doris nudged her in passing. 'I should hang onto that one, if I were you.' Her smile was brittle as she turned back to Keith. The band-leader announced a ladies' 'excuse-me'. 'Thank Gawd for that,' came the heartfelt whisper. 'Bye, Keith.'

For the rest of the evening the slug clung to the bar, looking morose.

Whenever they gave him a break, Joe made a bee-line for her. But he seemed reluctant to dance and, when she succeeded in getting him out on the floor, she could see why. The music in his veins stopped well short of his feet. But he held her close and, in his own unstrict tempo, just about avoided tripping and barging into other dancers, and that was all she asked. She liked it that he didn't sing in her ear, like some. Or nibble it.

Instead they talked. About the farm and the Hoopers and the animals, working in the fields in all weathers, the trials of milking. But she had to probe to find out what he did. A gunner, he admitted, at last.

So . . . what did that entail?

Well, it varied. Fighter planes and bombers. Mostly he went on raids over Germany but that day he had been high over Germany, with photo-reconnaissance. Sitting ducks.

Her blood chilled and she stopped dancing.

'I'm sorry, Joe,' she said quietly. 'Whatever must you think of me? Going on about my tin-pot little job, and all the while you're up there risking your life.' Her eyes swept the hall. 'And all these other men are, too.' She blinked, as the room shimmered and everything went quiet, like the moments before an air-raid. A muted horn continued to play a mournful, contemplative solo. In the mirage she saw gaps in the group at the bar, the slug gone, the band depleted, girls dancing alone.

She wobbled.

He took her back to the table and went off to fetch her a glass of water while, as she shook her head, frowning, the volume increased and the room was full again. Back to normal.

119

God, that was weird, that flash of – what? Premonition? Better go easy on the gin.

When he came back, full of concern, she turned the conversation to his family. There was so much she wanted to know. Until he told her: that he had an older sister who was a nurse, that his mother had been a teacher until her marriage. His father was a doctor. Joe himself had been at university when he was called up, studying geography. Hoped to finish his degree after the war. Then? He puffed on his cigarette. He didn't like to look too far into the future. But he was thinking of an academic career.

When he went back to the band he left her staring moodily into her glass. That would teach her to get her hopes up.

It was his name that had thrown her. He was Joe, not Clive or Desmond. And he travelled third-class on the train. You'd expect that of a Joe.

True he was only a Flight-Sergeant, not a Wing Commander, but his sister was a nurse. Not a shorthand-typist, not a Land Girl: a properly qualified nurse.

His mother had been a teacher. Not a washerwoman, not a cleaner, who dropped her aitches and saw ghosts. A teacher, with letters after her name.

His father was a doctor, alive and practising.

They probably lived in a big house in the country, with gun-dogs and a woman who 'did'.

They were rich, educated. Middle-class. Probably Tory. Out of her league.

She could say goodbye to that rash of little red-haired children.

But the music wouldn't let her be miserable for long, and any regrets for what might have been were soon chased away with a twinkling *Lady Be Good* and *Kalamazoo*, and another man, another gin and lime.

Towards ten o'clock the dancing became more boisterous and confused. What began as the *Palais Glide* and twirling around under a thin Lance Corporal's arm, turned into the *Lambeth Walk* and strutting with a Bombardier, and the *Conga*, sandwiched between two dapper little chaps with 'tashes', went from bad to *Knees Up, Mother Brown*, with all the Land Girls linking arms. She caught sight of him standing on the side, a beer in his hand, looking moody. She kicked her legs higher, showing her stocking tops. No, you don't want me, darling. Working-class Walthamstow. Common as muck. Like me Ma. Not the sort of girl you'd want to take home to Mummy.

Amazingly, he was still there when the music stopped, watching her over the top of his glass.

He claimed her for the last dance, reminding her that he'd promised her that ride home. Very decent of him. But then he'd been well brought up.

Or maybe . . .

And her heart sank, remembering Roy. Remembering Hooper.

Maybe Joe was the same. Maybe all men were. Only interested in one thing. Not in whether she would make a suitable wife for a don, a suitable mother for his intelligent children, a suitable daughter-in-law for a doctor. None of that would have occurred to him.

Of course. That was what he was after. What Roy called 'relief'.

Well, she would show him! Not all London girls were fast. Furious, maybe . . .

And as they rocked from one foot to the other, while everyone else twirled by to *Goodnight Sweetheart* her anger bloomed. What if he was good-looking and thoughtful, what if he did have lovely, laughing speckled eyes, what if he was holding her so tight his brass buttons were permanently impressed on her skin? He was a man and he wasn't to be trusted. She wriggled out of his arms as the music came to an end.

Looked around for Doris and the others. But they all seemed to be in various stages of smooch with airmen. Oh blow. They wouldn't be going home in the baker's van, then. How was she going to get back? She couldn't go with Keith by herself. That would be asking for trouble. Nor could she walk five miles in these shoes. And there was milking in the morning.

Only one thing for it.

\* \* \*

121

Her arms were round his chest. She could feel his heart beating, feel the song vibrating in his bones, though the engine drowned his voice. He was very happy.

More fool him.

The cold wind in her face, streaming her hair at thirty miles an hour, added to her chill resolution.

She would tell him. Thanks for a lovely evening. Thanks for the lift home. But she wouldn't be seeing him again. A cool handshake should do it.

But as she turned towards him at the farmhouse door, she caught a movement over his shoulder. Someone was watching them. Standing by the cowshed, watching them. Someone had been waiting for her to come in.

'Who?' she murmured, though even as she said it, she knew. She had heard the scrape of the boot on gravel, caught the glint of blond hair shining silver in the moonlight. Her cheeks burned hot now. How dare he spy on her? How dare he?

'Who is it?' whispered Joe against her hair.

'Oh, just Mrs Hooper, I shouldn't wonder. Take no notice.'

But he seemed doubtful, holding back. She had to wind her arms round his neck, run her fingers through his bright hair.

Up at the window, Mrs Hooper dropped the curtain and hopped quickly into bed.

# Chapter Thirteen

Lucy was chief executioner, swinging the chopper and separating heads from necks, hands from limbs.

'Anyone I know, dear?'

'Audrey!' She flashed, caught out by the bulk in the doorway. 'Oh, come in out of the wet for goodness' sake. What a day!'

Audrey shook out the umbrella, and left it open to drain onto the woodshed's brick floor. She looked around for somewhere to sit and seeing only the saw-horse, wedged her rump between the struts. Then she took off her glasses and dried them with a hanky. When she was comfortable she tilted her moon-face in line with Lucy's.

'You look a bit browned off, dear. Not a lover's tiff already?'

'No, no.' She lifted the chopper and laid into another log. 'I . . . I'm not sleeping very well, Audrey. I . . .' But it wasn't at all the thing to share with your supervisor, no matter how approachable. She pursed her lips, sighed and lied. 'Oh, it's just the damn rain. Looks like it's set in the for the week! I hate being cooped up indoors. Still, I don't suppose they'll send the planes out in this weather; there is that.' She lifted the log with the blade, and bang, bang, banged it on the block until it split.

Audrey looked unconvinced, and Lucy flashed her a reassuring smile, hoping it would mask the dark shadows she knew circled her eyes, bring some real colour into her wind-scoured cheeks. Audrey's struggle with her need to know resulted in a suspicious squint. Looking more like a plump mother hen than ever, with her hair, under the red felt hat, permed and dyed a Rhode Island henna, she clucked curiosity, and Lucy felt guilty.

Audrey's work was her life. Her little black Ford beat a bumpy path to the doors of most farms between Colchester and Norwich, but the box of money, Land-Army wages (forty-eight shillings each, less-a-pound-to-the-farmer's-wife-for-bed-and-board), locked in the boot, was the least of its load.

The back seat groaned with her concern: great-coats that really fitted, warm ex-Army underwear, new boots for old. Papers and letters explained rights and sorted out disputes; magazines and books, Audrey's own private lending library, provided for lonely evenings in. When Lucy once complained of a wheezy chest, Audrey immediately raised her finger, 'Wait a tick,' and, broad beam wagging, burrowed beneath bunches of carrots and bags of swedes from grateful clients, bowls of butter (bowl to be returned next week), and envelopes of red-triangles to be sewn on sleeves for six months' service. She surfaced with a jar of Vick's Vapour Rub and while she was at it, some Vaseline for her chapped hands, and could Lucy use some tickets for a dance in Brand End or a whist-drive in Whittleton? Going cheap?

Empty-handed, she'd have been welcome. You could share a joke with Aud, share your sandwiches, share confidences. But not today.

Neither woman spoke, attending outwardly to the chopping and splitting, and the chink of sticks falling onto the hard floor. The smell of new wood filled their nostrils like incense. Lucy knew Audrey was waiting.

'Seen Ma, have you?' A carefully chosen remark.

'Fleetingly at breakfast. She looked a bit tired. Out late again last night, at a meeting.'

'No message, I suppose?'

Audrey's mouth corrugated with regret and her chins shook sadly, as they had on each of the last three Fridays.

Lucy knew that her thoughtless words had gone very deep. But how was she to know? Mothers aren't supposed to take offence, to have feelings. They are meant to be an inexhaustible source of hugs and comfort. 'Never mind,

124

dear,' is what they say. But Nora hadn't even replied to her letters.

'Why don't you try phoning her?' Audrey suggested.

'She's frightened of phones.'

'Go and see her then. Look, I'm driving back tonight, I'll give you a lift.'

'Would you? Oh Aud, if you could . . . I do need to talk to her.'

'Course! I'll call for you, shall I? Between five and six.'

'Audrey, that's really nice . . . Oh damn.' Her hopes and her grin faded. Mrs Hooper wouldn't take it kindly. 'No, that's no good. No, forget it.'

'Lucy, dear, I can bring you back again in the morning if it's work you're worried about. Really, I don't mind at all, not if it's going to help you get things cleared up with your mum. I'll have a word with Mabel. You'll have to miss milking but I'm sure she won't mind, just this once.'

'She will, but if *you* put it to her . . . Thanks, Aud, you're a pal.'

'*Who'm this "she"? Cat's mother?*'

A tall hooded figure stood framed against the slanting rain: Mrs Hooper with a coat over her head, spongy jowls a-quiver.

Like lightning, Audrey flashed, 'I'll be back tonight, Mabel, to give Lucy a lift into Clacton. Her mother's not well. Half-past five all right, Luce? Lovely.' The farmer's wife was still blinking as the next bolt earthed. 'She'll be stopping the night, Mabel, so you'll be short-handed for milking. All right?'

Mrs Hooper stood her ground, considered, breathed hard down her nose and frowned, but when she opened her mouth, it was to say something completely different.

'You'm wanted at the house, Towngirl.'


The heavy air in the farmhouse had been disturbed. Ripples stirring a stagnant pond. She sensed the visitors' presence before she heard the low murmur of their voices.

There were two of them. Policemen, drinking tea. One, a Sergeant whose name she promptly forgot, she'd not seen before, but the one with the helmet and the ears was the

125

village bobby, Eric Stone. She'd had a run-in with him about leaving her bike outside Hettie Fitzell's shop. The pavement was narrow just there and she'd blocked his stately plod. More helmets and capes clustered in misery outside the parlour window, like something the weather had brought with it. PC Stone's appraising eyebrow was designed to unnerve her, and when he flipped open a notebook, and scribbled importantly, it was as though he were making a quick sketch of a villain.

'Oh God,' she said. 'Is it Ma?'

'They'm lookin' for a runaway, some young soldier,' drawled Mrs Hooper, gratified to see Lucy's scalp tighten, widening her green eyes. Excitement mottled her throat pink. 'You en't seen un, have you?'

'We'll ask the questions, missus,' said the Sergeant, and Lucy shot him a grateful glance.

Audrey, bustling in behind, declared that one soldier looked much like another to her and she'd already seen scores of the dear boys this morning, passing along the coast road, both ways. And airmen. And sailors.

But they weren't asking her. They passed a photograph to Lucy, who rocked as she recognised the earnest pose, the soulful gaze, the blond hair.

His regiment was being posted overseas at the end of the week, they said. He had had his request for leave turned down and had gone missing.

'Coward!' Mrs Hooper hoisted one indignant breast, then the other.

Lucy bit her lip to stop them quivering. 'No,' she managed to say. 'Roy's not a coward.' She turned to the police. 'You think he's round here somewhere, do you?'

'Well, after what you told his CO, miss, 'bout him bothering you, stands to reason we'm gonna start by lookin' round 'ere.'

Mrs Hooper sat up, antennae jiggling. 'What's this? What you been up to, Towngirl?'

Lucy held tight to the edge of the dresser. She suddenly felt very weary. 'I haven't seen him, not for ages, not since that time in Doddingworth.' They didn't need to know everything.

126

'You want us to leave, Lucy?' Audrey included Mrs Hooper in her gesture.

Oh yes. But they'd never forgive her, and it was wiser to have them for her, than against. Numbly, she shook her head. 'Stay! Please.'

'You best have a sit, Towngirl,' said the farmer's wife, suddenly kind. 'Here, have my chair.'

She told them about the parcel. The one that came last week. Containing, well, certain items of clothing.

Could she be more specific?

Underwear.

Oh?

This was very hard. Were policemen bound by some sort of Hippocratic oath? Mrs Stone was a regular in Hettie Fitzell's shop.

Two pairs of knickers and a brassière. She had missed them from her laundry a couple of weeks back, but assumed she had left them in the bathroom at the pub. She thought the landlady must have sent them on and wondered why. Stupidly. Then it dawned on her that she knew the handwriting. Tight little letters that, months before, had formed words oozing love, brisk wedding arrangements, rosy glimpses of their future in the Lake District, after the war, when he would be managing his father's factory, and she, the large house that went with it. But why send her her own underwear? And how had he come by them?

Then came the first real stab of fear. She knew how. And it wasn't the action of a sane man. While she'd been in the tea-shop, laughing and shrieking with her friends, Roy had been sorting through the wet things that she'd left on her bike outside.

The Constable was writing furiously.

'Was there anything else in the parcel, miss? A note, like?'

She shook her head. Her skin prickled. Her shoulders trembled when Audrey put her arm round her, and tears sprang to her eyes. '*Go on*,' Audrey communicated with a hug. '*Tell them! Tell me!*'

'I can't.'

'*Go on.*'

'He had . . .' She took a breath. 'They were stained, the

127

clothes, stuck together, like he'd been . . . I . . . I don't know. They smelled a bit. Unclean.'

Mrs Hooper shut her eyes and muttered under her breath. Then she took Lucy's hand and stroked it with her thumb.

'Don't suppose you still have the . . . um . . . the articles, miss?'

'What? No, of course not. I burnt them. Threw them on the fire.' All eyes turned to see the ghostly ashes blowing up the chimney. Mrs Hooper released her Land Girl's hand in order to massage her own throat. But the younger hands continued to need comfort and Lucy found them wringing each other, just as though she were washing them.

'What else was I supposed to do?' she said.

'You should have reported the matter, miss. Brought the evidence to the station.'

'He's got a disease,' she explained. 'It's why I couldn't marry him. It's contagious. I didn't think . . .'

'Ah.'

The Sergeant had to help the Constable spell it.

Audrey caught Mrs Hooper's eye, raised hopeful eyebrows and jerked her head towards the kitchen.

Mrs Hooper got the message.

'Fetch you a nice cup o' tea, shall I?' she suggested. 'Poor young maid.'

The police were convinced he was hiding somewhere on the farm.

'Oh, my Lord,' wailed the farmer's wife, on her return from the kitchen. 'He'll murder us in our beds!'

'Bain't been no talk o' murder, missus,' said the Sergeant, frowning, 'We don't want to frighten the young lady. Now, with your permission, we'll have a look around. Flush the bugger out.'

'What – now?' said Lucy. The tea was hot and strong and very sweet and she was able to consider practicalities. 'It's raining.'

They assured her that police work went on no matter what the weather, or how difficult the circumstances. They'd try not to inconvenience anyone but they had their duty to do. If

Mrs Hooper would just oblige them with the keys to the outbuildings . . .

'In that case,' said Audrey, 'I'll be on my way – lot of calls to make – if you don't need me any more? Lovely. Lucy, dear, you'll be wanting this.' She drew a small brown envelope from her briefcase. She winked cheerily. 'Buy yourself some new knickers!'

Mrs Hooper glared at her, but Lucy smiled. She felt quite light-headed.

'Thanks, Aud.'

'Just check it's all there, would you, dear? And sign the book. Good, good. Well, if you gentlemen wouldn't mind moving your cars so that I can get Florrie out – Florrie the Ford,' she explained. 'Though whether she'll start is another matter. Might need a bit of a push . . .'

'They went through the place like a dose of salts. Thought the old man was going to burst a blood vessel!'

Lucy's face was still flushed from her mad ride through the rain, her lashes glued with the water, her legs splashed with mud. She'd taken the short cut along the bridle path. The police hadn't been going to let her come but as the afternoon had worn on and Roy still hadn't been caught, Mrs Hooper had insisted. Best for Lucy to get out in the fresh air. And the eggs had to be in the shops in time for the Saturday market!

Things did look better now that there were other people involved. 'A problem shared . . .' Mrs Hooper had said. She, of course, shared all her problems – and everybody else's. 'Nasty things, kep' in the dark, do stink worse'n pig dung.' Here, too, she was an expert.

There was no time for a bath when she reached Doddingworth, not and be back for half-past five. Perhaps she could have one at Clacton? It would be good to get right with Ma again. She had such a lot to tell her.

The other three girls leaned on the table, their tea getting cold, their eyes bigger as Lucy got into her stride. Her old flame deserting, being hunted by the police. True romance, real drama. Better than pigs farrowing or the latest Thin Man film.

'First of all he was complaining they were upsetting the animals,' she said, 'poking round their pens. The poor things thought it was feeding time. Then they were traipsing over the beanfield, in the rain, with their "*gurt flat feet . . .*".' She mimicked the sour-faced farmer's distress. None of them had met Mr Hooper, but they knew the type. Not that they couldn't all see it from his point of view. You don't want all that fine aerated tilth flattened, the life pounded out of it, collecting puddles, souring the soil.

'Then they were plodding over the parsnips. "*On'y jest bin singled, they!*"' she wailed, giddy with relief. The police had assured her that they'd catch Roy in no time. He wouldn't bother her again.

Helen made a face. Singling was a fiddly job, down on all fours, sacking tied round your knees, grubbing out unwanted seedlings and weeds.

'Then he was worried in case they found out he'd been watering the milk, and then he was running around like a wet hen, trying to find papers to explain all the machinery in the outbuildings. God knows how he came by it all. Potato-planting machines, all sorts of gadgets, brand-new. I wouldn't mind but he hasn't the slightest intention of using them. Stan, one of the men, he reckons Hooper wangled them on some government scheme. Anyway, there he was, steam coming out of his ears, papers flying around. And, of course, it was all my fault. "*You and your fancy men, Towngirl!*"'

'Cheek!'

'That's what he calls you, Towngirl?'

'They both do. "*They come for I in a Black Maria, Towngirl, be all down to ee!*"'

'I'm Townie,' said Ruby. '"*Can't 'spect no more from Townie, I s'pose, comin' in all hours. Teasing they poor menfolk. Fast, they girls from Lunnon!*"'

Helen said, 'Well, they think I'm utterly hopeless. Too posh for words, coming from Cheltenham!'

Silence. Three pairs of eyebrows raised in confirmation.

'O-oh!' she wailed, not really comforted by their laughter.

'So they ain't found him yet?'

'No, but they will. They were sure of it.'

'Mmm.' Doris sounded doubtful. 'Suppose they don't,

though. Suppose he comes back, Luce. You gonna shop him?'

'Shop him?' She hadn't thought of it like that.

'Whyever not?' Ruby was indignant. 'Bleedin' deserter. There's my dad and my bruvver giving it all they've got, for King and country. And us lot, working our fingers to the bone, much thanks we get for it. And all them at Sowness. And your Roy's bloody skiving off! Oh no.' She took no prisoners. 'String him up, I say.'

Put like that . . . If he came back, and he wouldn't, but if he did, she really didn't know what she would do.

She couldn't help feeling sorry for him, having to rough it in this weather. Well-heeled, spoiled, he liked his comforts. And all for her. She owed him something. He was part of her history, after all. Turning him in would be rather like betrayal, like turning in one of her brothers. Not that any of them would do anything so daft, not even Siddy. But Roy had done her no harm, not really. Made her a bit jumpy, but that was nothing. And that parcel. Showing off because she was going out with Joe. That was what *that* was all about. Very childish.

Anyway, he was probably drying off in a nice warm police cell at this very minute.

She turned off the main road without bothering to signal. There was nothing behind her. She never came this way as a rule. The road to Great Bisset was a long and lonely one and the hill was a killer. But the bridle path would be a quagmire by now. And she had to get back by half-past five. So she lowered her fisherman's hat to the stinging rain and pedalled on and up, and up, until her muscles cried out and she dismounted and walked the bike over the hill.

Stopped, gasping for breath and wiping a drip from her nose . . .

. . . Blinked at Audrey's car, poor Florrie! Slewed off the road into the ditch, its front wheels pawing the air.

. . . Flung her bike onto the grass and ran across the road, crying, 'Audrey?' and shaking rain out of her eyes.

Not a sign of her.

Had she swerved to avoid someone, something? Had the

131

brakes failed? Had she walked back to the village?

She must have left the doors unlocked. Someone had been having a fine old time, scrabbling through the stuff in the back. There were coats and jumpers strewn around on the road, sopping, and papers, vegetables . . .

'Oh God,' she said. The ditch-water gurgled down the hill.

Audrey had been waylaid! The rep's worst fear. That's why the boot-lid was gaping open, like the beak of a hungry cuckoo baby, why the starter handle was lying on the road, wrenched out of shape. She'd been attacked and the Land-Army wages stolen!

Where was she then? Lying in the ditch with her head bashed in? Lucy ran up the hill and down, her oilskins swishing through the wet grass, wild and bloody thoughts darting through her brain. She climbed the gate to the field, but there was no bedraggled heap of Audrey tucked into the hedge.

'Audrey!' she yelled. 'Where are you? You all right? Oh, say something, you silly woman!'

Her wellies squealed and slipped on the pedals, her throat ached, as she cycled down the cart-track, over ruts and potholes, mindless of the khaki mud that splashed her, of the driving rain that sluiced her clean again. Yet even in her race against time and murder and goodness knows what atrocities, she noticed that the police cars had gone from the farmyard.

Good, they'd got him.

She hopped and skidded to a halt, spraying a foul-weather goose with liquid dung. And fell in at the door.

Sloughing off her oilskins, puddling the floor, she dived for the phone. She had already dialled two nines, and was flicking wet hair out of her eyes ready to speak, when the parlour door swung open.

'Come you in 'ere, girl. You never guess what 'appened!'

There by the fire, swaddled in a beige bedspread, steaming gently, like a pudding on a plate, sat Audrey.

Speechless, Lucy let the phone drop.

The rep was clearly shaken but prepared, in spite of it all, to tell all. Again. Mrs Hooper settled down to watch Lucy's face, to add the odd affirmative nod, an eager accomplice, vicarious victim. Mr Hooper sat at the table, still busy with his papers.

132

'I should have known,' said Audrey. 'Bumping down that blasted track, I could hear the money chinking in the boot, and the springs creaking. I'd not noticed the springs before. Got out into the lane, fine, up the lane, fine, stopped at the junction and put the handbrake on. It's a job to see round the corner, with those blasted trees in the way, and the rain.'

She shook her head and glanced over to Hooper, implying that *someone* ought to do something . . . but Hooper's back didn't flinch.

She went on, 'And you know how the traffic whizzes along that top road. Damned dangerous.' Still no reaction. She gave up.

She had leaned forward, she said, trying to see through the wipers. And then she had heard something moving in the back of the car. A coat slipping off the seat, she thought, or papers. Blasted leather seat. Everything always finished up on the floor. But, before she could turn round, there was this thing wrapping itself round her throat!

'I thought I was going to die, Lucy. My heart pumping away, trying to get my breath. Because whatever it was—'

'An arm,' explained Mrs Hooper, not herself having the storyteller's love of suspense.

'Because the *arm*,' said Audrey, with a touch of annoyance, 'whoever's it was, was strangling me. Muscles of blasted steel. I was clawing at it, trying to bite it. I nearly passed out.'

'Nigh on passed out,' affirmed Mrs Hooper.

'I had to lean back to try and slacken the squeeze and as I did so, I just happened to glance in the mirror and saw—'

'Saw a flash o' khaki, didn't ee, Aud?'

'Mmm. Did I hear you mention a cup of tea, Mabel? Just before Lucy came in?'

Almost unable to bear it, the farmer's wife dragged herself to the kitchen. But she hovered in the doorway, unwilling to miss any of the story, or to resist the punchline. 'Your Roy, weren't it, Towngirl?'

Had to be. The lead weight had returned to Lucy's insides. He must have seen the police coming up the track and nipped inside Audrey's car before they reached the farmhouse.

''Fraid so.' Audrey looked so apologetic, you'd have

133

thought it was her fault. 'Same chap as in the photo Constable Stone showed us.'

'I . . . I didn't think he'd hurt anyone.'

Audrey made a wry face and pulled down the bedspread exposing an inch or two of chubby neck. It was red and sore.

'He said he didn't mean to hurt me, just to make me a bit more pliable. His idea was that I should drive him out of danger. Well, I wasn't going to argue. He loosened his grip but he was with me all the way. I assumed we were making for Doddingworth. Then we came to the hill.'

Lucy sat forward. Yes, what had happened at the hill?

'Well, I changed down. Florrie's never been very fond of that hill, needs coaxing up it. Otherwise she overheats. Temperamental little madam.'

'Should've called her Lucy, not Florrie,' chortled the lady from the kitchen.

Mr Hooper gave the girl a toothless grin. Both women glared and he turned back.

'Carry on, Aud.'

'Maybe it was nerves, maybe the plugs were damp, maybe we were going too slowly, I dunno. Anyway, just before the top of the hill, we stalled. Conked out. Oh, that did it. I was a bloody woman. I'd done it on purpose. Lucy, take it from me, you can't say you really know a man until the car goes wrong! I took it that the perfect gent wasn't going to do the honours, so out I got, in the pouring rain, to crank her up with the starting handle, while he sat tickling the choke. Lovely!'

'And it wouldn't start?'

'Oh *yes*!' Mrs Hooper came in with the tea. 'Started right away, didn't it, Audrey?'

Lucy was surprised.

Audrey said, 'She was ticking over nicely. "Must have been dirt in the distributor," I said. I could see he had no idea what I was on about.'

Lucy shook her head. Roy didn't drive.

'Anyway, I waited for him to get out of my seat and he wouldn't. He pushed me away.'

'Tol' you to sling your hook, didn't he?' Mrs Hooper said.

'Well . . .'

'He told you to go?'

134

'In so many words. Said he reckoned he could manage from now on. "Can't be much to this driving lark, if a woman can do it," he said.'

'Huh!'

'Didn't need telling twice, did you, Aud?'

'You walked all the way back?'

'Ran. Like the clappers. Didn't look back. I heard the engine stall. Florrie's never been good at hill-starts and a non-driver wouldn't have a clue. Then I could hear her coughing and spluttering, but I had to leave her to her fate. Didn't want him catching up with me.'

'Soaked to the skin, she were. Called the police. They'm on their way back now.'

'But you left the keys with him?' Lucy couldn't understand why he'd had to force the boot open.

Audrey felt inside the bedspread and brought out a small key on a tape round her neck. Waved it ridiculously, over her bedragglement.

'Key to the boot,' she said. 'Always keep it separate, for this sort of eventuality. Don't have to make life easy for the blasted little tea-leaves, do we? They get to the boot over my dead body. It's not a lot but my girls deserve every penny and I'm going to get it to them come what may.'

'Ah.'

'What?'

It sounded a hefty sum. When the police asked Audrey for a rough estimate she told them: 'Forty-two girls still to pay. Tha-at's forty-two times forty-eight shillings. That's . . . forty-two times fifty is twenty-one, divide by twenty is a hundred and five. Take off two forty-twos is eighty-four is four pounds four, from five pounds . . . One hundred pounds and sixteen shillings. Exactly.'

They were more impressed by the mental arithmetic than the sum, although Mrs Hooper said, 'Don't believe I ever 'ad 'undred shillin' let alone 'undred poun'. Happen he'll get a long way on that.'

'With any luck,' said Lucy, strictly to herself.

# Chapter Fourteen

So there was no lift to Clacton. Florrie had suffered a broken axle, and Hooper towed her to a garage. The police had checked Doddingworth Station before putting Audrey on the train (*'Blasted good of them!'*) but there was no sign of Roy.

They gave Lucy progress reports from time to time. He'd been sighted in Beccles, and in Whittleton, too. They were hard on his trail. It wouldn't be long. Not that Lucy really held out much hope.

He wasn't daft, he was determined. He was cunning, wily and he wouldn't let them catch him – especially now he had money in his pocket.

And then the sun came out and it was hard to think about anything but the spring.

In Walthamstow it had been a change of light, a change of weather, privet in bloom and sparrows waking you at dawn. Now her senses were bruised with it. She felt duty-bound to draw Mrs Hooper's attention to the fields, brushed with pale washes of colour, to the distant thickets in a daze of soft new growth, fluffy as a Persian cat, all tortoiseshell orange and brown and black. Had she seen the old hazel, out the back, its bushy catkins busy in the breeze? And the blossom in the orchard? Had she noticed the daisies in the grass?

'What you take us for, Towngirl?' Mrs Hooper said at last. *"'Oh, come an' smell the primroses, Mrs H.'"* she mimicked, *"'just breave 'em in! And the varlets. Bloomin' lovely!'"* (If that was supposed to be how Lucy sounded she hadn't come as far as she'd hoped!) 'As if I en't been doing just that, every spring, for over fifty year. Just I never made no song and dance about it. Country I might be, don't mean I goes round wi' me eyes shut. See a lot more'n you think!'

Lucy blushed as their eyes met, thinking she meant the loving on the front porch. The women were in the dairy, the gentle motion of churning butter lending itself to idle talk.

Too casually, too softly, the other woman said, 'Seed that chap o' yourn, that pervert.'

'What!'

Her hand froze on the handle but her heart churned on in the silence.

'Thought I better tell ee. He'm back, right enough. Seed him getting off the bus when I were in town, last week, shopping. Knowed 'im from that photo Eric Stone showed us. He never see I, though. Doubt he'd know I, anyhow, lessen he seed us round and about the farm when he been spying on you. Never told no one, though. Thought it best comin' from you.'

For that Lucy was grateful. The woman could keep her mouth shut when she chose. No one knew about Roy's parcel, of that she was sure.

She was a strange one, Mrs Hooper. Lucy was in no doubt that the 'Lunnon' ways were resented, or had been when she first came to the farm. Her every word and action had been seen as a threat or a challenge. There were still times when she took pleasure in Lucy's failings. She'd laughed herself silly to see Lucy chased by the bull. And then she could be kind, like now.

On the way back to the house, she pointed out the blue and pink lungwort all along by the pond and, with incredible patience, reeled off the answers to Lucy's questions.

'That blue one? Periwinkle. And that yellow'n be celandine and that'n's butterbur.'

Lucy played with the names, rolled them round her tongue as though they were honey, soothing the soreness of Roy's return. Somehow she had expected it. She hadn't really trusted the power of money.

The geese made her smile, strutting the yard, turning in their toes, their seven fluffy goslings rippling along behind like dirty water. What were deserters to them? What did anything matter so long as they had enough to eat and

137

somewhere to swim? They didn't care that there was a war going on not too far away. That both sides were mounting a spring offensive. Rather like Mrs Hooper.

When she saw the curtains blowing on the washing line, the colours faded in sun-stripes, Lucy couldn't believe her eyes. 'Good grief!' she heard herself say. 'You're not going to clean the windows?' And had immediately bitten her tongue. How very rude.

But Mrs Hooper wasn't really offended. Though she had to grumble. As if she didn't have enough to do, she said. 'Still, can't have no Towngirl looking down her nose. Stood there rubbing holes in the dirt, if ee don't mind, saying her can't tell if the sky'm blue, grey or if 'tis piddling down of rain. And the face on 'er! Enough to sour the milk.'

Lucy's grin was answered by a brittle smile. It was a start.

The morning had gone in a blur of work. Air clear as ice. Scouring the nostrils. Muscles flexing and stretching. Planting potatoes in the top field, while the mind went away singing. Breeze pretending to be warm. Fighting a losing battle with the North Sea.

Every now and then Lucy glanced up to see one more window blinking at the sun. Mrs Hooper was no more than a tiny toy now, a pink plastic dolly you could hold in your hand, sitting on one window-sill and then another, the bee in her bonnet carrying her right around the house. Only it wasn't so much a bonnet on her head as a pair of old red drawers!

'What ee gawpin' at?' she'd demanded, noting Lucy's astonishment after breakfast. 'They'm clean! Keepin' out dirt and pests, same as always!' And she had made a dignified, clanking exit, to make a start on downstairs, with her bucket of hot soapy water in one stringy hand, and another of vinegar water for rinsing.

'What's all this, then?' When Lucy came out to pull on her boots she found a pile of old newspapers, held down with a brick. '*News of the World*? Mrs Hooper! Kidding us you're going to clean the windows! You're coming out for a quiet read in the sun, aren't you?'

No, no, she spluttered, unused to a bit of joshing. She never *looked* at them papers. Not her. Just scrunched them up for the final polish. All that scandal and stuff. No time for all that. And then she realised and jerked up her chin at the girl's fooling.

Lucy looked up, alerted by another sound than the irregular beat of Hooper's hammer on a nail somewhere, and the seagulls screaming, following the tractor in the next field. A different sound, an ominous sound. Far away. A buzz like a bluebottle caught behind the curtain, an angry buzz that got louder, became the distant roar of engines. A ragged swarm of Luftwaffe planes came over the hills, heading towards the sea with a single thought: to make it safely back to Germany. Avoiding Sowness, if possible.

Then one of the buzzing insects detached itself from the others and, as it dropped, its voice could be distinguished from the rest. A sad mosquito whine; a whine that hiccupped, whined and hiccupped. It was coming this way.

The woman in the crossover pinny raised her red raggy head to squint under her hand, as the plane came limping into view – lost, quite lost – abandoned by the rest which were already crossing the coastline. Over the hills it came, down and up, scooping the air like a bluetit, over the trees, over the fields, over Lucy's head, down, across the lane, over the hedge and out of sight. The engine puttered and stopped.

Mrs Hooper had a grandstand view, as she told them, when they came scurrying in for a cup of tea. It seemed the celebratory thing to do. They'd brought their sandwiches. A little break from work was called for. Not every day an enemy plane spreadeagles among the cowflops. They felt as proud as if they'd brought it down themselves. And maybe just a little wary of Jerries on the loose.

She hadn't stopped out there on the window-ledge, she hastened to add. She hadn't fancied being a sitting duck for enemy bullets, dying with her wash leather in her hand. Lucy realised she was looking through clean glass to imagine the sight. She thought of Mrs Hooper's terror. Thought she must be so glad she cleaned the windows today.

She had wriggled back inside, she said, banging her head on the frame. (She would continue to rub the lump, in rueful

139

recollection, later that day, two days later, two weeks later, in Hettie's shop.) Saying her prayers . . . she glared at Lucy who quickly lowered a disrespectful eyebrow . . . Saying her prayers she had peeked over the window-sill, and seen the cows leaping about in terror, as the plane loomed over the treetops. They bucked like 'they broncos in the cowboy films,' their poor old udders jiggling, before breaking into a gallop across the meadow, tails up like periscopes, herded by the spread wings of the aircraft as it slid on its belly to the middle of the field, and stopped, spattered with bullet holes, streaked with grass and cowpats.

The bellowing of the animals had brought tears to her eyes, she said, but the worst was to have to look on helplessly as they rammed the hedge, broadside-on, scrambling to mount it, and each other, trying to get out to the lane. When they found they couldn't, they went running round the edge of the field, shitting in frenzy. Took them a good five minutes to calm, to decide that the monster was dead. Then they tossed their heads and swished their tails and did the sensible thing. They got on with eating the grass.

She had waited. Hooper, armed with his hammer down there by the gate, also waited. Good job he did. She saw him duck back behind the hedge as a long zippered flying boot broke the symmetry of the aircraft. Then another. The soles flattened against the side of the plane and a figure, in grey dungarees, sprang clear and down to the ground. One of *them*! A Nasty! She had seen a real Nasty!

Her audience was agog, unable to speak, their mouths full of cheese and bread and home-cured pickled onions. They watched her eyes growing rounder, her hands pressed to her cheeks, like Dorothy seeing the Wicked Witch of the West flying past the window on her broomstick. 'Oh, my!' she had whimpered. 'Oh . . . we'm all gonna be killed in our beds.' As she repeated the words now, the thought somehow reminded her of the red drawers on her head. She removed them and patted her hair tidy.

She went on, explaining with an air of disappointment, that the German had decided against paying them a visit. He had made for the opposite side of the field. The cows had watched him go, incuriously, and so had Mr Hooper. Showing a bit of

140

sense for a change, she thought. No use getting himself killed. Who's to say there weren't more in that cockpit, armed to the teeth, just waiting to blow his brains out?

A shadow darkened the doorway and there was Hooper. The tomfoolery was at an end. There was work to be done.

Some went back to the potato field, a couple to the stables. Hooper had a job for them, he said. Lucy stayed behind to wash the cups.

She heard the bucket handles squeal and the slosh of black water tipping into the 'bombie'. That was the window-cleaning done for a year or two.

The ringing of the telephone made her jump.

The farmer's wife came in, flapping her hands at it. Strange creatures, telephones. So Lucy answered. It was PC Stone, who were just wondering, like, whether, be chance, an enemy aircraft had crashed in the vicinity?

Hooper was at the door, mouthing, 'Who?' She mouthed back, 'Stone,' and watched his face darken with cunning. He banged the side of his nose with his forefinger. What did he want her to say? She couldn't deny it. His popping eyes were full of meaning but quite unreadable.

'Um . . . not exactly crashed, Mr Stone.'

He came in then, put his face close to hers and snarled a rancid, 'No-o-o!' in her face.

She snarled back, cheese and pickled onion, 'You talk to him!' Knowing he wouldn't.

Only, Eric Stone was saying, a plane had come over that looked to be in trouble, like, but there weren't no explosion nor smoke nor suchlike . . .

Turning her back on Hooper, Lucy explained that a German plane had belly-flopped into the cowfield, scaring the shit out of the cows and ploughing up the grass, but otherwise doing no great harm. It was a two-man fighter plane and Mrs Hooper had seen one of them running off, over the fields towards the woods. There were no other signs of life.

'What, you reckon he'm had it then, this other?'

'Mrs Hooper, Constable Stone wants to know if the other man in the plane is dead.'

Mrs Hooper looked at her husband's livid face, at his fat

141

fingers flexing and unflexing with fierce longing, and first she shook her head, then she nodded, shook it again. About to burst into tears.

'Um, Mr Stone? Right, well, Mrs Hooper didn't see anyone else get out of the plane. She thinks he must be dead.'

'Hooper there?'

Hooper shook his head vehemently in answer to the proffered telephone.

'Be along, shortly.'

'You tell Hooper, don't ee go poking round. Likely they'll have a tank o' fuel – well, half a tank, leastways, for the return journey. And guns and that. Make a tidy old bang, that lot go up. Stay well clear, is my advice.'

'I think we'll probably have to move the cows then, Mr Stone. But we'll be careful. Don't worry.'

He thought about it. Said he'd get on to Sowness for reinforcements and they'd be right along, soon as ever. Within the hour, likely. They'd maybe come cross-country, through the woods, see if they could pick up the German on their way.

'Perhaps you could keep to the footpaths then, Mr Stone. All the fields are newly seeded.'

Hooper nodded. That was the right thing to say.

Stone mumbled inaudibly then he said, 'Oh, Miss . . .'

'Yes?'

'No word from Private Sykes?'

'No.'

'Let us know, won't ee? If he trouble you again?'

'Of course.'

When she relayed the bit about the fuel, Hooper's eyes narrowed to sly little slits.

'Us best be quick, then, Towngirl,' and he stomped out as the horse and cart clattered into the yard.

When the farmer told them his plan Lucy was aghast. She'd have no part of it: it was wrong. She'd never knowingly broken the law before in her life.

'Bain't breaking the law, girl. 'Tis salvage. Waste not want not.'

'It's stealing,' she insisted.

142

'Bain't stealing, not from the Nasties. Take what you like from Nasties; we'm at war, bain't us? They got no more use for un, anyhow.'

'Suppose we get caught? They'll put us in prison.'

'Us won't get caught,' Hooper assured her, as if he was an old hand at this sort of thing.

He and the men went back to the cowfield, armed with shotgun and hoses, while Lucy and Mrs Hooper loaded the cart with spare milk-churns.

It was a Heinkel, too small somehow, despite its long tail, for all the damage and misery it must have caused that day, the painted swastika on its tail-fin, too ordinary. The dead man's head was thrown back, his mouth open, as though he was snoring. The lack of blood from the bullet-hole in his forehead helped perpetuate the illusion of a sleeping passenger, and Lucy found herself whispering so as not to disturb him. The front seat, of course, was empty.

There were blinkers on the horse; even so she objected to being brought close to the plane, and Lucy had to hold her head and talk to her while the men managed the churn. The farmer was standing on the wing with one end of a short length of hose stuffed into the fuel tank.

'Ready?'

'Aye.'

He sucked the fuel through the hose, placing his thumb over the end between breaths, and then lowering it into the churn. He let go, and the petrol piddled in, deep and resonant against the metal sides.

A mirage shimmered from the neck of the vessel.

When it was full they put on the lid and the two men heaved it onto the cart. One more and they let Lucy go while they filled another churn.

Mrs Hooper was waiting by the barn, her face marsh-mallow-white instead of its usual pink. Lucy jumped down and, tight-lipped and speaking with eyebrows, the two women rolled the churns from the cart, down the back board and into the barn. They handled the twelve-gallon churns easily. It was a job they did every morning.

'This is a fire-risk, Mrs Hooper,' muttered Lucy darkly, as they covered the churns with sacks and arranged bales of

143

straw to hide them.

'Mabel . . .' said Mrs Hooper, after some thought.

At last. Mabel! After five months, Mabel! Friends in adversity.

'Mabel . . .' But she didn't smile. 'You're asking for trouble, you know.'

'Barn's a fire-risk any old how.' The older woman shrugged. 'Bain't no one gonna smoke in a barn, they got any sense. Safest place for'n, you ask me, Towngirl.'

'Lucy . . .' said Lucy, but she didn't hold out much hope. Mrs Hooper, Mabel, didn't take kindly to change. Lucy climbed back into the driver's seat, flicked the reins and clicked to the horse, from the side of her mouth.

As she and the horse careered up and down the half-mile track that morning, their hearts beating wildly, the cart racketing around the corners on two wheels, Lucy considered her position.

Who'd've thought it? (*Mind the pot-hole!*) Lucy Potter, typist from Walthamstow (*Was that churn secure?*) fuel-running for a gang of thieves? She cursed the day (*Quick, quick!*) she had learned to drive the horse and cart. Not that she'd had any choice. (*Out of the way, pheasant! Stupid creature!*) You did as you were told.

She had a choice now, though. No question. She knew what she ought to do. (*What was that – that flicker of movement in the beanfield! Someone coming?*) Dig her heels in. Walk out. (*A March hare! Fancy that!*) She must be mad, getting into this. Walk out! (*Nearly there!*) She'd get another job, easy well. Land Girls were gold-dust. The farmers were crying out for help.

But she didn't want to. (*Slow for the gate!*) It was all right here. (*Keep to the same cart-tracks, gently now . . .*) Hooper was a rogue but he knew his stuff, and Mabel Hooper, well, she was a funny old thing. (*Whoa, horse!*) Beneath those smelly old cardigans there was a sensitive woman. (*Watch them swing those churns, so easy . . .*) Ma would like her.

She flapped the reins; one more trip would do it.

When the police arrived, the German had gone to ground and the plane's fuel tank was empty – explained by leak-holes where an oversized bullet, the size of a shotgun cartridge, had gone in one side of the tank and out the other. Hooper's workers were all back in the topfield, planting potatoes. The farmer and his wife, between them, had driven the cows up the lane to another field, so that the Heinkel could be disposed of.

Cart-tracks? Ah yes – well, the cart had been brought in to stop the cows jostling the aircraft. Thanks to your warning, Constable Stone. All thanks to you.

The German didn't turn up until the first week in May.

It was Lucy's half-day. She and Joe had taken a picnic lunch, her usual cheese sandwiches, four rounds instead of two, a bigger bottle of tea, plus a couple of wodges of Mabel's seedy cake.

'Way to a man's heart,' she had winked. The picnic was her idea.

'What about the eggs?'

'I'll take 'em this time, on the bus. Time I went to town, try that hairdresser's you was on about. Can't be doing with all this hair on me neck, not this weather.'

What was the world coming to?

They'd been going to see *Lilacs in the Spring*. Any excuse to sit in the back row.

'Don't know what you'm thinking on, Towngirl, cooped up in the pictures on a day like this. An' you telling me you'm so fond o' fresh air. Your young man need to get out, he been flying them airyplanes all week. Want to stretch his legs . . .'

Stretching legs had been their intention. She had put on her walking shoes and socks, and a skirt and blouse in his honour, 'casting clouts' in all directions, for the may blossom was out and the day promised to be warm and bright and wonderful.

They stepped out up the lane, a long-legged pair, matched in that if nothing else, she thought. She realised she was getting too fond of him. It wouldn't do. Today she would tell him.

Sun glinted off the brilliantine in his hair. He had taken trouble today. Haircut, clean tie. He put his arm round her but

145

soon broke away to take off his jacket and that tie. It was too hot. Hand in hand was better. They hung over the gate and she introduced him to the cows: Marigold, the one with a sense of humour, whose favourite trick was to stick her foot in the bucket. Hebe, and her calf. Old Pansy, whose last year as a milker this would be.

'Then what?' asked Joe, and gave her a squeeze as her eyes filled with tears. She hadn't realised how attached she'd become to the creature.

When they reached the footpath along the side of the beanfield, they were forced apart by its narrowness. She went in front to show the way and to point out her handiwork, the new stile, the bridge across the stream, the cutting back of brambles and nettles, the felling of a tree. He drew her attention to weeds she'd missed among the beans and she hit him. They waved to Stan and Derek and the Italian prisoners of war, hoeing beet, knotted handkerchiefs on their heads. They whistled to see her in a skirt. Joe hurried her along. He was getting hungry, he said.

In the woods they sat, primly, in a shady clearing to eat their food. Halfway through the seedy cake she decided the time had come.

'Joe . . .'

'Mmm?' He turned his face to her and the sun, dappling through leaves, lit up his strange, speckled eyes. He was lying propped on an elbow, and tracing her leg from sock to knee with a grass-stalk. A lock of copper-wire hair had fallen across his forehead.

'There's something I ought to tell you.'

'Oh don't, not now. You're married with half a dozen kids?'

'No-o-o!' she laughed.

'Well, that's all right then.' He stopped tickling her leg and shaded his eyes to look at her properly. 'Go on, what?'

'I . . . I . . . well, I need to know how serious you are about me.'

'What? I thought that was the heavy parent's line.' He suddenly became much older and, for some reason, Northern. 'I'd like to know, young man, what your intentions are towards my daughter.'

146

'Well?'

'What? Oh, very serious. Very, very serious!' He pushed up her skirt and kissed her knee.

'Joe!' She straightened her legs and tugged her skirt down over both knees. He rolled around and lay with his head in her lap, squinting up at her.

'I have to spell it out, do I? I'm barmy about you. Always have been. Well, that's what it feels like. That I've known you for ever. I sort of recognised you on the train. I knew I had to see you again.'

'Oh!' He had never said so much before.

'And so?' he prompted, uncurling her hand and kissing the palm. The blisters were gone now, thanks to nightly applications of Vaseline.

'Oh, I . . .' What had she been going to say? She made a real effort to concentrate. 'Well, the thing is, Joe, I . . . I mean, I love you, but I'm sorry. I don't think it's going to work.'

The laughter drained from his eyes. 'There's someone else.'

'Oh no, no. I mean, I'm not right for you.'

He crushed the grass-stalk in his fist, and flicked it away. Waited.

'Don't look at me like that,' she said. 'Oh dear, I should have said all this before.'

She took a breath, removed a ladybird from his hair and told him in a rush that she had no posh education, no social graces, and a lot of bad habits. She told him about her mother. Up the pole, talking to ghosts, earning a living from it if the truth be told . . . so there was madness and well, dishonesty, in the family, and . . . and the point was that she wasn't nearly clever enough for Joe. She wouldn't be able to discuss politics and philosophy with professors, she wouldn't be able to hold sophisticated tea-parties for students and discuss plays and music. She'd never been to the theatre in her life. Or a concert hall. They'd all laugh at her and she'd let him down. His parents would despise her, think her a common upstart, on the make, and she'd hold him back and he would come to resent her and they'd just better stop it all now, before it got out of hand.

147

She waited.

But he said nothing. Didn't move. When she expected him to jump to his feet, brush off the crumbs of their friendship and walk away, he stayed quite, quite still.

Then he said, 'I can hear your dinner going down.'

'Joe!'

'What?'

'Weren't you listening?'

'Oh yes. I agree.'

She blinked. Her heart sank. 'Oh.'

'Well, absolutely. You're quite right. Chalk and cheese, I'm afraid.'

He sat up, made her wait while he lit a cigarette.

'I knew it all along.' He blew out the match. Took a deep drag of smoke. 'It was hopeless from the start. I mean, what can you have in common with a bloke with two left feet? A thirty-a-day man, who's scared of cows. Oh yes, I admit it. I bet you like to eat shell-fish, too, don't you? Well, I don't, you see. It says it all.'

She couldn't believe he was laughing at her and turned her head away.

'Lucy . . .' His voice was faint, across a chasm.

She opened her mouth to speak again but realised that he would not be able to hear her.

'Lucy, I couldn't give a . . . I couldn't care less how many school certs you've got – as long as they're not in politics and philosophy! I'm a geography man, for God's sake. Wide open spaces, me. Couldn't bear to be cooped up in a university. And don't do your mother down, sweetheart. She's a wonderful woman. You're a lot like her. So much energy and—'

'Spirit?'

She took his cigarette and stubbed it out in the grass. Clasped his hand and kissed his kippered fingers.

'Oh Lucy, you're . . . you're such a dope. Fishing for compliments, that's all this is, isn't it? All right, so you're the loveliest person, body, mind and . . . yes, spirit, that I have ever met and I am convinced, positively, one hundred per cent, that there is no one more right for me. Mum and Dad will love you. They'll see straight away that we were made

148

for each other.'

'How can you tell?'

'Oh shut up, woman. You *suit* me, for God's sake. Down to the ground!'

And that was where she found herself, joyfully flattened beneath him, kissing him hard. His mouth tasted of cigarettes and seedy cake, his skin smelled of sun. She wanted to breathe it for ever, his smell. She found his fingers groping with the buttons of her blouse and herself helping him. He fumbled with her brassière. She sucked at his ear-lobe, then helped him. She heard him groan as her breast fell free, felt his hand close over it, knead it, explore it. It felt new to her too. A strange thing to be so desired. Her nipple hardened under his thumb. His mouth left hers, bent on another quest. She felt his tongue flicking the nipple hard, felt him take it in his mouth. Her hands fluttered wildly about his head and her pelvis rose up to meet him.

She heard him croak in her ear, 'Oh God . . .' and roll off.

Her heart was thumping under her hand. 'What?'

'It's no good,' he groaned. She couldn't see his face; he had turned away, his arm flung over his eyes.

'What's the matter? What have I done? Oh Joe, I'm sorry.'

She was too 'fast', that was it. He was disgusted with her. He had said she was lovely and yet he had stopped loving her. In the space of a few seconds, it had all changed. So now he knew. She really wasn't good enough.

She leaned up on her elbow and prised his arm away. There was pain in his eyes. And something else.

'Joe, don't.'

'God, I love you.'

She kissed him. That was all she needed to know. Her nipple touched his shirt. She unbuttoned it. Horrid little khaki buttons. And found tender skin. She licked his nipple, a tiny bud on her tongue, tasted his sweat, teased the hairs on his chest.

'Lucy, stop. Please, love, stop. I . . . I can't stand it.'

He told her again that he loved her, that all he wanted to do was love her. Properly. All the way.

'Go on, then!' she pleaded. 'Go on!'

He explained what it would mean. That this was how

149

babies were made, that it might hurt, that she would no longer be a virgin, that if they weren't careful she could become pregnant and that once started there was no going back, not for him. He loved her to death.

'And that's the other problem,' he said. 'Lucy, I want to marry you but, well, suppose I'm killed?'

'Do it, Joe, please.'

He took her hand and guided it to the hard bulge in his trousers. 'This is it, then,' he said. 'Let me introduce you.'

Afterwards she reached into the carpet of yellow flowers on which they had been lying, picked one and held it under his chin.

'Well, that's another thing we have in common . . . we both like butter.'

'That's not a buttercup.'

'Margarine, then. It looks like a buttercup.'

'Same family, *Ranunculaceae*, different leaves. This one's called Goldilocks.'

She chuckled, threading the flower into his pubic hair. 'Good old Auntie Maud. She knew what she was talking about.' And then, of course, she had to explain. By the time she had answered all his questions about the ghosts and her mother, about Roy and the break-up, she had made a chain of flowers, which she wound around his limp penis. It looked so beautiful, curled up, asleep, in its nest of copper-beech hair, she had to kiss it. And it awoke, bursting its bonds and springing free.

'Good grief!' she said, seeing it, as opposed to feeling it, for the first time, in all its glory. 'This *is* serious.'

They found the German half-in, half-out of a hawthorn bush at the edge of the woods, the musky smell of may blossom almost masking the stench of decaying flesh. His flying boot was sticking out from a cocoon of stitchwort and goose grass, a starry winding sheet, and as Joe tore away the weeds, exposing grey overalls and flak jacket, as the flies buzzed at the disturbance, Lucy had a strong feeling, before she fainted, that they were meant to come upon him thus, after their first serious spell of love-making.

150

To have it spoiled.

That they were meant *not* to find him until his face had been well and truly gnawed by foxes and rats and other little carnivores, reduced to a mess of rotting flesh and maggots and white bone within a flier's helmet. That it had to be them, she and Joe, the lovers, who found the body. It was apt, it was just, it was how he had planned it.

Because, of course, she knew that the pilot had been killed and by whom. How, was not apparent; there were no wounds from knife nor bullet, no evidence of strangulation or garotting on what was left of his neck, no sign of suffocation. But Roy had done it. There was no doubt.

When she came round, she found that she had been moved further off. Joe had dragged her or carried her. He would not let her look at the body again. He kept apologising, as if it were all his fault.

'Poor chap,' he said. 'Terrible way to die, starvation. He must have crawled into the bush for shelter and never come out again. If he'd had any sense he'd have given himself up, but these Jerries, you know . . . very proud race.'

She had been picking long strands of goose grass from his trousers. Now she looked at him in astonishment. Starvation? You don't die of starvation in less than two weeks. (It was a little over a month since the plane crash and the body must have been in the hawthorn bush for at least three weeks, from the state of it.) But she didn't argue. Let him think the man starved to death, despite clumps of potatoes and swedes along the sides of the fields, despite milk-cows in the field down below, despite birds and rabbits and all the food that a desperate man would soon lay his hands on, and a farm nearby. Let him think anything he liked except that someone murdered him. Though perhaps the authorities wouldn't call killing a German 'murder'. Mr Hooper was always saying that the only good German was a dead German. They wouldn't hang you for it. Probably give you a medal. If you weren't already a deserter.

The police had another theory. They discovered abrasions across the back of the man's head. Must have happened in the crash, they said. He had managed to run across the fields before collapsing, crawling into the bush and passing out.

151

Mrs Hooper, when she arrived back, light-headed with perm, thought he might have eaten something poisonous. Bryony or nightshade. But it didn't really matter how it had happened, did it, not really? The important thing was that he was dead, not roaming round the countryside, murdering people in their beds.

So Lucy kept to herself the news that Roy had killed the man for her to find, as some sort of terrible warning. She kept to herself the fact that he was still hanging round. That she had seen him.

Where he was holed up was a puzzle. She had searched all the outbuildings, stables, cowshed, pigsty, hay-loft, barn. She had been up in the attic, down in the cellar. Not a sign of him. She had a feeling he must be living rough in the woods. Or round about the village.

How he was surviving, she had no idea. Unless he had laid in a stock of food, bought with the money he'd stolen from Audrey's car. He looked all right. A bit rumpled, but fairly fit. Apart from that hard-done-by look in his eyes. *He* certainly wasn't starving.

What he wanted, she didn't know any more. He didn't say much, if anything, these days, no more pleading with her, no more tasteful little parcels through the post – she left her laundry at the pub and collected it when she was ready to go home – no threats, nothing. He just turned up at odd moments, to let her know he was still around; once, three or four weeks ago, when she was on her own in the cowshed, a couple of times before that, when she was working in the fields, but mostly in the tracks and lanes around the farm, appearing from the shadows, from behind trees and around corners. He didn't expose himself, nothing like that. He'd just stand there, 'like two of eels', a silly smile playing round his lips. She supposed he thought he was looking sexy.

That time in the cowshed, she had asked him, without breaking the rhythm of the milking, leaning into Marigold's side for strength, what he would do if she gave in, if she said, 'All right, Roy, you win.' Would he go to the police? Would he spend however many months or years in the glass-house that it took to repay his debt to society? Because she couldn't marry a wanted man. Would he? Would he do that for her?

152

He frowned, his hand on the cow's knobbly haunches. Looked at Lucy hard as if really considering the matter. Then he muttered, in his thin voice, 'You got me going there, Luce.' And kicked over the bucket of milk.

She had been so angry. 'If you won't go to the police, Roy, I will.'

'Do it, Lucy. By all means. And while I'm on fatigues, cleaning bogs with a toothbrush, or whatever, I'll be thinking of you . . . thinking of seeing you again, thinking of all the lovely things we'll do together when I get out.'

And then that smile. At the time, not understanding, she had thought it pathetic. Now that she knew what he meant by 'lovely things', knew how lovely they were with Joe, she was sure she would rather die than do them with any other man, Roy least of all. Now when she thought of his smile, she shivered.

# Chapter Fifteen

It had been a long session, with Nora doing the lion's share, and Eric and Iris spelling her, in Mr Whittaker's absence. The poor old man had had one of his 'turns' and Doris had made him stop at home. Eric was a good substitute, though, getting better and better. He seemed to be taking his lead from her, letting the words come from the spirits, not attempting to put in his own two penn'orth, like some. Like Iris, with her auras and her flowers and her plucking names out of the air. But never mind, she got the job done.

At the end they all sang '*I'm H-A-P-P-Y!*' with gusto and really seemed to think that they were. As they trooped out for their tea and biscuits they were all smiling and there were tears of real joy in their eyes.

But what about the medium, Mrs Potter? Was she happy?

Couldn't rightly say she was.

What with all the worry about Jack. She hadn't heard from him in blooming ages. All the others was a bit slow with their news but that only to be expected. Jack was different. Him and Luce was a pair of letter-writers. And they'd been coming thick and fast till just before she come away. Where was he? Little toerag. He wasn't dead, she knew that much. None of 'em was dead. No young Potters in the spirit world, thank Gawd. She kept thinking he might be a prisoner somewhere, fed on bread and water. No, most likely he'd got hisself a girl. Too busy courting to write home. But somehow that didn't sound like young Jack.

She was beginning to feel her age, that was the top and bottom of it. Tired out, most of the time, bleeding knackered tonight. Sowness had more than its fair share of dark forces, she'd say that for it! They was always there, of course, souls in torment, mostly, and generally, it was just a matter of sliding away from them. They got the message. And, more often than not she spotted them before they saw her. Say so herself, she could tell a bad un a mile off, so she'd close herself to it and Bob's your uncle. Tonight, though, she had been aware of a very determined something, nagging away on the edge of her psyche. Each time she finished a 'reading' it'd be there. She knew better than to pay it heed. Do that and, like one of them nasty delinquent brats, it'd make your life a misery. No telling where that could end. But it was a distraction and she finished up with a splitting headache.

What with that and her indigestion, a pain that went right through from her ribs to just below her left shoulder-blade, she was not on her best form. The doctor called it 'nervous stomach' but she put it down to Marjorie's cooking.

'A nice steak and kidney pudding tonight, Nora. Line your stomach, keep out the cold.'

Lie on your stomach more like, like bleeding lead. But she got very sniffy, Marje, if you didn't eat what was put in front of you. Nora would have given the world for a bit of toast and dripping, now and again, or a lightly boiled egg.

And standing all that time was doing her ankles in. She'd tried conducting the meeting sitting down but they couldn't see her over the rail.

What she wouldn't give to be able to go home at the end of the day. Soak her feet, loosen her stays, take her teeth out if she wanted. In Marje's guest-home, you had to behave yourself. Like a guest. You had to make polite conversation.

'How's the baby? I heard him crying last night. Teething, is he? Poor little mite . . .'

'Lovely weather we're having. Just look at the sea. So near and yet so far, eh? First thing, when they tell us the war's over, I'm going to wriggle me toes in the sand and have a paddle.'

'Heard from your son, have you? Richard, ain't it? Oh, Rodney. And where is he now?'

'What a pretty pattern. Is it for yourself? Oh yes, you suit that colour. Don't know how you can keep track, all those knit-two-togethers.'

Variations on a theme. She could hear herself saying the same things, over and over. Even bored herself. But what could you do? Organise a sing-song or a game of Consequences? Get up on the table and do a fan-dance?

The other guests was well-to-do more often than not, no company. Once they'd had their fortunes told they made strangers of themselves. And who could blame them? They was officer class and she was ranks. She knew that. And she wasn't going to start sounding her tees and aitches for Tom and Edna from Maida bleeding Vale.

Marje was all right but she was either busy in the evenings, totting up her takings, or she had her nose in a book. In fact, she seemed to prefer her books to a good old chinwag. That's education for you. You don't hold with gossip. You don't hold with going down the pub for a Guinness. You don't hold with a bit of a flutter on the dogs. A dull old stick in her way, was Marje.

And what was the alternative? Listen to stuff on the wireless you didn't understand. Concerts and talks, mostly about the war, and you lost track. Many's the time she started out with good intentions, and finished up sound asleep.

Time she got upstairs, all she wanted was her bed. There was Mum, bright as a button, all ready for a natter, and Nora couldn't keep her eyes open. Any case, you had to keep your voice down or you'd have them banging on the walls. Poor Mum got the ike, more often than not. Got to taking herself off to Great Bissett. That was why she'd come, wasn't it? Keep an eye on her lovely Lucy.

What would Lucy have made of that, eh? Didn't believe in ghosts and there was her Gran hanging over her bed, night after night, like a blinking guardian angel!

Oh Lucy.

She'd sort of expected the girl to be there, in the audience tonight, seeing it wasn't all that far from Great Bisset. There had been a few Land Army girls, and the uniform had made her heart jump, but none had been her Luce nor any of her mates. Knowing how the girl felt about the sidekick stuff, she'd probably boycotted the place on purpose.

That awful row. Dirty money, she'd made it out to be, like Nora was some old prossie or something. Terrible things

156

she'd said. And them letters, saying she was sorry, she never meant to hurt her . . . Not worth the paper they was written on. Because what hurt was that she really believed it. That Nora was a quack and a parasite. Some words you can't take back. They go too deep.

So what if Lucy didn't believe in it, clairvoyancy and that? Why was she *so* anti?

Nora didn't believe in Father Christmas but a lot of people did very well out of him and nobody said *their* money was dirty.

And . . . whisper it very quietly, but she didn't think God was all He was cracked up to be. What sort of a God let all this killing go on? All this suffering? And *she* saw both sides of it. Talk about impartial. He couldn't give a toss. And the Church was raking it in.

Mum was nagging her ragged and all.

'You didn't oughta charge for it, Nora, that's the top and bottom of it. She's quite right, the girl.'

'I don't. It's a silver collection, that's all. Give what you can. Some goes on overheads and some they give to me and the others. And I have to keep a roof over *my* head, and all. Two roofs.'

'If you're daft enough to keep two places going . . .'

'I have to. Can't let strangers take over number 41 while them lot's in residence.'

'Get yourself a different job, then. Take in washing again.'

'Leave off!'


All the same she had found herself wondering, after the set-to with the girl, whether Matron would have her back at the hospital. That was real work. She missed the other cleaners, and the nurses, and the patients and the porters. You could have a laugh with them. What the hell was she doing with all these boring old farts, anyway? In bleeding Clacton, of all places?

Running away. That's what preyed on her mind. That's what gave her headaches. She'd run away.

All right, so everyone said she done the right thing. There was a war on and London was getting the worst of it. Silly to take risks, they said. Well, yeah, but all the same. You don't

157

desert your post at the first whiff of danger. You stay and fight.

And she longed for Walthamstow. With her bones and blood. The smell of chimney smoke and cheek-by-jowl living, the narrow streets, the High Street shops, the dirty sparrows, the people. She needed to scuttle down the shelters when the purple siren sounded, to listen to the bombs falling all round her. Own up, she found it exciting. She missed gasping at the damage in the light of day, shouting at the kids looting, and oohing and aahing with the neighbours over who had copped it, who escaped. She wanted to be part of it. Her place was down home.

She would go back, she decided, soon as she'd finished the circuit. Finish the circuit first, though. Can't let people down.

Old George cou'n't rightly say where Miz 'Ooper got to. Only knowed what 'er tell'n. 'Er were in a dang-fire rush for the bus, all he could say. And her wou'n't be back till late. So they'd 'ave to manage the milkin' atween 'em.

Mr Hooper was hardly more forthcoming. Apart from being nonplussed that his wife had dared to go out after he'd told her she couldn't. Mixing with uppity Londoners was giving her ideas . . .

Oh, something over in Sowness, it were. Hettie at the shop'd phoned her arter dinner, saying they'm getting up a coach-party and would her like to make up the number? Blessed mothers' meeting, far as he could make out. Back in Great Bisset round nine or ha'-past.

So after a supper of warmed-over rabbit stew, Lucy washed up her plate and Mr Hooper's and while he snored under the newspaper, she settled down to read *Gone with the Wind*, one of the books she had borrowed from Audrey. It had done the rounds. The pages were falling out and the battered cover was hanging by threads, but Lucy was soon back in Tara where Mammy was running up a dress from the velvet curtains so that Scarlett could go a-calling on Rhett Butler.

The clock on the mantelpiece groaned and whirred, getting ready to chime the quarter-hour. Lucy looked up. Quarter-past nine. She would go and meet Mabel. She marked her place in the book and, slipping on her jumper against the sun

158

going down, called Bella for a walk. No need for a torch. Thanks to double summer-time it wouldn't be dark for ages.

As she passed the cowfield, the dog trotting at her heels, she hardly noticed the Heinkel, still there after a month, a shell of its former self. The cows had been returned to the field and were now happy to shelter from summer storms beneath the spreading wings. The corpse had been taken away and disposed of decently, as had any useful working parts. Old George, she knew, had two new leather chairs beside his cottage fire, low but comfortable. Someone had half-inched the radio and Milly, in the pub, was doing a roaring trade in underwear made out of parachute silk. There wouldn't be much left for the Ministry of Works' men by the time they got round to it.

They met on the top road. Lucy felt a twinge of alarm to see Mabel scurrying towards her, her podgy face agitated, a sickly orange colour in the evening sun, her hat awry, her new perm snagged and snarled with bits of twig. She smelled of fear overlaid with something sweet. She must be wearing perfume, Lucy decided.

'Oh, Towngirl!' she cried thankfully. 'Oh, deary me!' glancing over her shoulder as though the trees' long shadows contained devils.

'What? What's the matter, Mabel?'

'That young man o' yourn.'

'Joe?'

'No, t'other one. The pervert. I see him!'

Lucy caught her breath. 'Where?' She stamped her foot as first fear, 'Oh hell,' then anger, 'Oh shit,' caught up with her. 'Where?' Her eyes darted around, expecting to find Roy slouched by the hedge, with his face of brooding menace.

'He'm gone *now!*' She spoke as to a silly child. 'I see him coming along here, large as life, five minutes since.'

'Five minutes? What did he say?' Now she noticed scratches scored into the dough of Mabel's face and arms. 'Oh Mabel, what's he done to you?'

Was it the disease, she wondered, affecting his brain now and making him violent?

'Don't be daft, Towngirl,' said Mrs Hooper contemptuously. He hadn't laid a finger on her. She explained that she

159

hadn't exactly waited around to find out whether he would. She had spotted him way off in the distance. There had been a gap in the hedge and she had crawled through into the field. And there she had stayed, sprawled among the field beans (the sweet smell!), panting like a cornered hind, and saying her prayers, of course, until she had heard him trudging past. He could have had no idea she was there.

'Look at the state of you!' Unclenching her fists, Lucy picked twigs and bits of leaf and tiny black caterpillars out of Mabel's grey curls. 'And your shoes, Mabel – they're sopping!'

She had stepped in the ditch on her way in, and out, of the hedge.

'You sure he didn't see you?'

'No. No, he never see us.'

'But he did put the wind up you, didn't he? Oh, I'm sorry!'

A resigned shrug acknowledged that the blame did lie with Lucy.

'It *was* him, was it? It was Roy?'

'Yellow hair, brown soldier uniform. Cou'n't be no-but else.'

Lucy nodded sadly. She'd seen him, herself, the night before last. She had been out in the yard and, startled by Bella's frenzied barking, had looked up from grooming a suddenly skittish horse, to find him leaning against the cart, just staring at her. Brushing Molly's flanks always had a calming effect and although her heart lurched she was able to control her words.

'You're taking a chance, aren't you?' she'd said.

And he had just smiled that same knowing smile, making her want to take a pin and burst him. In any case she was too busy hanging onto the horse's head to pay him any attention. Molly, usually such a docile old nag, was on hot bricks. And Bella was threatening to rip her chain out of the wall, her eyes glowing red, her teeth dripping rage. Lucy turned to tell him to bugger off but he'd already gone back to his lair.

'Wonder where he was going?'

'Well, he was crossing onto the footpath, when I come out

onto the road again. Goin' down village, likely.'

She gestured, with her head, towards Great Bisset. Sure enough, the rows of beans arrowed down to a young soldier heading down towards the church spire. His hair shone pink in the light. That was Roy all right. Who else would be prowling around the fields at this time of night? She shouted after him, 'Bloody pest! Get back to the Army!'

He didn't seem to hear her.

They walked the rest of the way with their own thoughts, helping Bella to round up foolish chickens that had taken advantage of Mrs Hooper's lateness, to hide. The collie nosed them, cackling and complaining, out of the massed grasses and cow parsley onto the farmtrack, whence they were made to skitter smartly through the gate and back to the henhouse. A roost in the open air might be good for morale but hungry hunters would never believe their luck.

'I think it's time we told the police, don't you, Mabel?'

'Up to you, Towngirl. He'm your young man.'

But Mr Hooper wouldn't hear of it. Silly old woman, serve her right, he declared, acting daft, getting herself all scritched. Shou'n't go out nights if she were going to bolt through the hedge first turntail she come across. Weren't doing no harm, jest walking up the road, minding his business. Not like he were one o' them sex rapists. Prob'ly helping hisself to a few peas and carrots and early strawb'ries but no more'n that. Long as he left the chickens be . . .

No, police were the bother. Snoopin' round. Three times they tromped over his parsnips, with their big, flat feet. Three times! First the turntail, then the airyplane, then the body in the may. Wonder they was any parsnips left. And they was just waiting for a reason to search his barn again. 'Cause they knowed he got petrol. Sure as them eggs he give Eric Stone of a Friday over a pint. Three on 'em, reg'lar, wrapped in paper. But he were a crafty old cuss. Biding his time, likely. Making him sweat.

So no police. Not another word would he hear on the subject.

No police.

Now. He had stayed up long enough for stop-outs and was

going to his bed. And them as had work in the morning be wise to do the same.

Mabel made them both a cup of hot milk and while they drank it, Lucy moved a chair beside the open window for the farmer's wife to sit in while Lucy set her hair. The evening sun gave a better light than the oil-lamp. And she needed fresh air. Milk and setting lotion and Mrs Hooper's kitchen made a heady brew.

It was only then that she remembered to ask about the meeting.

The joke was that the poster must have been there in the post-office window for weeks, among all the others for whist-drives, League of Health and Beauty classes, bring and buy sales, knitting bees, films, tea-dances and concerts, and bikes for sale, but the symbol of the cross, designed to draw attention to it, had simply caused her eye to slide on past. Mabel hadn't made the connection, either. Potter was a common-enough name, after all.

'Your *mother*?' she squealed, almost missing the saucer with her cup. 'Well, I'm blowed. Course, you said, di'n't you, she were in Spiritualism? Never knowed she were Nora Potter, though. Why, she'm *famous* round 'ere, Towngirl!' Lucy gently, firmly, twisted the grey head to the front and down, but Mabel continued muttering into her double-breasted pinny. 'Oh my, wait'l I tell Hettie. She be over 'ere like a shot, see Nora Potter's girl!'

Like a shot! thought Lucy, and half the village with her.

Head up again, Mabel sipped her drink and dreamed of fame while Lucy stood, breathing hard in the summer night, combing Amami setting lotion into the front hair and clamping it with vicious metal waving claws.

'Ow!' Milk slopped onto the pinny.

'Oh sorry, was that you?'

'Oof!' she said, rubbing the sore spot, ignoring the stain among so many on her lap. 'See, I allus pictured your mum being long and skinny like you. Not though, is she? Nothing like.' When the cup was secure in its saucer again, Lucy applied more downward pressure to constrict Mrs Hooper's throat. But she persisted. 'And you never knowed she were

162

doing Sowness tonight? Likely slipped her mind, busy woman like that. Pity . . . you could o' sat aside us. Give Hettie summat to think about. So that were your Ma, then. Well, I never . . .'

Lucy wound the slippery hair onto curling wires and bent the ends in to the middle. Tight. *She* wished she had known. But Hettie wouldn't have thought of telling her. A suspicious hush still followed the *ping*! of the shop door when she went in, lasting until she had made her purchases and gone out again. And it hadn't even figured on Audrey's list of 'Forthcoming Events for June'. Why not? Had it escaped her notice, too? Or had she been sworn to silence?

'Whyn't you tell us she were good? Old Donald, he come through clear as a bell,' Mabel gushed.

Lucy's ears started to burn as though she were hearing something she shouldn't. Donald was the son the Hoopers never talked about, though the sideboard was a shrine to him. Donald, the sepia baby on a rug, Donald, the urchin at school, Donald, aged about ten, beside a sandcastle. But when she had asked about him, Hooper had only grunted and Mabel had always frowned a warning, shaken her head. Donald was not to be discussed.

Perhaps the service had done some good, then, if it had lifted the veil on that particular taboo.

''Aving the time of his life, he said,' his mother reported happily. 'Allus did see the funny side. He'm dead, see,' she explained, 'that's the joke. Cheered me up no end, 'earing he were enjoying himself. Said he'm learned to dance and making new friends. That were summat he never had time for 'ere. Too much to do on the farm, 'elping his Dad.'

'She tell you that? About the farm?'

'No, I told *her*.'

'Mabel! You gave it to her on a plate!'

'Eh?'

She shook her head in despair. 'You're supposed to let her do the guesswork.'

'Her don't need to guess, Towng— um . . . Lucy.' As though putting a face to the mother gave status to the girl. 'He was standing right by her.'

'Mabel, Mabel . . . None of it's true!'

163

'Oh, 'tis,' she said firmly. '"Someone here comin' through for Mabel," she say, and then she'm telling me 'twere my Donald. How she know his name – eh? lessen he tell her? And how she know he favour me in looks? How she know him an' his dad never got on?'

All this was news to Lucy. She shrugged. 'Inspiration?'

'Oh, her were inspired, right 'nough!'

So somehow Nora had known that Donald was shy and fat and prematurely balding with a complexion like pink blanc-mange.

Lucy snorted. 'Getting a bit personal, isn't she? She really say that – shy, fat and balding, with skin like pink blanc-mange?'

'Say again?'

'I said Ma's got a cheek, picking on those sort of details. And what made her choose blancmange?'

A fraction of a pause.

'She di'n't.'

'You just said . . .'

'No, I never. I said 'e favoured me in looks.' She swivelled round to stare hard at her hairdresser, suspicion squeezing her eyelids. 'Now then, Towngirl, who you been talking to about my Donald?'

'I dunno. No one. I . . .' She shook her head helplessly. She couldn't remember. One of the farmhands, maybe. But she'd obviously hit the nail on the head. Gently she turned Mabel to the front again.

*Shy, fat, and balding . . . and blancmange? Where* had *that come from? She had just made it up. Hadn't she?*

With fingers that shook a little, Lucy tucked in the ends of the headscarf that Mrs Hooper would wear in bed.

The only photo on the sideboard of Donald as an adult showed him taking part in a tractor race in the Young Farmer's Show 1937. Then he was a slim seventeen-year-old with a full head of hair. But surely she had seen a more recent photo. Or something. She had a clear image now of Donald Hooper: nice boy but shy, plumpish, thin on top and dressed in white.

White?

Mabel followed her gaze. 'Poor old Donald. He were a tub

164

o' lard at the finish. Put on near three stone in two years.'

Lucy wobbled. The kitchen smells were beginning to get to her. Mabel must have put something in the oven. The smell of meat-pie was overpowering. Silly to stand for so long when she was tired and had a period due. Bound to feel faint. She sank thankfully onto the chair that Mrs Hooper vacated.

*There had been an argument between father and son. In this very room. Stinging the air with their raised voices.*

'A nancy job for a nancy boy!' Hooper's voice dripped with derision.

'It's what I want to do.' Pulling nervously at his ear.

'Why don' you join they other girls in the ATS and 'ave done wi' it?'

'Leastwise then I wou'n't have to kill no one!'

Split-second silence.

'Not *kill*!' His voice rising to a scream. 'We'm fighting Nasties, boy! They'm kill *you* soon as look at you. Burn us farm round our ears, rape your mother . . . And what you do about that, eh? Toss a few pancakes?'

Nervous snigger.

'Can't do much about'n, laying dead in a burn-out farm!'

Hooper lunged at his son, who ducked.

'Don't ee gi' me your cheek, boy! You'm a dang coward! A coward and a nancy-boy and I can't abear looking at you!'

A door slammed, making her blink.

At the back of the humming in her head she heard a drawer open and close and Mrs Hooper's slippers scuffling back across the redbrick floor.

'He were too soft-hearted by 'alf, old Donald,' she said, her creaky voice quite untouched by bitterness or scorn. 'Cou'n't bear to harm a living thing. Not a man's man. Sucked his thumb till he went in the Army and then turned to food for his comfort.'

*Toss a few pancakes?*

'Him and his dad never see eye to eye 'bout that. Mr Hooper can be a bit . . . hasty, time to time.'

'Hasty?' Not how she would describe a mean-minded, overbearing bully.

165

On the table, Mabel had spread out four official Service photographs. Ranked white paper cut-outs. Only the faces were different.

'That's my Donald,' she said, poking her grubby nail at a roly-poly figure in the second row. He wasn't smiling. He wasn't even looking at the camera. They were all in boiled white linen. White . . . the universal uniform of the chef. White . . . sanitised, hygienic. White jacket, trousers, apron. And black boots. The Catering Corps.

'Lovely cook, my Donald. You never tasted nothing like his steak and kidney pie!' Her eyes misted in fond memory. 'Your mum say he'm still at it, slaving over 'ot stove, making food for angels, now.'

Lucy couldn't take her eyes off the photo.

Those in the back row and at either side had got to wear their chefs' hats, with the pouched top tilted to rakish angles. The others were bare-headed, holding their starched headgear in the crook of their right arms, so as not to obscure the faces behind.

And Lucy, with a flutter of her heart, was able to see, quite clearly, that Donald Hooper *was*, in fact, prematurely bald.

# Chapter Sixteen

'*Putting you through . . .*'

'Hello, Marjorie? It's Lucy Potter . . . Yes, fine, thanks. And yourself? Good, good . . . Mmm . . . Um, Marjorie, I need to speak to Ma, urgently.'

So urgently, so many things to sort out. All night she had worried at it. All through milking she had rehearsed it in her mind, squeezing the cows' teats in emphasis and persuasion. It was generally impossible to get any sense out of Ma on the phone. She was as bad as Mabel, reduced by a disembodied voice to a bag of nerves. She hardly listened to what you said, only answering, if she had to, in squeaky monosyllables. She was as frightened of the phone as other people were of ghosts. But if Lucy could just get her to understand how sorry she was to have missed the meeting, and to make some sort of firm arrangement to see her . . .

Her mother wasn't there.

Marjorie's words dropped like stones into a bottomless well. After the meeting Nora had stayed overnight in Sowness. Alone.

What are friends for, Marjorie?

'We all rather abandoned her, I'm afraid. I had to get back to settle Connie's account. Phil is being restationed, you know. Oh, I shall miss them, and their dear little baby. But I couldn't leave Tom and Edna to do all that. Poor old things. They try their hardest but I can't expect . . . well, you know what I mean, don't you, dear?

'Sorry? Yes, well, Eric was to have stayed with her . . . Oh yes, you do. Young chap with a stutter? That's the one. Yes, he was to have gone on to Whittleton with Nora but when he checked with his unit last night they ordered him back to base. Very abrupt. Some sort of balloon going up tonight, I gather. Oh, he didn't say that, of course, and you mustn't breathe a word, dear. But reading between the lines, I think there must be some sort of a "push" on. I do feel so sorry for our dear boys, don't you, Lucy? All so very *physical* in the services. No time at all for things spiritual. So, *reluctantly*, and I do emphasise his reluctance, dear, he decided to squeeze in with the rest of us, Ernie and Iris and Ted and me, and come back to Clacton straight away, rather than wait. Saving on the train-fare. Because it all comes out of his own pocket, all this, you know.

'Sorry? Yes dear . . . Well, I suppose it would look like that to you . . . Well, not in the lurch, dear, no. Not completely alone. You're forgetting the Great Spirit. With her at all times.

'Sorry? Oh, I'm sure she can cope, someone of Nora's mettle. She's looking forward to it. Meeting new people. John and Irene are picking her up from Sowness after dinner and taking her on to Whittleton. Very capable people. Very strong in the Spirit.'

Who? Where?

*What*?

Marjorie peg doll bandied names about like bread for ducks, inviting Lucy to peck up and digest before they sank into the sludge.

She tried both numbers that Marjorie gave her. Bay View, at Sowness, was engaged and the girl at The Grand, Whittleton, said they weren't expecting Mrs Potter until after high tea.

'*Sorry, caller, your Sowness number is still busy. Will you hold?*'

As Lucy put down the receiver, it pipped and rang. Not her mother.

There was a warm burble of men's voices, waves of raucous laughter washing over rocks of dread. Cutlery rattling, crockery rattling more than necessary . . . Joe's mouth was close to the phone, trying to block it all out.

'Oh Lucy, Lucy,' he growled. 'God, I've missed you. Three

168

whole days.' His hand, she knew, was cupping the mouth-piece, as tenderly as he took her elbow or a breast. The warmth of his breath was making her ear glow. 'Look, love, I'm afraid something has come up.'

Her giggle surprised them both.

'Something else, I mean.' He groaned. 'Jesus, what you do to me!'

'Ditto,' she said softly, her fingers tracing the curve of his lips in the greasy dust of the hall table, lips that would part and gently suck her finger end . . . She shivered.

'Get a hold of yourself, woman!' he chuckled. 'A big, strong gal like yourself! There are fields to be ploughed, pigs to be mucked out.' His speckled eyes would be twinkling, but his face would settle into anxiety. Something was worrying him. It was uncanny, she realised, how in tune they were, even over distance.

'What's the matter, Joe?' But it could only be one thing. 'You can't get away tonight?'

He sighed. 'All late passes cancelled. And for the foreseeable future.'

'Oh, Joe!' She didn't ask why.

Silence.

'Does that mean that Tuesday's concert is off, too?' she said hopefully.

'Well, I won't be able to go, but there's no need for you to miss it.'

Damn, she thought.

'Shame, I was looking forward to it.' He went into his villainous Mr Hyde mode. 'The Tchaikovsky *Torture*!' He pronounced it Tawchah and she had to smile, seeing him as he rubbed his hairy paws together in evil anticipation. 'I wanted to watch you *squirming* in your seat, my *deah*, and stifling your screams, propping open your eyelids!' And then in his own soft voice, 'The Violin Concerto's such a good one to start with, I think. I'd be surprised if you didn't get something from it.' He couldn't resist it; 'Someone as grossly insensitive as you!'

'Come over here and say that. I'll show you how insen-sitive I am!'

'Is that a promise? It does grow on you though. That's the

169

magic of it. The second time, you'll soar. The third time – pow!'

'A bit like sex, then,' she suggested in a low voice. The quiet in the parlour was ominous. The Hoopers either had their noses in the *News of the World* or their ears to the door.

'Oh, Lucy.' He cleared his throat, suddenly brisk. 'What I'll do, I'll come over with the tickets this afternoon. I don't know when else I'm going to be free. Maybe you can get one of your friends to go with you, Helen or someone. All right? Have to go, there's a briefing. Bye, love.'

Bugger, bugger, bugger. She should have asked him to pop round to Bay View with a message for Nora. Why did these things never occur to her until a split second too late?

She hadn't wanted to go to the concert in the first place. Only to be with him. And to keep her side of the deal. She was teaching him to dance and he was introducing her to Tchaikovsky.

Good grief! Tchaikovsky!

*Swan Lake* was pretty, in small doses. She'd heard bits on the wireless in *Forces' Favourites*, but that was music you could dance to. He had warned her that this other stuff wasn't like that at all. A Violin thingy. She hated violins. Nasty screechy instruments.

And who could she get to go with her? Who would want to? And how? It was at least ten miles to Lowestoft. If they biked it, they'd sweat and snore all through the concert. A bus, then? To Lowestoft? It would take all day, changing here, there and everywhere. And getting back would be a nightmare. If you missed the last bus . . .

Better just forget it, eh, Luce?

Gladly.

Chairs scraped next door and she heard Hooper give his post fry-up belch. Must be getting on for eight. Automatically she glanced at the grandfather clock. Stupid. She still did it. Even if she'd been able to see its face under the film of dirt, it wouldn't have done her any good. It had stopped at twenty to three, years before.

The farmer, grease on his chin, stumped out into the hall in his wellington boots. Caked with mud and goodness knows what, yet he never seemed to take them off. When the mud

170

dried, Mabel simply went round with a broom.

Lucy found herself wondering what happened when he went to bed. He had to take them off then – *Surely?* Good grief, the stink would be unbelievable. How could anyone get passionate about a bloke with smelly feet? And a mouthful of gums? And those thick fingers? Yet Mabel must have. Once.

Now they slept with a bolster down the middle of the bed. She knew because she had popped some of Audrey's magazines into their bedroom recently, when Mabel was thinking of changing her hairstyle, and seeing the lump in the bed, thought it was Hooper lying there and backed out in confusion, falling over the mat and dropping the magazines. Even while her eyes were stinging with embarrassment, she couldn't quite believe what they were seeing: Hooper in bed at eight o'clock in the morning! So she'd gone to have a closer look, and lo and behold, a bolster.

That explained a lot.

Perhaps she should blame his unwilling wife for the unwelcome advances of her employer. Who'd have thought it, though? That the pink marshmallow mouse, who squeaked whenever the lion roared, was capable of making a stand like that, of setting boundaries. You never could tell.

Funny the people we pick, she thought. Like her and Roy. Big mistake.

'Gi' yer a penny . . .' he said.

'Eh?'

'Bleddy miles away, Towngirl! Thinking about gettin' back to they peas in the Bottom Field, shou'n't wonder. Go at 'er like you was yest'day, us'll be outa there be dinnertime.'

Praise, indeed. A goad, but a compliment, too. She was beginning to recognise them now. Not that they flew about. He had never forgiven her for not lying quietly beneath him while he stuffed her full of his proprietary rights. And failing that, for not being a man, with hefty shoulders and powerful arms. Her shortcomings in both these areas gave rise to a certain mutual coolness. There were one or two things, however, at which even he had to admit, she excelled. She, who couldn't swing a sack of spuds for the life of her,

171

'couldn't 'alf pick peas!' They were about to exchange a gruff smile, man to man, when she told him she'd catch him up. She must just try, one more time, to reach her mother. At that his eyes receded under a thick scowl and he muttered about bleddy soft women.

Bay View weren't answering at all now. So, on a whim, and a pang of conscience, she got Audrey Bibbings out of bed.

'Lucy!' she protested, between yawns. 'Ordinary mortals appreciate a blasted lie-in on Sundays!'

But she said she adored Tchaikovsky and had nothing planned for Tuesday and would pick Lucy up at six. Lovely.

Damn, thought Lucy. She'd rather hoped . . . Still, he'd be disappointed if she didn't go. And he could think of her and the music and the 'Tawchah' while he was dropping bombs on Germany.

No, not Germany. There had to be sea. And ships. Destroyers. Bombardment from both air and sea. Germany was landlocked.

(*Sea? Where had that come from?*)

'Lucy? You still there? I was wondering, dear, when you've finished *Gone with the Wind*, they're crying out for it at Brand End . . .'


Half-day mornings always dragged. And this one, blindingly blue, with its niggling clouds labelled Ma, Joe, brother Jack, Roy and Tchaikovsky, though not necessarily in that order, resulted in a thumping headache by noon. Blacker shapes lurked just below the horizon, second sightings of Donald Hooper and some Italian island . . . *Italian what!* . . . but she didn't even want to begin to think about them.

She took her bottle of cold tea back to the farmhouse, and lay on her bed with the black-out drawn. She heard Mabel come in from church and start banging about in the kitchen. Sunday's was a dinner worth waiting for. Until three, generally, by the time the rabbit was stuffed and roasted, or the unlikely chicken.

She closed her eyes and saw peas.

Rooted in the dry crumbs of earth, their delicate leaves fluttered at her waist, pods nudged her hands, like friendly little animals, and tendrils curled around her fingers, her

172

arms, up into her hair, pulling her down and binding her to the bed.

The ringing of a telephone pierced her pea-green dream, splintering its images and scattering them like smithereens. She was wide awake and whatever the angels of her unconscious had been trying to tell her, now they were gone, along with her headache, and all that was left were a few green leaves fluttering at the back of her head, a vague sensation that reminded her of the smell of pear-drops, and a feeling of foreboding.

Downstairs a smoky haze of roast meat layered the air, stifling all the usual staleness, and settling in a sort of patina on the heavy furniture. There was no one about. Lucy took a deep breath and submerged, heading through to doors and windows and flinging them wide.

The phone rang on. And on.

Mabel was in the garden, picking mint. She looked relieved when she saw Lucy. 'Please,' she begged.

'Hooper's Farm.' Flapping her hand before her face and coughing a bit.

'That the Land Girl?' It was PC Stone. ''Fraid I got bad news for ee.'

Lucy's heart missed a beat. 'Ma?'

'Still worried 'bout your Ma? No, no, she'm all right far as I know.' He sounded quite kind. ''Tis that soldier-boy o' your'n, that Private Sykes.'

'Roy? What – is he dead?'

It was what she expected.

'No. He'm just bin seen. In the village.'

She sighed, with awful disappointment. 'Oh.'

'Six-footer, yeller 'air. Acting suspicious. Sounds like'n, don' it?'

'Well, possibly. What was he doing?'

'Rootin' through young Eileen's pram.'

'What!'

'Eileen were raisin' a stink, like.' He had to chuckle at his little joke but, getting no response from Lucy, quickly turned it into a cough. 'The young lady were creatin' a disturbance and 'er mother, Mrs Cosgrove, see this fella turnin' stuff out

173

the pram so she 'ollered at'n to stop. Time she got to'n, he run off.'

'What was he . . .? Why would he do that?'

Surely he wouldn't risk capture for a toffee?

'Her never rightly saw where he went. Too busy sortin' out the girl.'

'With a stick and a sweetie.'

'She got 'er work cut out, poor soul.'

'Too true.'

'But us reckon down 'ere, he'll be up your way afore long, you bein' the attraction, like.'

Tell me something I don't know.

'Thought you best be on your guard, like. Any sign of him you get on to us. Don't ee do nothin' foolish. We'll get him, don't ee fret.'

Lucy and Mabel sat on kitchen chairs in the sun, to shell peas for dinner. Bella flopped down in their shade, her chin on her paws.

'You en't afeared on 'im, then?'

'Afraid? No. Well, a bit, perhaps.' Her strong thumb popped a pod and pushed the swollen peas into the bowl on her lap. The empty shell went on a pile between them. 'I'm just so sick of him, Mabel. Wherever I turn there he is, Mr Mean and Menacing. Seen too many gangster films, if you ask me. But, apart from what he did to my knickers, which was disgusting, and very silly, showing off really, he's not done anything desperately scary. Though he's not sane, all this hanging about.'

'Mad wi' love.'

'Love! That's not love. If he loved me he'd push off and let me get on with my life. It's like a schoolboy crush he's got. No, it's not even that.'

The juicy popping of pods was the only sound while she thought and Mabel waited.

'See, Roy has to be the one pulling the strings, the one in control. He can't bear it that I've got away. That he no longer has any hold over me. He has to prove that he can still make me jump. Literally!'

'All men be like that.'

174

'Joe's not. My brothers aren't. Well, not all of them. One or two are quite nice.'

'They'm 'ard to find, the nice ones.'

There was a sigh which Lucy couldn't ignore. Their eyes met and then dropped to their work. Lucy braced herself for what Mabel had to say.

'He'm a bugger, my old man.'

Well, we all know that, thought Lucy. In the pause she bent to grab another handful of pods from the bucket.

'Why do you stop with him?'

'Can't do a lot else. Wou'n't last five minutes on me own. No money, no family.'

She was trapped, then.

'Know where he'm at?'

Lucy assumed that Hooper was downing pints in the Bull and Crown in Great Bisset with the rest of the bald old men. But no.

'He'm with his fancy woman.'

Somehow Lucy wasn't surprised. But that Mabel should know and condone it, that was revealing.

'Go over there most Sundays he do, afore dinner. "Pay his respects to Annie," like . . .' Her mouth twisted. 'And see that poor blessed child of his.'

'You sure you want to tell me this?'

'Needs to be aired. Fair crippling me, keeping secrets all us married life. Cou'n't tell no one 'ere, though. Go through the village like wildfire. But you won't go blabbin', that I do know. You got secrets of your own.'

Lucy assured her that it would go no further.

Mabel nodded. 'Wou'n't want the child to suffer no more. Well, her bain't a child no more. She'm well growed. Well growed. Must be all o' sixteen. Bodywise, that is.'

'Bodywise?'

'Body growed up but left her brain behind. Eileen Cosgrove. Her that sets under the tree. Her with the pram.'

So that was Hooper's child . . . Poor Eileen.

'Blames hisself, he do.'

'Really?' Who else? Well, Mabel, of course. No doubt she came in for the blame somehow, somewhere along the line.

'Her being simple, I mean. He blame hisself.'

175

What could she say? She picked out a pea from the bowl, noticing the tiny bore-hole, and flicked it away. A goose pecked it up and waddled closer, honking happily.

'It's the in-breeding,' said Lucy. And stopped. Why had she said that? *In-breeding*? How had that nasty little thought popped into her mind? Small, tight-knit community . . . was that what she'd been thinking of?

Tighter-knit than that.

Slowly she said, 'She's his sister . . . Eileen's mother, Mrs Cosgrove. Hooper's fancy-woman's his sister. Isn't she?'

Mabel leaned across and righted the bowl on Lucy's lap. The peas were dribbling out between her brown knees and bouncing on the stones. The dog's eyes danced with interest but she didn't move.

The goose was in clover.

'Told you that, did 'e?' said Mabel. 'Trying to impress a young maid. Well, tha's his lookout, dirty old devil. They'm both as bad, though. Dogs on 'eat. Hoopers never could keep their 'ands to theirselves. No, nor nothing else neither!' she sneered.

'Mabel, he didn't—'

'Oh, I bain't complaining, Towngirl. Tell the world if 'e wants, and go over there every Sunday till kingdom come, all I care, and all t'other days of the week, long as he leave me be when he come back 'ome.'

That was the bolster explained then. But was it chicken or egg?

'Mabel, he didn't tell me honestly. I just guessed.'

'Good guess.'

A pause, as the same thought occurred to them both.

''Appen you'm takin' after your mother, like'n or no, Towngirl.'

'Oh, rot! I don't see ghosts.'

Mabel shrugged. 'Mebbe 'tis takin' you another way.'

'I'm not seeing things, Mabel, I'm just—'

*What? Good at guessing? Inspired?*

'Can't stop'n if's meant to be.'

Oh no, definitely not.

'Come on. We must have enough peas to feed an army. I'm going in.'

176

'Sling they shells on the bombie, Lucy.'

Then, picking out two or three whole pea-pods, green and smooth and bulging ripe, from the pile of empty shells, she joked, 'Shan't ask for your 'elp again, Towngirl. You'm slinging good peas away there.'

'No,' said Lucy. 'Those have got maggots in.'

Mabel pouted in disbelief. She split the pods, one by one.

Bewildered by sunlight, the maggots waved their tiny black heads among the curds of destruction.

# Chapter Seventeen

Unearthed, they lay exposed to the sun for the first time, the pale eggs of a secretive mother. She marvelled at how cleanly they came, and held one in her hand for an instant, enjoying the weight of it, the satisfying shape and sheen of it, before tossing it into the bucket.

The tractor was already two rows ahead, relentlessly lifting and scattering four-foot swathes of new potatoes down the hill. Unlike the main crop, earlies weren't put into clamps but loaded straight onto the cart ready for market. Workers bent along the row, filling buckets for Stan to empty into half-hundredweight sacks, held open by Mr Hooper. Stan was a tall, skeletal man whose looks belied his strength. He could swing a heavy sack up onto the cart as though it was filled with feathers. Not a grimace, not a grunt; only the twitching and ticking of the sinews in his neck and long, brown forearms showing that it was any effort at all.

There were six pickers: two women from the village, far more friendly since their little chat with Mabel in church yesterday, three Italian POWs and Lucy. They had begun cheerily enough, the bending-picking-throwing, bending-picking-throwing setting up a kind of rhythm, to which a song had lent momentum. By the end of the first row, they'd exhausted George Formby, the Italians finding *Me Little Bit of Blackpool Rock* and *When I'm Cleaning Windows* very hard going. Like their jolly little Italian ditties, something was lost in the translation. You couldn't do Vera Lynn justice when you were bent double, and our Gracie's high notes needed too much puff. *Keep Right on to the End of the Road* seemed more appropriate as they worked their way up the hill again, but as their thigh muscles were pulled and stretched and their backs began to ache, and the sweat dripped off the ends of their noses, and down their backs, they had fallen silent, become the well-greased human pistons in some age-old machine.

Strangely she didn't feel too bad, after a night in which she had been woken several times by imagined noises, and night-mares where Mr Hooper, in a white chef's hat, stirred pink blancmange in a pot which, upon closer inspection, turned out to be his sweaty wife and blubbery son, and where doors opened on a room where the German pilot lay on a slab, his head a huge maggoty pea. Roy was winkling the maggots out with a pin and eating them.

Thankfully, he wasn't her worry any more. The police were redoubling their efforts, patrolling the lanes of Great Bisset, beating the footpaths with shiny black boots.

It was all the worry about him, she was convinced, that had caused the 'funny' turns, the prescience, or whatever it was.

Though long days in the sun didn't help, not to mention long sessions with Joe.

Yesterday afternoon, in the barn, had been exhausting. Talk about the concert had led naturally, it seemed, to sex. Though thinking about it afterwards Lucy couldn't quite see how. Nevertheless, that seemed to set the pattern till supper-time. One way and another . . .

They covered a lot of ground, in their nest of straw: books, films, politics, the war, their families, their hopes and fears, all punctuated with sighing and panting and squealing and grunting. And groans.

Three hours was hardly long enough to say and do all they needed to say and do. To find out all there was to know about each other.

In case there wasn't another opportunity.

The straw rustled and ticked but had no ears to hear their soft murmurings.

Every now and then they emerged blinking, for Joe to have a cigarette. You don't smoke in a barn.

When he had gone, back to bombing Nazis, she tried phoning

179

her mother again. But she had just missed her. She left a message to say she had called.

She was really annoyed about missing that damned meeting. More so than she liked to admit. Things could have been put right if she had gone. She had hurt Nora, goodness knows why, and the longer the wound was left to fester, the less likelihood there was of it healing.

And it was all over nothing. Lucy couldn't believe how petty and priggish she had been. A stupid, stupid point of honour. When would she ever learn? When pressed, Mabel had told her that she had put sixpence in the box on the way out, and felt that the evening had been worth every penny. Some people put in more, some less, some nothing at all. What did it matter anyway?

She had never worn the dress. Couldn't bring herself to unwrap it, even, and hang it up. It lay in her bottom drawer along with sanitary towels and a couple of wedding presents Ma had found at home and sent on: a set of baking tins from one of her old schoolfriends: '*For getting buns in the oven!*' and beautiful lacy bed-linen from Jack: (*Don't wear them out too quickly!*')

Meaningless words. Kiss of death.

The 'prescience' was easily explained. She *must* have overheard someone talking about the Hoopers, father and son and sister and daughter: the gossips in Hettie's shop, who knew a lot more than Mabel gave them credit for, or Old George wittering on to the cows when he was milking. Sweet nothings that helped the milk to flow, he said; grumbles, in other words, that helped him sort himself out, more than the cows. She hardly listened any more, though unconsciously she must have absorbed it all.

She didn't want to think about the peas.

Down the field and up again, twice, and potatoes were no longer beautiful. She would never eat another, mint sauce or no. The bald smoothness of them, the sound of them drumming into the bucket, the look of them blistering the earth like a pox. A bucketful weighed a ton. She was soaked in sweat, and longing for dinner-time. From time to time she

180

had stopped for a drink, gingerly slotting her vertebrae back together as Stan came round with the tin cup. But even the water had tasted of potatoes, warm and starchy.

What she did find refreshing were the colours of the day. It was a treat to look out and see, from the top of the hill, the land stretching away in rich cabbage-greens and pea-greens and beet-purples and mustard-yellows, acid against a sky so blue it would suck you into it. When she bent to the work again the colours in her eyes muddled together, like dirty painting water, becoming slug-grey and bloodless tubers again.

By eleven o'clock the tractor had laid bare the entire crop, the hands had cleared a third of it and Molly was trotting back from the farm with an empty cart.

At about eight minutes past eleven, they heard the hum of a plane. Lucy straightened up and ran her fingers through her wet hair. Her skin glistened brown in the sun. Not for the first time she sent her thanks winging over the hills to Ruby, for advising her to cut the legs off her 'issue' dungarees. How could those women bear to work in skirts, or the men in heavy cords? She arched her back to ease the ache and saw a thin thread of white smoke dribbling across the sky, a flaw in blue silk, spoiling it. A skylark trilled in a pretence of ecstasy, a decoy soaring higher, and a blue butterfly beat its wings and disappeared.

The tiny plane scribbled furiously, took a fortifying breath and swooped low. Becoming a German Ju 88 with a potato field in its sights.

Bullets and workers hit the ground together. Lucy heard the loud ping of metal on metal beside her head but didn't dare turn to see what had become of her bucket. Potatoes jiggled and exploded all around her, spurting a juice she didn't know they had. Clods erupted and loose earth leapt like pelting rain. *'Look, Luce,' Granny Farthing said, 'when the storm was at its height. 'See the little soldiers marching down the street!'* But the rain's drumming hadn't been so loud, nor so insistent.

In an instant it had gone, skimming the hill neatly, heading in slow motion down to where the farm buildings stood. Transfixed with shock, Lucy struggled weakly to all fours and, spitting dirt, saw what was going to happen . . .

'The barn! Oh, Jesus – *he's* in there,' she whispered, horrified. 'He'll be roasted alive. No-o-o,' she breathed. 'Oh Roy, don't just sit there. For Christ's sake, get out, you bugger – *get out!*'

As the roof blew out and the building was engulfed in the billowing flames of a petrol fire, a toy soldier shot across the barnyard, slapping at his sleeve. She watched him roll on the ground, over and over, between buildings and then she couldn't see him any more though she watched until her eyes hurt. He had got out in time. He had heard her.

Distant milk-churns rose on their own explosions, like jet-propelled rockets or vessels of the gods pouring golden flames. Spent, they rolled slowly in the violent thermals and fell back soundlessly. Smoke clawed at the sky, a black beast pulling it down in heavy folds. Lucy could just make out the enemy plane creeping off through the disarray, out to sea, shaken by the enormity of what it had done.

'Bet he never expected that to 'appen!' drawled Stan in her ear.

'Who?' snapped Lucy. How long had he been there? What had he seen? And heard?

What exactly had she said? She knew though. She could see Nora sitting slumped in the chair doing her Uncle Harry impression. Somehow Lucy had dredged up his words of warning from the time of the Blitz. The words that had sent them all diving for cover. Of course, they had survived that air-raid. The words had been meant for now.

She sat back on her heels, shaking. Being shot at was nothing at all, compared with having saved Roy by telepathy. Her silent warning had carried over three fields and a farmyard, and all on dead Uncle Harry's say so. What the hell was happening?

Stan hadn't seen Roy. He had meant the man in the plane. 'Bet he never thought he'd hit jackpot. Her's gone up like a bleddy bomb.'

Slowly, people were getting to their feet. Agnes, from the village, was screaming, blood dripping from her hand. Mario, who had thrown himself on top of her, had been nicked by a bullet and blood had soaked his trouser leg.

182

Amazingly, no one else was hurt, though they could hear cows bellowing in fright or pain. The other Italians gave the wounded bandy-chairs to the cart.

The door of the farmhouse opened slowly and a small figure stood there. Turning her face away from the boiling heat, she unchained Bella and dragged the cringing animal inside. The door closed.

'Oh poor Mabel, she'll be frantic!'

'Better get down there, I 'spose. Get some water started. Bring your bucket.'

But Lucy's bucket, when she examined it, was useless. There were two holes: one where the bullet had gone in, one, on the other side, near the bottom, where it had come out before burying itself into the earth, six inches from where her head had been. She sat down again, hard, her legs suddenly boneless.

The column of smoke had been seen for miles and firefighters came from Doddingworth, Whittleton, and a contingent from Beccles Air Base. From Great Bisset, itself, farmworkers arrived with their wives, clanking with buckets and curiosity. They came across the fields, to leave the roads clear for the fire engines.

There were three main sources of water: the tap in the yard, the duckpond and the stream that ran along the bottom of the cowfield and under the lane. None of the hoses was long enough to reach the stream, so people with nothing to do, a score or so, formed a bucket chain from the yard, up the cart-track to the gate, up the lane, into the field, to the stream. The hoses alternated the play of water between the barn, when they could get near it, and the farmhouse. Not that it was in any real danger of catching fire. There was only a light breeze off the sea, blowing the smoke towards the high ground. The only damage to the house was scorched brickwork, blistered paint and cracked windowpanes on the side.

Mabel was in tears. It weren't fair, she kept telling people; she hadn't long cleaned them windows.

And were it true, they asked her, that the Land Girl were that Nora Potter's daughter? Could Mabel ask her to get in touch with their Billy? Did she do fortunes? Did she know when the war was going to end? What were she named, anyway, when she were at 'ome?

The fire raged well into the afternoon, so intense that the June sun felt cool. The weak went to the wall and had to be revived with cups of hot sweet tea and cold wet flannels. Above the crackle and roar of fire came the cries of animals crazed with fear, and the banging of the bull trying to break out of his pen. The barn walls burned like bones, blackening and collapsing, with a hiss, into the dark lake that spread out across the yard. The roof fell in, charred and burning beams crashed down in a shower of sparks. No one could explain its incredible ferocity. Terrible smell of petrol, Lucy heard a policeman observe.

Well, Mr Hooper reckoned he'd might have had a couple of cans in there and, of course, there was the threshing machine, that mess of glowing metal, which had had a full tank on her. The Nasty scored a direct hit, likely.

And all the blackened milk-churns?

A pity, agreed the farmer, deliberately misunderstanding. Wou'n't be able to use'n again.

But straw alone couldn't account for a furnace like that. And stocks must have been running down given the time of year . . .

Oh aye, thank the Lord it hadn't happened in September. No, Mr Hooper had to admit, 'twere a mystery. One they'd likely never get to the bottom of.

'See,' said the policeman, 'nobody saw no bombs dropped, no incendiaries.'

'No, nor they did. You'da knowed if'n one o' they buggers landed, right enough.'

The young man aired his knowledge about the white magnesium flash and the blistering sound of the silver canisters as they made contact. They'd have seen it up on the hill, no doubt about it.

Mr Hooper wondered if perhaps the Nasties had invented some new device? And did the Constable happen to know anything about claiming for war damage?

Lucy frowned hard to hide a smile, as she passed a bucket to Stan. The buckets were only two-thirds full by the time they reached her end of the chain and pitifully inadequate.

184

She waited for the spidery man to fling water, long-armed, over roaring red fireballs of straw that tumbled into the yard. But Hooper stepped in front of him, and made a show of taking the bucket one stride closer to the danger. He was almost on top of what was left of a bale, his pink head streaked with valour, his sweat sizzling.

As she collected the empty bucket from Stan he caught her eye and jerked his head backwards at Hooper. 'Get him!' his woolly eyebrows seemed to be saying as they met the peak of his greasy cap. They both knew that Hooper would get away with it, probably make a profit out of it, crafty old devil.

By late afternoon the fire was spent and the barn reduced to a smouldering, blackened heap of rubble and ash.

Hooper came into the kitchen as Lucy and Mabel were wrapping eggs in newspaper.

'Just a few,' his wife begged, 'just to thank them as come over to help.'

'Twere throwing good money after bad. Hoopers'd do the same for them, ever'onc knowed that. And with the barn gone and the straw and the thresher, they'd have to tighten they belts. Starting with eggs. Far better she and Towngirl made theirselves useful and fetched the cows in. Them as were left.

So everybody had gone home, bone-tired, dirty, stinking of smoke and sweat, and empty-handed. But more than eager, Lucy imagined, to spread their version of events, thick and slab as the crab-apple jelly they ladled from the jar. No doubt 'petrol' and 'milk-churns' and 'serves the bugger right' would have been among the words and sentiments to get an airing over the supper-tables that night.

Two of the cows had to be put down, much to Hooper's disgust. He felt sure that at least one of them could have been saved, with splints and plaster of Paris to set the broken leg. The vet had to point out to him that without constant watching, over the next week or so, making sure she kept off her feet, the animal would have gone mad with pain. And as Hooper was forced to admit, no one could be spared. Plus there was the problem of milking. Plus the vet had never

185

known plaster casts to set bovine bones successfully. Far better to put her out of her misery.

Like a spoiled child Hooper ranted. All that money he was losing. Two of his best milkers and no compensation. He'd go and fetch a bucket now and milk them, dead as they were.

Lucy saw him trudging up the track with bucket and hose and somehow, according to the milk book, he actually carried out his grisly threat, but *how*, she never discovered. When she went in for supper an hour later, he was on the phone to Harkness, the Doddingworth butcher who sold their eggs and Christmas chickens, arranging for the man to come over in the morning to give them a price for the two carcasses.

'First thing, mind,' he was saying. 'Sky's redding up out there. Be another scorcher the morrow. They'n need get inside that afriginator o' yourn pretty quick, stop'n going off.'

At last the Hoopers were settled, he, at the table, with his bits of paper, licking his stub of a pencil and working out losses and gains and insurance claims, and she listening to a crackly *Sincerely Yours* on the wireless. Lucy went and fetched her soap and flannel.

'Just popping out for a wash,' she announced. Since the start of the hot weather, she had taken to 'slooshing' herself down at the tap, last thing at night. Sometimes the geese came out to join her, paddling in the puddles and stretching their necks and flapping, but they'd had enough excitement for one day and regarded her grumpily from the muddy hollow that had been the pond. It wasn't dark but, if either Hooper or Roy or anyone else took it into their heads to spy on her they wouldn't have seen very much. She only undressed a bit at a time, and by careful management of her towel kept fairly decent. In a houseful of boys you get into the way of it.

The water was freezing, coming directly from an underground spring, but though she gasped, the flannel took away the worst of the shock. And plenty of dirt. The state of her! Black from the fire and there was ash in her hair. She should really wash that, too, but she couldn't go to bed with it wet. That was how you caught pneumonia, according to Ma.

The night clouds were massing on the horizon by the time

186

she was retying her bootlaces, and the sky was mottled with the pinks and purples of the dying sun. She shivered. There was coolness coming off the sea. A movement of air. It occurred to her that she ought to check on the barn to make quite sure the fire was out.

The air hung warm around the cinders and smelled sour and sad. It reminded her of coming down the morning after Bonfire night, and being unable to tie in the cold, bleak ashes with the roaring excitement of the night before. Breathtaking showers of silver and gold reduced to a cone or a tube of singed and sodden cardboard. All that was left of Guy Fawkes, an old shoe, perhaps. Fire and ashes. Life and death. No wonder Ma tried to make out there was more to it.

She was glad he had got out in time. She could never have borne the guilt if he had perished and it was her fault. Not that she felt anything for him now. Apart from fear.

Though she'd told Mabel she wasn't afraid, she was. Not that she thought he would harm her. But every time she saw him now, or heard his name, her heart sank under a ton weight of despair and she would tremble, break into a sweat. It was for that she feared him. As she would fear an insidious recurring nightmare.

She caught her breath. There among the charred timbers and over-baked clinker, were a dozen or so blackened tins, some gaping open at the join, some exploded. He *had* bought food, quite a store. There was a knife with the bone handle burned away, a buckled tin plate and mug, a spoon, the remains of a torch. He hadn't just ducked in here this morning. He'd been living here.

And had he been at home yesterday afternoon, when she and Joe had come calling? Had he watched and listened? He wouldn't have done the decent thing and sat with his eyes squeezed shut and his fingers in his ears, not Roy, not for three hours.

Oh dear.

A quickening breeze tried to revive the embers but the reddish glow quickly reverted to dull charcoal.

Her eye was caught by a wire-worm wriggle of brightness in a nest of black dust that might have been straw. It sketched the outline of some small regular shape. A pocket-book or a

187

wallet. It was, unbelievably, his wallet – the one she had emptied onto the draining board. Burned silver and missing a corner but bulging so tight with papers that air, carrying fire, had not been able to penetrate. He wouldn't want anyone to find that.

She fetched a rake and shovel from the woodshed and drew it towards her, leaving a combing of ash behind. It was too hot to handle, hot as coals. A rime like red frost kindled around the edges when she blew on it and it sizzled under the tap. When it was cool she wrapped it in the damp towel and took it up to her room.

Drawing the Army-blanket curtains that served as black-out, she stifled immediately in the heavy warmth. Since May she had been leaving curtains and windows open. It was generally still light when she stumbled across the room and fell into bed and a deep sleep, often before dragging off her clothes. Tonight, though, she lit a candle and set it on the bentwood chair beside her bed, undressed to her knickers and slipped on her pyjama top. It was too hot for anything else. She wanted to look at that wallet.

It broke in half like a biscuit and there was all the old stuff, burned round the edges like a treasure map, but recognisable: her photos and letters, the Appointments card, with the last date, the 21st April at 2.30. Hadn't he told her, before Christmas, that he was cured? The bugger! Train tickets, leave passes and a lot of pound notes. As she put it all away again she found herself yawning.

*Lucy and her mother were replanting the duckpond. It might have been a large muddy bomb crater but they knew it was a duckpond because there the men were waiting to turn on the hoses to refill it. They had to hurry. Squelching around, sliding in the ooze, they planted crackly five-pound notes in holes they made with their fingers. Some had already started sprouting, long fronds uncurling like bracken. They would grow up through the water and bloom on the surface like white water-lilies. Well worth the trouble.*

*Then out of the sky zoomed a bi-plane. It looked very friendly, a big smile painted on the pilot's shop-dummy face but, as it passed over the duckpond, it changed into a huge dragonfly, that grabbed her mother with its spidery arms and hovered with her over Lucy's head. Nora seemed delighted. She kicked up her fat little legs and swam away through the air. And then it was she who was wearing the wings, and a beautiful dance dress, shot with blue. As she flew away, five-pound notes fluttered down from her handbag. The air was full of them. Hundreds snowing down.*

*Lucy knew it was wrong. Nora shouldn't be so happy. Lucy had to get out of the pond to save her, out of the mud, but it was slippery. The more she struggled the deeper she sank. Now her legs were so tired they wouldn't move. She was up to her waist in goo, her breasts, her neck. It was closing over her mouth, stopping her crying out. And there was something in the mud, low down, some loathsome, crawling pond creature, probing between her legs. Her breath came quickly.*

A sweet old voice close to her ear was telling her to wake up.

'Open your eyes, duck. You gotta wake up.'

That smell of pear-drops, a tinkling piano.

Not another air-raid!

'Wake up, Luce!'

Not her mother. No, it wouldn't be: she was away with the fairies.

She thought she knew who. She wanted to see. So much. But she had to stay in her dream. To get out of the mud.

'Wake up, there's a good girl. Come on now, open your eyes for Granny.'

That made her eyelids unclamp. But she needn't have bothered. She couldn't see a thing. The room was black as black. But there was something blacker looming over her face. Someone. Someone had his hand over her mouth. Someone straddling her, rough material against her legs, a knee on either side. Someone whose other hand was moving inside her knickers.

She groaned, caught at the sleeve and, charred, it ripped easily.

'Take it easy, duck,' said Granny Farthing. 'We'll get you out of this. Keep breathing slow like you're still asleep. You gotta surprise him. Think what you're gonna do. You got

189

teeth, knees and hands. Work it out, then do it. But do it quick. You ain't got long.'

Logically she knew it couldn't be her grandmother, despite the pear-drops she'd forgotten Granny loved, despite the Chopin. It was her own instinct for self-preservation. What the hell? she thought. It's good advice.

In one movement she bit deep into his finger, wondering whether you could catch VD from swallowing someone's blood, while other parts of her brain were directing knees to jerk up into his back with enough force to knock him off-balance, ordering strong elbows to jab, muscled arms to push away, lithe torso to twist and wriggle out from under, feet and legs to kick, fingers to tear hair and rip flesh, fists to punch and work-hard sides of the hand to chop. He didn't stand a chance.

As she fell on the floor on one side of the bed, she heard him land on the other side, heard the clatter as the chair went flying, the thud across the floor to the window and the scrape and slither of him climbing through. She heard the clank of the drainpipe as loose bolts grappled with their moorings, heard his boots strike the flagstones as he landed and the dog barking and geese honking and Hooper yelling out of the window of the next room and the gun firing, blamming away as the running footsteps became fainter and fainter. And all the while she sat there on the floor, feeling her heart beating in her throat, blinking into the darkness, trying to see the old woman who had saved her.

'You will, you will. Give it time,' said Granny Farthing. Or her remembered voice in her own head. 'It's early days, duck. Early days . . .'

Then Mabel was in the room with her candle.

'You all right, Towngirl? D'e hurt you, poor young maid? It were him, weren't it? Blasted pervert.'

Then, as Lucy fell into the woman's strong arms, she realised that though he hadn't spoken, though she hadn't been able to get a look at him, she hadn't questioned his identity, not for a moment.

She sat down heavily on the bed, her legs giving way for the second time that day, and saw, caught between her trembling fingers, four or five damp golden hairs, pulled from

190

his scalp. She retched emptily and wiped her hand off, and off, on the bedspread, but they were wound tight and wouldn't come. Seeing her distress, the farmer's wife picked them into her own hand and got rid of them out of the window.

Then she righted the chair and, from the candle, relit Lucy's.

They sat side-by-side without speaking, watching the play of shadows on the walls, listening to the distant rumble of the Sowness Air Force taking off to do war against the enemy. When Hooper returned, banging around and cursing, his wife went downstairs to fill him in on events. A few minutes later he was berating Eric Stone on the telephone.

'Damn deserter, murdering us in our beds, and what you doing about'n? Where'm your men now, eh? Swarming over my land all day, making a bleddy nuisance of theirselves, bleddy tucked up in their bed when's really wanted!'

Mabel came back with a bottle of rhubarb wine and two glasses, to find Lucy on her hands and knees.

'It's gone! He's taken it.'

Mabel joined in the search but there was no sign of the wallet now. Just a streak of charcoal across the chair, and black crumbs of burned leather and paper on the floor.

That's what he had come for. She'd just been the cherry on the cake he'd been unable to resist, after the titillation of Sunday afternoon.

When she finally blew out the candle, she had a glass and a half of Mabel's patent rhubarb wine in her belly and the dog on the rug beside her.

She closed her eyes and saw again the black-on-black darkness bending over her. Felt the warm hand moving over her, fingers worming into her, juices flowing. She shivered and bit her lips guiltily.

Had she groaned? She seemed to remember groaning but she had thought it was Joe.

She blinked into the darkness again and muttered, 'Thanks, Gran.'

# Chapter Eighteen

When she clattered down the stairs the next morning, with Bella at her heels, the cows had been milked and escorted back to the field, the books had been done, the two carcasses carted away, the chickens fed and it was almost nine o'clock.

'What ee fancy? Scrandle eggs or porridge?'

'I don't have time, Mabel, I really don't. What we doing, top field again?' She was half-way out the door.

'Sit ee down, Towngirl,' said Mabel, pink and flustered, 'sit ee down, do. Always in such an all-fire rush. Got summat to tell ee.'

All this pampering. She'd have to get 'nigh on ravished' more often.

As Mabel cooked the eggs she told her quite the most marvellous news ever:

Nora had telephoned. (*Thank You, thank You, thank You, God!*), leaving a message with Mabel (*of all people!*) about an unscheduled meeting in Sowness – a repeat performance – if Lucy would like to come, next Saturday afternoon, the fourteenth. It was all there in indelible pencil, the purple still on Mabel's tongue.

'Nice woman, your ma. Us got on like 'ouse on fire! Or a barn!'

How they had managed to communicate at all, Lucy found hard to imagine, with them both holding the receiver at arm's length. However, in a frenzy of hero-worship, Mabel had apparently promised to get the girl there by hook or by crook.

'Saturday? Well, how can I? I'll be working.'

Mabel winked and nodded. She had something up her sleeve.

And Joe had phoned to say he were all right, she added. Just off for a spot of shut-eye. Couple more nights should do it, he said. Sent her his love.

Joe. She'd have to tell him about last night . . .

Mabel had news about that, too. The police were closing in on the pervert. A 'cordon', them called it. Reckoned to have'n behind bars by tea-time. Rat in a hayfield.

The man from the insurance was coming to look at the damage and all were going right with the world.

'Four telephone calls? Mabel, you're doing really well!'

'Five,' said Mabel, holding a loaf to her greasy pinny and buttering busily. 'Granny Newsom's girl, from the village? Been picking spuds. *You* know, 'er's got shot by the Nasties, yesterday?'

'Agnes . . . I never thought to ask. How is she?'

'Well, 'er can't work, poor soul. Stuck at 'ome today, arm in a sling, dosed up wi' Aspro.'

'I'll pop over there later. It's my half-day.'

'Said you might, only . . . Lucy . . .'

Lucy looked up from her scrambled egg. How often did Mabel call her by name?

'What?'

Mabel had the loaf in a firm grip, so intent on slitting its throat her cheeks had a feverish flare. As she placed the slice carefully beside the girl's plate and patted the jar of jam towards her, she shot a glance under her eyelids to gauge Lucy's temper.

'*What*, Mabel?' Lucy had been feeling rested and calm. But the woman's behaviour was worrying.

Mabel took a defiant stance, her bread her defence.

''Er was asking if you could . . . if you would, like, tell 'er fortune.'

When the shrieking subsided and the plum-jam and the glass had been cleaned off the floor and the dog put outside, still barking at the commotion, Mabel sat down, at a safe distance, to explain.

'I told her you'm likely be workin' s'arternoon, seein' you

be wantin' Saturday off, go and see your mother. I know Mister want that barn cleared off soonest. Get a new one up be Harvest-time.'

Lucy blinked. Oh no, Mabel, it wasn't that easy.

She informed her treacherous friend that she had arranged to go to a concert with Audrey that night and didn't intend turning up garmed with soot and stinking of smoke. Tuesday was her bath day and she wasn't giving it up for anyone.

'But . . . what about Agnes?'

'That's your problem, Mabel.'

'She'm en't on the phone.'

'Phone Hettie. I'm sure she'll be happy to pass on the message!'

A compromise was reached.

Lucy spent what was left of the morning picking potatoes and, instead of going to Doddingworth, lent a hand after dinner, shovelling ash into sacks and heaving charcoal timbers onto the cart. By five o'clock she was black, and ready for the bath that Mabel had waiting for her in front of the kitchen fire. Flying in the face of government regulations, Mabel had filled the tin bath so full, she had to bale out before Lucy could get in.

The curtains were drawn, the door locked and Lucy lay soaking in luxury. Hooper and the men were out at the tap. She could hear them, scrubbing up for supper. Not a shred of humour among them. Walthamstow folk laughed more, she was sure. There was more than houses in between town and country. But she and the other Land Girls were making bridges.

When she had first come to Hooper's, no one sang in the fields. Work was serious.

'What they send *you* for?' had been one of the first things Old George had said to her. And jealous Mrs Hooper, peering at her husband's new Land Girl (for Land Girl read 'handmaiden', 'concubine', 'tart'), driven to exhaustion by a day's muck-spreading, had told her, in all sincerity, 'Bain't no job for a young maid. Won't be able to 'ave no babies!'

Well, that remained to be seen. Anything like her mother and there'd be no stopping her. ('Child-bearing *lips*', was

194

how Nora had once described herself!) And what if they were red-heads, her children? There were some colours that would suit them. Like green . . . There were all sorts of greens. She pulled a sour face and massaged the last of the shampoo into her scalp.

Now Mabel was a friend, making up for the lack of loyalty with hot water when it counted. Lucy dipped her jug into the bucket beside the bath and swilled it over her sudsy hair, disturbing the bathwater's grey crust. Mabel was planning on getting in after her. Tough.

When Audrey arrived Lucy was still damp, wiping rice pudding from her mouth, but ready. Audrey gave her a funny look and said she smelled nice. Lucy supposed it was because Audrey hadn't seen her in 'civvies' since she'd left Clacton.

Mabel waved her off at the door, as though she were a daughter. Times had certainly changed.

As they drove by the village green, someone waved to them from under the tree. No pram. Eileen would be indoors having her tea. Two people. One of the Italians and a woman.

'Stop a minute, Aud.'

Agnes Newsom was holding Mario's hand. Her other one was in a sling. Last place I'd sit with a bloke, thought Lucy, providing early-evening entertainment for the village. Last place I'd sit full stop, after Eileen has had her smelly bottom on it.

But Agnes's life was not cluttered with such considerations.

'Off out?' she yelled.

Lucy hesitated. It still went against the grain to shout.

'Lowestoft. Going to a concert.' Enunciated as clearly as *'For now we see through a glass darkly . . .'* from the front of the school hall. The Bible-reading competition . . .

Agnes had her hand to her ear.

'Eh?'

What the hell? She gave it full throttle.

'I'm off to a concert, Agnes!'

'Big band?'

'Tchaikovsky!'

195

'Foreigner, then?'

Lucy smiled and nodded. Then she remembered her manners.

'How's the hand?'

'Which one?' she grinned, holding up the one clasped in Mario's big brown paw. 'Can't pick no spuds for a while. Thank God.'

'Mario all right?'

'Oh yeah, he'm all right ... Don' ee reckon, Towngirl? Don' ee reckon he'm all right?'

'I'll say!'

''Ere, Towngirl! Can I come over tomorrer night? 'Ave me fortune told, like?'

Audrey snorted.

Lucy took a deep breath. Mabel hadn't told her – so she would have to. And anyone else that was listening.

'Agnes, I am *not* a fortune-teller! I don't have an ounce of second sight, no psychic gifts, nothing! Come over, by all means, but there'll be no fortunes, no crystal balls. I'm just an ordinary person. *Very* ordinary!'

Faces appeared at windows, eyes at door-slits; people in their gardens looked up, boys on the other side of the green stopped their game of cricket.

'That told 'em,' said Audrey, putting the car into gear.

'Hope so,' said Lucy.

As they drew away, she looked back to see the curtains drop into place, and Mario taking leave of his girl, hurrying away to make it to the prison camp down the road before curfew.

A sudden movement, high in the oak tree. A quiver of leaves, as though a branch had sprung back. A blackbird flying out, with a startled 'pink, pink, pink!'

Of course, she should have guessed. Where else was he to sleep, now that the barn was burned down?

The concert hall was, in fact, the Lowestoft Drill Hall, and it was packed.

'Didn't think there were this many concert fans in East Anglia!' she whispered to Audrey.

'Don't think "fans" describes them exactly, dear.

196

"Aficionados", perhaps.'

You live and learn.

All sorts had come to the 'Tawchah'. Rich and poor. Elderly ladies with fox-fur stoles and pearls, their husbands with old-fashioned walrus moustaches, and gold watch chains holding their port-bellies in. Farmers and fishermen, cheeks ruddied by fresh air; their women in flowery frocks. Pale professionals and their wives. Long glamorous dresses, and dinky little evening hats. *Every* kind of uniform. Children, even, in slicked-down hair and best bib and tucker. Lucy began to wish she had put on her really posh frock – the contentious blue one.

Everyone clapped when the orchestra came on. She waited for them to start, but first they had to shift their chairs and their music-stands, settle down and tune up. Some of the audience watched, most fluttered their programmes and continued chatting. They knew what to expect. This was a happy ritual.

'It's really special, isn't it?' she said, seeing all the dinner jackets and black, off-the-shoulder dresses onstage. You'd have thought they were going to a dance. There were a lot more dresses than suits. They didn't let men off the war to play the French horn.

Audrey smiled in a motherly way. Or it could have been smug. Lucy wished she'd tried harder with the nail-brush.

Then came the conductor and more clapping. Lucy took a breath to comment but Audrey had a warning finger on her lips.

The first piece was by Mozart. Some overture or other. Catchy. You could almost dance to it. She started tapping her foot to the beat and Audrey nudged her. So she wiggled her fingers on her knee and got a gentle dig. Nodded her head and that was wrong, too. In the end she was sitting ramrod still, not daring to move, just flicking her eyes over the different instruments: the huge drums caught her eye, and so many violins, big ones and small ones, and pretty-sounding flutes. She began to recognise their melodies, appreciate how they echoed and intertwined.

It was when she was really listening that she got the tickle. All that shouting. She cleared her throat and the people in

197

front turned to glare at her. It was still there. She swallowed. And again. With every breath that she took her throat became drier, fluffier, more tickly. Impossible to stifle. A spasm met with Audrey's reproving elbow. She had to swallow again. Her eyes were beginning to water. It was agony. Tears ran down her cheeks. Now she really was squirming in her seat.

And the blessed music went on.

When it ended, she realised that the tickle had got lost along the way, somehow, along with Audrey and the people in front, along with everyone in the hall. Along with the hall. She had been soaring, just as Joe had promised. With wings. On a current of music. Dipping and climbing, light as air, on air. Blown about. With Joe. Gaining power. Circling. And levelling off. *Steady now* . . . It had been dark up there. And double-dark below. The sea, sprinkled with smithereens. With danger. *Where*? Warm skies, warm seas. An island. *Pantelleria*. Poor little Pantelleria. Drums beating. *Not drums*. Big guns. Shells. Continuous, relentless bombardment. From cruisers, destroyers and from the air. Flying fortresses. Bombing. Bombing. Destroying utterly. Opening up Pantelleria. The way through to Sicily.

'Sorry about that, dear,' said Audrey.

'What?'

'They find it offputting, you see.'

'Sorry?'

'Beating time. It isn't done. Bad form.'

'Oh . . . right.'

'Good, isn't it?'

'What?'

'The music. Only you weren't applauding, dear. I just wondered . . .'

'Applauding? I was . . . God, Audrey, I was well away. Pantelleria. It won't be long now. They can't take much more.'

'Lovely,' her companion said with a slight frown. She was clapping again. A woman came onto the stage, to play the piano. 'Chopin,' Audrey announced, as the hall hushed reverently.

Lucy realised that she knew the piece. She had played it over and over on her grandmother's gramophone. Winding

198

up the handle and putting it on again. She had danced to it, twirling round the tiny front room, holding up the hem of her frock as the snow flew by the window, piled on the sill and the front hedge, and Jack coughed on the settee. The room was dark with snow. Dark and strange. But the music was light and lovely, rising and falling, swelling into bubbles that burst into bright tinkling cascades, and spirals and loops.

And here was Granny sharing the memory, silently offering pear-drops in a paper-bag. Lucy shook her head. You probably didn't eat sweets in concerts either. She didn't want another dig in the ribs.

Granny made a face at Audrey. A face that said, Miss Hoity-Toity. Music was meant to be enjoyed. Look at that big empty stage with just a piano in the middle. Made for dancing.

And somehow the old lady was up there on the stage, in front of all the people, in her funny long skirt and her shoes shaped by bunions, and she hopped and skipped and dipped and twirled, slowly at first and then faster and faster, her hairpins flying and her fine soft hair coming loose. Through the empty chairs and the music-stands she waltzed and waltzed, holding her skirt so she wouldn't trip. Round and round, through the piano, through the pianist. She was young again, smooth-skinned and tall and her shoes were foot-shaped and pretty and she looked like Lucy. Her cheeks were flushed with the joy of it, the sheer lovely joy. And she was dancing for Lucy, because Lucy couldn't dance, but had to sit there, ramrod still.

And as the music came to an end, Granny Farthing's eyes sparkled as, holding up her skirt like a real lady, she made a deep curtsey this way and that way and Lucy clapped and clapped, as tears swam in her eyes.

Audrey looked at her as if she were a stranger and Lucy pitied her because she had not seen Granny dance.

In the interval they had cups of tea and biscuits and Audrey went to the toilet.

The violinist is swaying, delighting music from his instrument. His bow touches the strings, his fingers fly, gentling notes, riding notes, squeezing notes, gouging and

199

ripping. Making music that hurts, so exquisite you roll back your eyeballs to catch it. Music that sobs, dropping big, fat tears on your programme. Music that carries you up and up so far you think you can go no higher, but then you do. Music that flies, that floats out of the top of your head. Notes so heavy they drop like quicksilver, perfect, right, necessary. All the notes there have ever been, merging, cancelling out prismatically into swirling white soundlessness. Round and round. Lengthening into a tunnel, opening out, a cone of it, of pure singing silence and timelessness . . .

And there at the end is Nora. Dumpy and dear. Ma. All alone in her tight shoes. Needing you like mad. Like mad.

Like the time she cried out in pain in the garden, with a splinter the size of a toothpick jammed down her fingernail. And you pulled it out. The time she caught the fingers of her right hand in the mangle and couldn't reach with her left to turn the handle back. And you released her. Like that she needs you. But she doesn't know how to ask. Keeps repeating tired old catch-phrases and clichés: 'All hands to the pump' and 'Man the barricades'.

*'All right, Ma, I'm here now. Lean on me, I'm young and strong. I can help.'*

And that was the Tchaikovsky. Not 'Tawchah' at all.

Lucy couldn't stop talking on the way home. It was wonderful, a discovery, a new dimension. Different from the wireless, different from other music. Like reading a wonderful book, you mulled over the beautiful phrases, remembered the imagery and lost yourself in it completely. Forgot where you were. So clever, so perfect, it had to be the nearest thing to magic. If there was a heaven it had to be full of such music.

Audrey smiled happily, her Billy Bunter glasses glinting in the moonlight. She was so pleased that Lucy had enjoyed it. She said she hoped they could do it again. She had enjoyed it, too. And she patted Lucy's knee. Several times.

Not that Lucy minded. She hardly noticed. She prattled on excitedly about Nora's meeting and the impression her mother had made on the ladies of Great Bisset, and picking potatoes and the strafing and the poor cows being killed and the injuries to the workers, and the fire in the barn and the mayhem at the farm, and Roy's appearance and the police, and Audrey nodded and made all the right comments and the closer they got to home, the longer Audrey's hand seemed to linger on her knee. Lucy became very conscious of the hand and its pressure, and didn't quite know what to do about it. Ignore it or slap it off as you would if it was a bloke getting fresh. Audrey was her friend. She shouldn't be doing this. Worrying her. Making her forget the music.

The lane from Great Bisset was very dark with overhanging trees, and the headlights, of course, were down to mere slits in the blackout. The car was creeping along and Audrey's finger was creeping under Lucy's skirt.

'Oh, what's that?' Lucy cried and leaned forward. Audrey's hand shot back to the wheel.

'Only a fox, dear,' she said, and changed gear.

Then Lucy felt warm fingers quivering along her leg, under the skirt, above the stocking top. She looked down. Her skirt was up to her knickers. And Audrey was staring straight ahead.

'Audrey!' Lucy squealed and grabbed the plump arm, not only to stop it doing what it was doing. A dark shape hurtled from the bank and across the road in front of the car. There was no way they were going to avoid hitting it. In a squeal of brakes and a sickening crunching and thudding, the Ford ploughed into the thing, stopped, and whatever they'd hit stopped too.

'Oh my God!' Audrey cried, squinting through the windscreen. 'Oh my *God*!' She buried her head in her hands. 'Oh God, oh God oh God oh God!' wiggling in her seat, like a naughty child who says I won't I won't I won't!

Shaking, Lucy wound down the window and croaked, 'Hey, you all right?' But the body lay there unmoving.

It had suddenly got very cold.

'Got a torch, Audrey?'

'Uh?'

'A torch?'

'Oh, um . . . glove compartment.'

'Right. You stay there, you've had a shock.'

'No, I—'

201

'Stay there.'

She got out, shut the door, and went round to the front of the car. Bent down. Touched the dark bulk that sprawled across the road. It was some sort of rough cloth, and lumpy, and gave off a horribly familiar smell. Earthy.

'Oh my –!' She played the torch over it, and gave it a nudge with her foot. 'Audrey, come and look. You'll never believe this.' She gave a short laugh. 'Of all the—!'

With sniffs and groans, Audrey squeezed out of the car. Crept around the door as though too much noise would awaken injuries and gazed, in trepidation and disbelief at – a huge sack of new potatoes.

'Blasted spuds?' she roared. 'How the hell?'

Lucy was just trying to explain, as much to herself as Audrey, how it must have fallen off the cart, landed upright and then, somehow, tipped over, coincidentally, as they had come along . . . when a noise behind made them turn. The engine revved, the door slammed. Audrey leapt forward to save her car.

'No!' she wailed and, as the car reversed away from her into the gateway of the cowfield, howled, 'Not again!'

Lucy attacked the passenger door. A hand came across to flick down the lock, a dusting of fine, fair hairs on the backs of the fingers. And the sleeve was scorched by fire. She stepped back, helpless, as the car swung round and away up the lane, out of sight, out of hearing.

'Blasted, sodding, bloody man!'

Cows came to the gate to look at women shouting and stamping and paddling the ground like terrible two-year-olds, kicking the sack of potatoes until their toes hurt. Then they had to start walking.

'Did you get a look at him?'

'Well, I could see it was a soldier.'

'Blond. Did you see his blond hair?'

'Was it him then?'

'Who else?'

'He was waiting for us.'

'Had it all planned.'

'There can't be that many cars come down here at night.'

'None.'

'But he was waiting, Lucy. Ready for us with his blasted sack of blasted spuds. See what I mean? How did he know?'

'Ah . . .'

'What?'

'Well, I did kind of tell everyone in Great Bisset that we were going to a concert.'

'So you did.'

'And . . . I think he might have been hiding in the tree.'

'What tree?'

'The tree on the green. He heard us.'

'Oh, come on!'

'No, really. The barn's gone, the place is crawling with coppers, the tree's the one place no one looks. He's been there before, of course. That was what the rumpus with Eileen was about.'

An owl hooted and the wind stirred the leaves as they walked, immersed in their own thoughts. An occasional 'Bugger, bugger, bugger!' exploded into the silence, or 'Bloody man!'

So dark was it in the lane that they almost missed the track. Audrey turned her heel in a rut and fell against the fence. She yelped.

'Damn and blast it, Lucy, that's all I need, a blasted twisted ankle!'

There were tears in her voice.

Poor old Audrey. Poor old mother-hen.

'Come on, Aud, lean on me. It's not far now.'

Audrey took her arm and snuggled in close.

'But Aud . . .' she warned.

'Mmm?' she grunted contentedly.

'Don't you go getting ideas. I've got one lover and I don't want two.'

'Yes, Lucy.'

*'Good girl,' said Granny Farthing, breathing pear-drops into the night. 'She needed telling.'*

The moon rumbled across the sky, caught in a dragnet of war-planes, dozens of them. And then it slipped free. When the rumble faded the women heard voices drifting over the field, and firefly torches winked through the fence. Cautious now, the moonlight picked out buttons and badges and pale

203

skin and slowly pieced together two policemen, walking in single file along the footpath towards them.

'Aye-aye,' said Lucy. 'The cordon tightening, if I'm not mistaken.'

'Pity the horse has bolted.'

When the theft had been properly reported, when all phone calls had been made that could be made at that time of night, and the policemen had gone home on their bicycles, they found that Mabel had put two armchairs together.

'Mister'll sleep down 'ere,' she explained. 'Won't be most comfy he'm ever been, Audrey, but needs must. You can come in wi' me. Don't ee fret,' her grin was wicked, 'I jest 'ad a bath in Lucy's dirty water but I'll put a bolster down the middle to stop any 'anky-panky!'

Audrey went a bright crimson.

Lucy frowned. What did Mabel know? Was this the village grapevine at work again? Or was Mabel good at guessing, too?

'I'm packing in my job,' Audrey said, limping up the stairs.

'Oh rot, you love it.'

'I'm fed up with having the blasted wages stolen, Lucy. I mean twice in – what? – four months? It's a bit much. It's like every time your Roy needs some extra cash he pinches my car. The Ministry'll begin to think I'm a bad risk.'

'Not you. Me, maybe. Me and my choice of bloke.'

'Hope he takes better care of poor old Florrie this time. She doesn't like rough treatment. Busted axles and the like. I bet the front bumper'll need fixing.'

'Damn. Someone'd better go and move it, that sack of spuds.'

'In the morning, dear, in the morning,' Audrey yawned. They had reached the landing. 'Mind, that was a good bit of driving. Neat reverse turn.'

They stared at each other.

'Audrey, Roy can't drive a car . . .'

# Chapter Nineteen

Nora couldn't face a kipper.

'I enjoyed me porridge and me bit of toast,' she assured the waiter, 'but I've 'ad quite sufficient, ta. Couldn't eat no more if you paid me.'

Gawd, the very thought made her heave. Kippers for breakfast! Whoever heard of such a thing? And it wouldn't do her indigestion no good at all.

Kept her awake most of the night. Worse at night than in the day. Not that she ever got a proper night's sleep in these hotels. Just be getting off and she'd have this hiccup of, like, fear, waking her up again. And then she'd lie there, worrying she wasn't going to sleep. Among other things.

The doctor had told her *not* to worry. Worry was the worst thing for nervous indigestion, but what can you do? You got a war going on all round you, your boys are away fighting, Gawd knows where, one of them you ain't heard from in six, no seven blinking months. And your daughter is acting up. A flaming prima donna. You worry, don't you? And then you worry about worrying.

She stared into her dismal cup of tea. Milky water, that's all it was. How they had the brass neck to call it tea . . .

'What's this, late breakfast or early lunch?'

'Marje! I . . . I . . .' She dabbed at her mouth with the napkin. 'Where'd you spring from?'

The tall woman hovered, anxious, trying to read her eyes. She supposed the strain was beginning to show.

'Bad night?'

'Not as bad as you, gel. You can't have been to bed!'

'Came on the workman's train.'

Nora regarded her with curiosity. And waited.

'Oh,' she finally admitted, 'no use denying it, Lucy made me feel thoroughly guilty. Said I'd left you in the lurch.'

'Lucy?'

'Mmm. She phoned, when was it? Sunday.'

'She phoned *you*?'

'Looking for you. *Urgently*. I told her to try Bay View or here.'

'She did.' Thinking about Lucy made her head ache. 'Oh, I'm pleased to see you! Sit down, Marje. Oh, that's lovely.' All her hard feelings, all her bitterness flowed away like weak tea poured back into the pot. 'The others ain't come?'

'Couldn't get away.'

'Ah well.'

'Everything all right then? With Lucy?'

'Getting there. Getting there.' A lot depended on whether she turned up at Sowness on Saturday. Probably wouldn't. She worked Saturdays, didn't she? Well, that would be her excuse, anyway.

Nora wasn't looking forward to Sowness. Not a bit.

'Waiter!' she called. 'More tea, duck. For two. That's one *full* teaspoon each and one for the pot, and *fresh* tea leaves – not twice brewed.'

She turned back to Marjorie, cool and ribbed, like a glass wash-board in a watery green silk knitted thing, and a hat to match, pulled down over the coils of plaits. Beside her, Nora's frock of hot-house flowers made you break out sweating.

'And a jug of hot water, please.' The hoods shuttered down over Marje's eyes. And up. A simpering smile.

Flirting. At her age! Oh Gawd, thought Nora. Don't frighten him away, Marje, please! His tea may be lousy but it's all we've got. Then Marje turned her attention to Nora once again.

'So how've you been?' The enquiry was delicate, as from a hospital visitor, expecting the worst. Nora was not going to disappoint her.

'Bleeding terrible!' she said with gusto.

206

'Oh, Nora! I'm so sorry. But I *had* to go back to Clacton. Duty called.'

Nora shrugged. Grumbled. 'It was still bleeding terrible. Didn't think I was gonna make it.' She frowned in puzzlement. 'Only someone stepped in, last minute, and helped me out.'

'I was praying for you. And I'm sure the others were.'

'No, this was real strong stuff.' She realised what she'd said. 'I mean, different from the usual sort of back-up. Like a surge of power. Just what the doctor ordered. Could've been someone in the audience, I suppose.'

'Congregation,' corrected Marjorie gently. 'Yes, John said it was a strong church.'

'John's a bleeding quack. I told you, Marje, when he come to ours. I said, didn't I? Him and his little wifey. Not enough spirit between 'em to light the lamp in my lavvy. No, it weren't him. Someone else . . . Mind you, they was only just in the nick. I thought I'd had it.'

'Oh Nora . . .'

'Like a *whoomph* it was. The dark forces didn't know what had hit 'em.'

'Oh good. I mean, I'm sorry. I came back as soon as I could.'

'Not soon enough.'

'Oh dear.' But Marjorie had clearly suffered enough recriminations. She reached into her tan-coloured bag, that matched her tan-coloured shoes and tan-coloured gloves, and pulled out a bundle of letters.

'Some post for you, Nora. I thought you'd want me to bring it.'

'Oh lovely.'

Post always cheered her up. There was a lot for just a week. She sifted through it quickly for the BFPO ones. Bother the cheques and the invitations to speak, bother the gushing thanks from grateful clients, bother the bills, she wanted news of her boys. One especially.

'Oh!' she said, her eyes feeding hungrily on an envelope. 'Is it from Jack?'

'Yeah.' Muttering, on the one hand, 'About bleeding time,' and on the other, 'Thank Gawd for that!' she held it close to

207

look at the postmark, moving her glasses into focus. 'Newcastle? What the 'ell's he doing in Newcastle? He's supposed to be in the desert.'

'Open it and see.'

After cleaning the butter-knife on her napkin, she slit open the envelope and with great care, as though it might crumble and blow away, she withdrew the few pages and unfolded them.

'Oh my good Gawd!' Her eyes transfixed by words.

'What?'

'He's in hospital! Oh, my boy, my poor boy!' She ran her eye over the first page, sucking out the sense of it. 'Oh Marje, he says he's had a nasty crack on the head or something, didn't know who he was for months. Marje, I'll have to go to him. Oh Jack!' She was bundling all her letters together again, collecting her bag, getting up to leave.

'Nora, sit down, dear.' Marjorie patted the seat, sensibly, as Nora's eyes darted about looking for somewhere to pin her thoughts.

She sat down. And got up again. Little cries of, 'Oh Jack . . . oh son,' like distant sea-gulls.

'Nora, you haven't read the letter at all,' said her friend sternly. 'Sit down, read it properly. He might not want you to go haring up to Newcastle. He might not even be there any more. It's a long way for a wasted journey.'

No, and there's two more meetings to fit in this week, thought Nora. But she did as she was told, she opened the letter again, but the words just swam around in panic. All she could see was Jack lying broken on that hospital bed. Suffering. In the end, she let Marjorie read it to her:

'*"Dear Ma. Thank you for all your letters. I have just been reading them, sent on by my regiment and piling up in my beside locker. It sounds like you have been having a fine old time, Ma, kidding everyone you are a medium and earning yourself a few bob. Can't be bad! Sorry I have not been able to reply. The thing is, I have not been all the ticket, Ma, since getting blown up by Rommel. Don't worry, I'm in good hands and should be out of here soon. What happened, I got a nasty crack on the head and lost my memory. What a joke! Didn't know who, what, where or why I was, plus a few odd broken bones. Only just come out of it and feeling pretty silly, I can tell you. They did say they told you where I was and every-thing, but the way you write it sounds like you did not know a thing about it. They must have sent the letter to W'stow. You and Lucy must have spent a worrying six months or more. Sorry about that!"'*

Marjorie took this as her cue to pour tea. Nora thought it looked no better than the previous lot. Nevertheless it was hot and she sipped it gratefully as Marjorie read on:

'*"No, seriously, I have a lot of catching up to do. One minute I am sweltering in this tank, seeing sand and sand and sand, next there's a big bang and I'm in the RVI with a pretty nurse on my knee. Do not ask me how she got there! Her name is Susan, by the way, and I think I must have got to know her very well in the time I have been here! That is what she says, anyway. I may just have to marry her! I will bring her to see you before we tie the knot, do not worry.*

"*What about old Lucy then? Last I knew she was working in the factory and all set to become Mrs Sykes? Now her letters are full of tractors and cows and spring mornings and this Joe bloke."'*

'Eh?' said Nora, sitting up. Joe? Must be someone new. The only Joe she knew was the one on the train. Not their sort, with his concerts and his red hair.

Marjorie gave a 'Search me' shrug, with eyebrows to match, and went on:

'*"What's he really like, Ma? She makes him sound too good to be true. Though she does have her doubts about his red hair."'*

It couldn't be.

'*"He sounds a decent sort of bloke. Better than Little Lord . . ."'*

'Hmm,' said Marjorie, puzzling over a word. She passed the letter to Nora, who adjusted her glasses.

'F . . . filling? Faking? Lord faking Roy? Search me.'

'Lord Fauntleroy!' said Marjorie in triumph.

Nora looked again, unconvinced. Then she fell in, and hid a smile behind her hand. Let Marjorie think it said Fauntleroy. It wouldn't do her any harm.

'*"Better than Little Lord Fauntleroy. What a prat. Excuse*

209

*my language, Ma, but whatever did she see in him?"'*

'Language?'

'Prat,' explained Nora.

'Oh. *"Anyway, tell her to get a move on, I could do with a Potter wedding – a good old knees-up, and seeing my big brothers again. Make sure they're alive and kicking. Because they don't write. I suppose six or seven letters, just to keep up with the family, is asking rather a lot of a bloke on active service. I know Lucy seems to find the time, but she's a woman.*

*"Saw Mick out in Aden, in October, seems like yesterday! I expect he told you. He had just got his stripes, jammy bugger. Full of it, isn't he? I have had a postcard from Arthur, sunning himself in the Med, getting ready for the 'big one'. All right for some, eh?*

*"Things have been moving on in the war, I gather. Glad I did not get blown up in vain. Seems like it is only a matter of time, now.*

*"Stroke of luck about Bampton Road, eh, Ma? I mean you and Lucy being well out of it when the bomb hit."'*

'Eh?' She grabbed the letter from Marjorie. 'What's he on about? What bleeding bomb?'

Jack's scrawl, which had started all bright and breezy, now assumed a sinister obliqueness as Nora took over the narrative. '*"I don't suppose you have had a chance to look at it yet. Billy Moffat came in to see me a couple of days ago. He got leave to see poor old Aggie and called in here on his way back. A bit out of the way, but you know Billy, nothing is too much trouble. It was good to see him. She does not sound too bad, Aggie, a bit shaken up, and cut about by flying glass, but on the mend. When she comes out of hospital she is going to live with her sister in Basingstoke. She will not go back to Walthamstow. Billy says their damage was worse than ours: where it only caught our front bedroom, and that bit of the roof, it took off the front of her house. Of course, she was in there, blacking her nose at the window! Blown back on the blast, poor cow! She swears she did not hear a thing, that there was no warning or anything. When you think, Ma, you or Lu—"'* The blue ink blurred and Nora's voice wavered. '*"Lucy could have been in . . . in bed."'*

She couldn't manage any more. The paper crackled, being handed back.

Marjorie held Nora's hand to stop it shaking and smoothed the letter on to the table between them. She took over.

' *"Billy says number 41 is still there, but shored up because of the gap where 43 and 45 was."'*

'Oh my Gawd! The Bannermans,' she grieved, 'and Old Man Harris!'

' *"Ted and Ada's was not touched, only the windows smashed. Billy said they took for ever mending the sewer, apparently, and was just getting round to filling in the crater in the road with the rubble from the two on our side and two over the road. Billy says someone has fixed corrugated iron over the hole in our roof . . ."'*

'That'll be Ted. He's a good neighbour.'

' *". . . to stop the rain coming in, and nailed up the windows against looters. So there is no need to go rushing back. There is nothing you can do, anyway. You cannot go moving back in until the landlord has made it safe. Anyway, you sound nice and cosy up there, why don't you look around for a cottage or something? I am sure one or two of your strapping sons will help you with the move when the time comes.*

*"Do not come up. I would love to see you but it is a rotten journey, just not worth it. Soon as they give me the All Clear, which should be any day now, I shall be down to see you. Susan is due some leave too and we could do with a week by the sea. Take care of yourself, Ma. Love, Jack."'*

'Oh Nora, my dear . . .'

She tried to swallow the lump in her throat. 'Well, that solves that one, don't it? No bleeding home to go to, now!'

'That's not what he says at all! It just needs fixing up a bit.'

'Well, Mrs Next-door's gone and Old Man Harris. Poor sods. Aggie Moffat's off to Basingstoke and what's left? What's left, eh? A blooming bomb site where me neighbours used to be. And what about the old folks, Auntie Vi and Uncle Harry and Dad and the others? They'll be having forty fits, won't know what's hit 'em. Oh, this war gets on my bleeding wick.'

'But the boy's all right.'

'I'll believe that when I see it. Why don't he want me up there, I'd like to know? Bet he's lost a leg or he's got hisself burned or something.'

'He said he's almost on his way home.'

'Yeah?' She got up to leave and stumbled against the chair.

'Nora, dear! Why don't you go and have a lie-down? You've had a nasty shock. Got to get you right for the meeting at Monk's Thornton tonight.'

'I don't want no blooming lay down!' Nora shouted, stamping her foot for the first time in fifty years, causing heads to turn and Marje to wince. Marje hated scenes and bad grammar, but Nora didn't care.

'I don't *want* to do no meeting in Monk's flaming Thornton! I want a taxi to the station so I can go and see my boy!'

This was Wednesday, ten-fifteen in the morning. It took two taxis, three trains, a few greased palms, almost ten hours, and a will of iron, but by the close of visiting time, she was sitting at Jack's bedside in the Royal Victoria Infirmary, Newcastle-upon-Tyne, nursing the first decent cup of tea she'd had all day.

At the same time, Lucy, unaware of her mother's mutiny, was at the table with the oil-lamp, and *Gone with the Wind* open before her. But she wasn't reading. Her eyes followed the print, came to the bottom of a page and her fingers turned it, but Lucy hadn't been with Scarlett at Melanie Wilkes's deathbed at all. She hadn't been anywhere near Georgia. She couldn't care less whether Rhett loved Scarlett or Ashley didn't, or what. She was in the car, Florrie, trying desperately to see the driver's face.

How could it have been Roy driving, when Roy couldn't drive?

How could it *not* have been Roy, when she had seen the sleeve, burnt in the fire? And the fair hair?

Between the black and white of words, she saw his image again and again. Appearing out of the fog, speaking to her, kicking the milk bucket, doubling up when she kneed him in the crutch, and lately, not bothering even to speak. Just standing there, like two of eels. It was Roy. Roy the police

212

were after. Roy who had come to her room for his wallet. Roy who had tried to rape her. To give her VD. Vindictive . . . No question.

So how had he learned to drive? Wild thoughts chased across her mind. She had visions of him, sitting up in the oak tree, studying some sort of How To manual. Perhaps it had fallen out of Eileen's pram and that's what he'd been hunting for when Mrs Cosgrove chased him off. Or maybe he'd been practising on the tractor, in secret.

Nonsense.

He'd probably learned in the army and forgotten to tell her. Even the best of drivers had trouble with temperamental old Fords and hill starts and wet April afternoons. Specially if they were panicking. Given a warm June evening and a flat road, they were fine.

Of course it had been Roy. And now he was gone.

She pushed the book aside. She was too tired to read. It had been midnight before they had got to bed last night, and she hadn't slept well, what with all the excitement. She had woken before dawn, listening for planes returning, trying to focus on Joe, and getting Nora and Audrey and Roy all swirling around together to the strains of a violin, like subliminal soup. When the cockerels had started up she'd been glad to get up and do something real.

*The Brains Trust* was burbling away to itself on the wireless. Hooper wasn't listening. He had his nose in the newspaper, horizontally. (It fluttered on the out-breaths.) Mabel was in the kitchen, chopping beet for jam. Gooseberry and beet, a concoction of her own. It sounded awful, but she said it wouldn't need sugar.

With care and cunning, Lucy got up, turned down the volume to avoid the telltale whistle and buzz of static and, with her ear close to the speaker retuned to the Third Programme, gradually turned up the volume again when the sound was clear. The *Radio Times* had Schubert listed, a string quintet, and, with the zeal of the recent convert, Lucy was determined to hear it. She rested her chin on her fists and watched as sad violin strains wriggled up the greasy black curlings of lamp-smoke, as a cello plucked at the pollywogs on the ceiling, as moths flitted on the notes between, drawn

213

irresistibly to the light. It was pleasant to pick out tunes and rhythms but, with nothing to look at, with the sound so small and centralised, she drifted off and thought about hoeing parsnips and looking for eggs. The hens laid them in the most unlikely places. Perhaps this was one that would grow on her.

*'Luce! Lucy! Come on, duck, Ma wants to get the tea. Ain't got all day to chase after silly little gels. Luce! Where are you?'*

*Lucy watched her slippers slapping up and down the garden path, behind, then in front of the big-bellied sheets, going on tip-toe, picking their way among the prickly bushes on the other side of the garden, to lean over Next-door's. Heard her rattling round in the outhouse, opening, shutting the lavvy door. Heard the back door slam.*

*She wasn't never going back in there, in that horrible house. She was going to stay out here, with the chickens. They didn't care if she crayonned 'L' for Lucy in her picture book, they didn't mind if she quietly peed in the garden, if she went through Dad's drawers, tasting the shaving stick, rubbing the cufflinks on her cheeks, smelling his scarves and gloves, trying to catch the man who had bounced her on his foot, going, 'Bumpety, bumpety, bumpety, bump, here comes the galloping Major,' and then went off to work and died.*

*Chickens didn't come out of the walls, with cross faces, and tell her off, shout at her, make her cry. Nasty ladies with smelly breath, telling her not to poke her finger in the cat's ear, not to spit out the nasty greens when Ma wasn't looking, not to put bits of paper on the fire, not to, not to, not to. And that man who kept looking at her when she was on the lavvy, that man with his nasty hairy smile and his red flicking tongue . . . He was there at night, and all, with his smell of dirty clothes and his hot eyes. She'd woken up and seen him, looking at her mary and she'd pulled the covers up quick and shouted for Ma and she'd come and said it was all a nasty dream, there was no one there. Not now there wasn't. He'd gone back in the cupboard when he'd heard Ma coming.*

*No, the chickens just looked at her with their one eyes, shook their floppy red bits and got on with pecking up stuff from the floor, purring and chirring their chicken chatter.*

*Then Jack was there, his face like a jigsaw behind the wire.*

214

*He wanted to come in, too, but she told him to go away. This was her place. And then she knew what he would do: he was taking a breath.*

*'Ma!' he yelled, his mouth all full of gaps where teeth used to be. Telltale tit, your tongue will split and all the little puppy dogs will have a little bit.*

*And there was Ma, muttering, with a sob in her voice and pulling her out of there and banging her head on the shitty perch, smacking Lucy's legs and shouting, in time with the smacks.*

*'You-stupid-stupid-little-girl!' and thinking up more to say just so she could do more smacks, while the chickens carried on pecking.*

*Next time she would run away harder. To the park, or to the trains; she would run away and run away until the people stopped coming out of the walls and spying on her.*

*It was Jack who told her what to do. He didn't see them any more.*

*'Just don't,' he said. 'Shut your eyes and don't see them.'*

*Simple as that.*

*But it wasn't her eyes she had to shut. It was something in her head and it was hard at first. Almost impossible. To take no notice when there was this old granny snapping at you, when there was this old man staring at you, blowing you wet kisses. It was uncomfortable, like having slippers on the wrong feet, or sucking two different fingers when you were trying to go to sleep and Ma had put bitter aloes on your two favourites.*

*But she had got used to it.*

*And, after a while, she had stopped running. She had stopped sucking her fingers, too.*

There was a sound like rice grains tipping into a pudding dish, on and on. Applause. People clapping. The music had ended. She sat staring at the lamp's pearly glass. Remembering. Chewing her lip and remembering.

When a man began talking, softly, over other murmuring voices, about Beethoven, she tiptoed over to the wireless and returned it to the Light Programme, realising as she did so, that she had missed the main nine o'clock news. The weather forecast was for rain in the East.

215

The telephone rang and Hooper snuffled awake, but Lucy was already there.

'Lucy!'

'Oh, hello, Aud. Got back all right then? They found your car yet?'

'Don't you know?'

'Sorry?'

A breathy pause.

'No, no, they haven't found it. Well, they haven't told me if they have. No, I don't suppose they'll give it another thought. They must have hundreds of stolen cars on their books. I've already put in my insurance claim.'

'But Roy was driving it. He's a wanted man.'

'Small potatoes! Oh sorry. No, Lucy, they've got enough on their plate. I'd forget it if I were you.'

It wasn't so easy to forget. Anything. Not now.

'You still there? Lucy?'

'Yes, yes.'

'Look, dear, what I was phoning about . . . Did you hear the news?'

'No, I missed it.' A sudden pang of alarm. 'What's happened?' Her mind flew to Joe.

'Oh, nothing to worry about, dear. No, I . . . well, I . . . I seem to remember, yesterday, at that concert, your saying something about Pantelleria.'

'Did I? Oh yes – that island in the Mediterranean.'

'How did you know about it?'

'Search me. It's where Joe went. They were bombing it last night.'

'He told you, did he?'

'No, of course not! He knows better than that. What's this all about, Audrey?'

'Well, I had a thought. See, they mentioned that place on the news tonight. Pantelleria.'

'Did they?' She wasn't surprised. It was an important victory.

Audrey rattled on, about the surrender at noon, about the four days and nights of continuous shelling by cruisers and destroyers, bombing by the RAF, sometimes for seventy-six minutes at a time, which had resulted in an outstanding

216

strategic victory for the Allies.

'Mmm,' she said in the pauses. 'Mmm.' Because she knew all this.

*But she shouldn't have known, should she?* That *was Audrey's point. This was news.*

Her hands were suddenly damp. The hair on her neck was wet and cold. Sweat trickled between her breasts, under her arms.

'Lucy, dear?'

'Yes. I see what you mean, Audrey. It *is* odd that I . . .' Her voice tailed off. She sat down heavily on the stairs. 'Aud . . . did they say about the airfield? That Pantelleria had its own airfield?'

'Well, that was the whole point of taking it, wasn't it? So that . . .'

Lucy completed her sentence '. . . So that they could station the Allied Air Offensive there, for a concerted attack on Sicily.'

'Which is . . .?' prompted Audrey, getting the idea.

'Sixty-five miles from Pantelleria!'

'And you're telling everyone you're not a blasted fortune-teller!'

Lucy drew a long, shuddering breath.

'You all right, dear?'

'Yes, yes, I'm fine. It's just, well, I suppose I've sort of known for a few weeks. Months. In fact, Audrey, I'm beginning to realise that it's something I've been suppressing for years. It's a bit worrying.'

'Worrying – why? I think it's brilliant. A great gift!'

'Do you?'

'You can tell me how much I'm going to get from the insurance.'

'See, that's just it. I can't do it to order. If I could I'd know why Joe hasn't phoned tonight to tell me he's back safe and sound.'

'Oh dear. Oh, I'm sorry, Lucy, I'll say goodbye and get off the blasted phone. I just thought you'd be interested in the Italian thing.'

'Oh, I am, I am. Thanks, Aud. Oh, and Aud . . .'

'Yes?'

'Keep it to yourself.'

As she hung up she realised her grandmother was sitting, higher up the stairs. If Lucy had put out a hand, she could have touched the toe of her crooked foot.

'So now you know,' the old woman said.

Somewhere a piano tinkled. It had to be Chopin.

'Yep, now I know.'

'Nora'll be pleased.'

Back in the parlour, the smell was overpowering. But it wasn't pear-drops, it was burning sugar. Hooper was opening windows!

She flung open the kitchen door in time to see Donald Hooper helplessly, hopelessly, tearing his figurative hair, dancing from one foot to the other, while, at the kitchen range, his mother, red in the face and running with sweat, continued to stir her seething pot.

Lucy nodded to him. He wasn't frightening. Just a bloke concerned about his mum.

'Towngirl,' she greeted her, passing a hand across her forehead, 'blessed if I can get this jam to settin' point. Bin boilin' for hours. Thought I get'n done afore us go abed, but summat's up wi' it.'

'It's burning, Mabel!'

'Eh?'

'Your pan, it's caught on the bottom. Can't you smell it?'

She sniffed. 'Can't smell nothin'.'

'Take it off the stove, love, you'll have us on fire again!'

With towels and cloths wound round their hands they lifted the big pan, roaring hot, onto the pile of newspapers Nora had set there ready. The jam continued to bubble and plop.

'I can't believe you didn't smell it, Mabel.'

'Don't seem to smell a lot o' things lately,' she admitted. 'Must be getting old.'

Well, that explained a lot, thought Lucy, spooning up the mixture and letting it dribble back. Even the late sunset could lend it no glamour.

'Whatever colour would you call that?' Mabel's gaze was doubtful.

'Puce?' Lucy offered.

218

'Don't look very appetising, do it?'

'What does it taste like?'

She blew hard on the spoon and took some with her teeth. 'Dunno. Beet, I s'pose,' she said, 'and gooseberries.'

'Well, it would. Is it sweet enough?'

'What you think?' handing Lucy the spoon.

Donald made a face in sympathy, to match her own. It was foul. Sour, burnt, with beetroot overtones.

'You can't taste either, can you, Mabel?'

'Don't seem 'ardly fair somehow, do it? Some people 'avin' six senses, seeing through pea-pods, and me only three.'

'I keep telling you, Mabel, I don't *have* a sixth sense,' looking straight at a fat man in a chef's hat, who winked and faded through the red-hot range. Mabel, in her affliction, had missed out on bluebells and fresh-mown hay and woodsmoke and creosote . . . not to mention burnt Sunday roast and pig-dung and Hooper's feet, but Lucy didn't feel so sorry for the woman that she would admit to seeing the ghost of her son. She'd never hear the last of it. Donald understood, she was sure of it.

'Come on,' she said. 'Bed. Leave it to cool. Feed it to the pig in the morning.'

'Give her squits.'

'Well, put it on the "bombie" then. Oh come on, Mabel, you look exhausted.'

But the smell of sweet burning bled through the floorboards and Lucy's dreams were of planes falling like fireballs, of crippled engines whining, of burning flesh, of red hair shrivelling, skin blistering, crackling like Sunday roast, speckled irises whitening like the albumen of an egg and, when her unconscious was shrieking, No more! she clambered up from that pit, forcing herself into consciousness.

Her ears hummed with sudden silence, and she lay stiff with horror, her pounding heart filling her chest, leaving no room for breath.

'Joe . . .' she shuddered, forcing her eyelids to open, though they were heavy and aching to dream on. She blinked hard to keep awake and a hot tear ran across her nose.

219

# Chapter Twenty

The 'bombie' lurked out of sight, downwind, over and against the low wall at the end of Mabel's kitchen garden. Corrugated iron sheets, on the other three sides, were designed to keep you from falling into the pit. This was where the bucket from the privy was emptied. Not to be confused with the dung heap – a huge steaming mound not far from the cowshed, where good, honest, uncontaminated animal waste rotted down ready for recycling, the 'bombie' was also the dumping ground for kitchen and garden waste. Pea-pods and nettles, rhubarb leaves and chickweed, steeped in the contents of chamber pot and privy bucket, thinly disguised with Jeyes' Fluid. When the pit was brim-full with the magic brew it was earthed over to ferment, with the soil from a new hole. Mabel's vegetables, fed regular doses of matured 'bombie', were superior to any in the fields.

Carefully Lucy set down the heavy pan, took off the lid, with which Mabel had covered it overnight, and tipped the burnt jam over the side of the iron sheet.

Do wasps never sleep? she wondered vaguely. They homed in on the sticky mess from nowhere, half-a-dozen buzzing the news, oblivious to the dread in her heart and the tear that slid down her cheek. She watched them absently, wondering whether there would be anyone sensible at Sowness, at four o'clock in the morning, to take her call. Perhaps she had better leave it until the Hoopers were up. They needed their sleep.

As she waited for the pan to empty . . . Waited . . .

Her eye was caught by a movement near the house.

Fear shrunk her throat.

A figure in khaki, a soldier, leaning against the house, with a menacing smile stuck to his handsome face, pushed himself off the wall and began to walk across the yard towards her. The dawn gleamed pink in his colourless hair.

'Oh my God!' she breathed; he was relentless. He'd come back, just as he always did. There was no getting rid of him until he'd got what he wanted. And she was so weary of him. So tired of fighting.

Come on then, Roy, she thought. Get it over with. Here by the bombie. As her body numbed for him, cold fingers released their hold on the pan. It was a heavy, enamelled heirloom, a Hooper hand-me-down, Mabel's favourite. They were going to scour it clean with Vim and try again. Still half-full of jam, it was sinking slowly in the quicksand of sludge. She'd recover it next year, in the spring, or the year after.

But there was a summerful of jam to make and Mabel would never forgive her. She leaned over the corrugated side to save it, couldn't reach, leaned further and the rusted metal crumpled, like wet cardboard, under her weight. Falling, she put out her arms to save herself and felt them sink into a soft mire of stinking muck.

'A-ah shit!'

It was fitting, it was just. It was the last straw. She would let herself drown in the stuff. She'd be rid of them all, then: Roy and the disease he was so keen to share, Joe who was too painful to think about, Nora, her psychic legacy, Granny . . . But when a wasp buzzed by her ear, she found she was scrambling backwards across the sheet, pulling the pan up after her. She flapped at the insect and there was another, three or four, targeting her, angry at having their treat fouled. Frantic, she reached up for a hand to pull her clear. Least he could do. He was supposed to love her, after all. But he had gone.

'Thanks, Roy,' she said.

Flight Sergeant Joseph Torrance was missing, they told her, when she finally plucked up the courage to telephone. Had been missing since Tuesday night.

'Is that missing, presumed dead?' She changed hands. Her arm ached almost as much as her throat. The smell of the vinegar with which Mabel had doused her wasp sting permeated the raggy bit of sheet in which her arm had been wrapped. Made her feel sick.

His plane had been shot down over Pantelleria, they said, the night before last, Tuesday the tenth. Just before they had lost radio contact the pilot had reported two men dead, and that the rest were baling out. Eye-witnesses thought they'd seen men parachuting clear, but couldn't be sure in the confusion. If he had escaped, if he hadn't been injured or killed, on or before landing, they would expect to hear from him within the next day or two. They would pass on any definite news. One way or the other.

'The island is in our hands now, you realise,' they said.

'Yes,' she said. But it hadn't been, on Tuesday.

'Be 'ome afore ee know it,' said Mabel, with more confidence than either her squeeze or her smile conveyed.

No, he wouldn't. Lucy jabbed between the parsnips with her hoe, making her arm throb. She was some sort of psychic, wasn't she? Seeing ghosts, making predictions? Clairvoyant. That dream couldn't have been clearer.

It was almost as though they'd known, that afternoon in the barn, that this was all they would have. And that concert. On the very night it . . . She had seen his plane over Pantelleria. What had that been, if not an omen?

How unfair. How hard. To have met such a man, the right man, to have known such happiness, so briefly, and to have had it snatched away.

And meanwhile, Roy had turned up again. The bad penny.

When she saw Mabel and Constable Stone dragging up the footpath she naturally assumed the worst.

'He's dead, isn't he?'

'Whassat?' He was puffing too hard to catch what she had said.

'Joe . . . Flight Sergeant Torrance.'

Mabel was shaking her head. The policeman had taken off his helmet, but only to mop his forehead. He squinted at her,

222

his nose and cheeks pink blobs of exertion.

'En't come about yer airman. Yer soldier's the one.'

'Roy?'

'Aye. They got'n.'

'Got him?' They couldn't have. Not so soon.

'Up Norwich way. Didn't get too far. Going round'n round, you ask me.'

'No road-signs, see,' said Mabel.

'They've *got* him? Really?' Her heart bounded. 'Well, that was quick! And thank the Lord!'

The policeman nodded.

'In the hospital. Drivin' like a maniac, they reckon. Smacked into a bus coming t'other way. Car's a write-off.'

'Oh no. Poor Audrey!' And, as an afterthought, 'Is he badly hurt?'

'Bit o' this, bit o' that. Head injuries, they do say. Knocked him out. But they reckon he'm had a good night.'

'A good night?' What was he talking about?

'So they say. Got no worse, like, in's sleep.'

'But if they caught him this morning?'

'Yest'day afternoon, they got'n.'

'*Yesterday*? No, that's wrong!'

She told him how she had seen Roy only five hours earlier. How he had stood and watched while she dunked herself in the 'bombie'.

The policeman stuck out his lower lip, and shook his head. Most definitely. Flipped open his notebook.

'Young soldier, in service of 'Is Majesty, answering description o' your man, Private Roy Sykes, were took to the King Edward Military Hospital in Norwich, following an accident on the Aylsham Road, involving a black Ford Ten, registration number HX 263, which 'e were driving, on the wrong side of the road, like, and a Green-Line bus. Yest'day arternoon, two-thirty.'

There was proof. In black and white. So Lucy must be mistaken. And, loyal as ever, Mabel was siding with the law.

'Happen you'm on'y *thought* you see'n, Towngirl.'

Like I'm losing my marbles, eh, Mabel?

She said, '"Answering the description". The bloke only looked like him.' She blinked as possibilities began to occur

223

to her. 'It wasn't Roy, because I *did* see him this morning and not a sign of any broken bones. So they've got someone else in that hospital. Perhaps he stole the car from Roy. Or . . . or maybe it wasn't,' she cleared her throat, 'maybe it wasn't Roy who took the car in the first place. Only someone who looked like him.'

''Twere you *said* it were 'im, miss,' the policeman pointed out.

'Look, Mr Stone, it was dark. I suppose we expected it to be Roy but it could have been somebody else with fair hair . . . and . . .' No, this was ridiculous. Of course it had been Roy. There was the burnt sleeve. 'Well, what makes them so sure it's Roy?'

'Papers and stuff in his wallet. Bit charred, they said, but good enough to identify'n.'

'Oh.'

The damned wallet.

'Well, Roy could have left the wallet in the car while he . . . I dunno, got out to, you know . . . and this other man stole the car and the wallet.'

It sounded very far-fetched, even to her. But the explanation must be something like that. A thought struck her then.

'If they've got his wallet they'll be able to see that he doesn't match his photo!'

'Don't say nothing 'bout no photo.' The Constable was looking perplexed, scratching behind his ear, flicking through the notebook for the magic words that would make Lucy . . . what? A liar? Mad?

She said, as calmly as she could, 'Well, there was at least one photo of Roy in his wallet, taken with me at the seaside. It was there the other night. I told you.' She bit her lips at the cheek of it. 'You'll have it written down.'

Mabel had been hovering. Biding her time. Now she made a suggestion.

'Whyn't you go up to Norwich and see'n for yerself, Lucy? I come wi' ee. Sort it out once and for all? Happen Eric'll lay on a car for us, ask'n nicely. Save 'anging about for buses.'

*　　*　　*

'Oh,' said Mabel, when she saw the man in the bed. 'Oh aye, that be him. That your Roy, ennit? I seed him in the lane that time, coming back from the meeting.'

It wasn't, of course. Even Constable Stone had to admit that it was nothing like the photo on police files. Squarer chin, higher cheekbones, broader forehead. The same fair hair, but long and unruly, poking out from a bandage, and a growth of beard. Shadows under his closed eyes, hollow cheeks, dirty fingernails, dry skinning lips. His arm was in plaster and there was a support round his neck, but that didn't disguise the fact that he looked as though he had been living rough. Whereas Roy had somehow always managed to keep himself looking fairly spruce. Even this morning, at dawn. A dusting of golden stubble but no more.

Two very different men.

They examined the uniform, which had been bundled in the bedside locker. Roy's penknife was in the trouser pocket – the one Nora had given him for his birthday, a fancy Swiss affair with half-a-dozen useful attachments, corkscrews, and things for taking stones out of horse's hooves.

Fascinated, she fingered the familiar scorch on the sleeve, remembering when she had touched it last, had pushed her thumb through the brittle threads to make the hole bigger, make a ragged flap of material.

There had been no such flap on Roy's sleeve that morning. No damage at all. Somehow he had acquired a new jacket. New trousers too, maybe. So when had he given, or thrown, the old uniform away, forgetting to take out the penknife in the pocket?

When?

They brought the wallet from the ward safe and examined it carefully. Broken now in two pieces, it was the one that had been in Lucy's keeping so recently. There were photos of her, worn with handling, but there were no photos of Roy.

Lucy's head buzzed. Why had this man been wearing Roy's old uniform, carrying his wallet, pretending to be Roy?

And for how long?

Ages? One night – two? Had this tramp come to her room? Oh God, she breathed.

225

She thought she knew but she had to be sure.

He knew the answer. Him. Lying there, out of it, with his stupid eyes shut. He knew.

Damn cowardly deserter. He couldn't just lie there.

She had to know.

Propelled by an unseen hand, she lurched forward, pushed her face into his. Drew back at the familiar rankness. And shaking with fear and loathing, rasped, 'Who *are* you?'

When he did not react, she grabbed him by his shoulders.

'Lucy!' Mabel dragged her arm. She shook her off.

'Who the hell are you?' she cried. 'Who?' Slapped his face. 'What's Roy got to do with *you*?'

He moaned and, as they went to restrain her, his eyes opened, feral grey, and he caught her arm in a strong grip, his nails biting into her skin.

'*Nein*, Towngirl. *Bitte!*' he said. His voice was harsh, gutteral. There was a a look of hurt in his eyes she did not understand. Then she remembered hearing a curse as her assailant landed on the floor in the dark. It hadn't been a word that she knew. Naturally enough. It had been German.

She was asked to be quiet as she was disturbing other patients, but she found it hard to stop laughing. And crying. She stuffed a towel into her mouth and Mabel tried to comfort her, to find a way through the sobs.

'Slap her face,' snapped a nurse. 'She's hysterical. Bring her to her senses.'

But Mabel was gentle, bustling her out, despite Lucy's struggle to stay, to know it all. Before the door closed she looked back, tried to read the eyes of the German, peering at her between uniforms, khaki, black and white. But all she saw there was misery. She must have hurt him somewhere along the line. Then they pulled the curtains round the bed.

They found a patient who spoke German and at least two policemen stayed to scribble down his statement.

Two hours later, in the car going back to Great Bisset, Constable Stone told them that the German's name was Friedrich Weiss.

'First he try makin' out he come down by parachute, livin'

226

rough, like, till 'e *find* the car abandoned, like, wi' the clothes inside'n and the wallet.'

'Likely story,' sniffed Mabel.

'Well, 'tis just possible, I s'pose. Stroke o' luck for'n, but possible. Sykes'd want to be shot of a stolen vehicle, like, soon as ever. But us cou'n't make out 'ow come, if he'd gone off, bought hisself new clothes, an' that, he left his wallet and all that money in the boot.'

'It was still there?'

'Just as he left it. No, top 'n' bottom of it were he done away wi' Sykes.'

Lucy drew a sharp breath. 'But I saw Roy!'

'An' 'ow come he knowed you be name of "Towngirl", when he come to? Fair giveaway, that were. He bin 'anging round yon farm! Us got it out on 'im, though. In the finish. Bit o' persuasion an' it all come out.'

After the crash he had made his way to the village and spent a day or two hiding out in the church belfry until the hue and cry had died down, but hunger had driven him back to the farm. He existed on root vegetables, which he had had to eat raw, milk from the churns and animal feed.

'Give'n squits, I don' doubt,' said Mabel, with relish.

He had, in fact, been seriously considering giving himself up when he realised there was another outlaw living in the woods, and this one had food. From his vantage point in the trees, he had seen the soldier, a deserter, crawling into a holly bush with a greatcoat over his head, and emerging with a tin of beans. He had watched, drooling, as the man had opened the beans with his penknife and eaten them.

When the man had gone, he, too, crawled into the bush, protected a little by his helmet.

'Like a tent, he said it were, dry an' cosy. Happen a bit prickly on your . . . on the floor, but the greatcoat woulda taken that off. Big thing were tins an' tins o' food, all in a pile round the trunk o' this 'ere 'olly bush. Fifty or more. And a tin-box of money. He reckoned our soldier-boy were diggin' in for a long stay. But not a tin-opener could he find. Well, he were desperate peckish. An' folk a bin killed for less.'

'Killed!'

He sniffed. 'Top 'n' bottom of it. Hung on there till young Roy poked 'is head back in, and then he brained him wi' a two-pound tin of plums! Bleddy caveman, pardon me, Miss.'

It would have been funny if it hadn't been so awful. Such a lie. Because it couldn't have happened like that. She shook her head.

'Not Roy,' she said. 'Roy's alive. I saw him this morning. I've seen him lots of times – and talked to him. You yourself have seen him, Mabel.'

Mabel nodded but her heart wasn't in it.

'Well, old Jerry swear he kill someone. Swop clothes on 'im, took his papers, acause he reckon a soldier in khaki stand less chance o' being shot than a Jerry air-pilot. Then he poke him under that may tree. Easy to find. Make it look like the pilot were dead an' us'd stop lookin' for'n.'

'The the c-corpse . . .' she swallowed, 'the one in the may b-bush, in the German uniform, with his f-face all . . . That was . . . that was . . .'

''Cording to old Jerry, 'twere Private Sykes.'

And the awful thing was, it all made sense – everything the Constable said. There were indisputable facts. Weiss had transferred to the barn, soon after the murder, as the woods became too busy. People seemed to be drawn there, by summer walking and picnics. They brought their dogs. Poachers brought their snares. Kids wanted to climb trees and build dens and play Robin Hood. Lovers wanted seclusion. It all became too risky.

He found the perfect hiding place, behind the milk-churns in the barn. All covered over with a tarpaulin and bales of straw. Fact. No one touched them or went near them. They were full of petrol.

Lucy and Mabel couldn't have looked more surprised.

'Fancy that! How did they get there, I wonder?'

Somehow he had escaped when the barn blew up, another fact, and knew he had to move on. He would steal a car. Fact. And then a plane, back to Germany. That was where his duty lay. Fantasy. If captured he thought he could play for time by feigning shell-shock, loss of speech. Fantasy. To do that, with any hope of fooling the authorities, he needed the wallet.

Fact. And the fact was, Lucy had taken it to her room. The German had been the intruder.

But the facts didn't explain the other undeniable fact that she had seen, that she had continued to see, Roy. Where did he fit in?

There was some reasonable explanation. There was, and she knew she knew it. But it fluttered out of reach, like an injured bird. She rubbed her forehead, squeezed her eyes and all her energies to get there. To focus, to get beyond ... Nearly, nearly.

Nothing. Sheer, blank, nothing.

Her head ached. Her wasp-sting stung. It was too hard.

She opened the window. There were fields flowing by, vibrant in sunshine, hedges, trees, cows, sheep. As her muscles relaxed, as her mind expanded, music flooded in. The strains of the Schubert quintet, slow and mesmeric.

Reason told her Roy was dead, yet she had seen him.

*And she probably would again.*

It came to her then.

She *had* seen him. Just as she had seen her grandmother and Donald Hooper. She hadn't seen Roy, in the flesh, since May. A ghost is what she had been seeing. A ghost. Silent and menacing. Not Roy at all.

Her head swam.

'Stop the car! Quick!' she said. And vomited.

# Chapter Twenty-One

The hall was packed, standing room only, all eyes on her, the miracle-worker. Where did they all come from? All these people, their eyes begging, 'Me, me! Make it my turn!' Marje reckoned some of the villages had laid on charabancs. Made it a proper outing, with a high tea thrown in. Not bad, eh, for a washerwoman from Walthamstow?

They were all there, in the front row. Guilty consciences after last time. Marje and Ernie and Ted, Eric and Iris, come down in Ernie's limo from his funeral business. Mr Whittaker was still laid up. Doris reckoned Ted's 'laying on of hands' had made a difference but he still couldn't stand up for long, poor old chap. So Marje was doing the prayers tonight in her no-nonsense schoolmarm voice.

She prayed for the usual stuff, the helmet, the buckler, the sword and shield, the shoes, the bulletproof vest, and everyone did the actions. But it never had the same ring as when Mr Whittaker done it. Please God it would do the trick.

Nora recognised some of the faces, their eyes squeezed shut, trying to get in the mood. Not easy on a Saturday afternoon in sunny Sowness-on-Sea. Some had come back for a third or fourth go. She felt sorry for their dear departed, having to think up something new to say.

Lucy wasn't there. A couple of her friends, that Ruby and that posh girl, but no Lucy. So much for Mrs Hooper and her promises. So much for Lucy. She and her daughter was finished, that was quite clear. She'd told Jack as much and he'd said, 'Cobblers.' But what did he know? Poor little sod hadn't known his own name for months on end.

She wished she had stopped up in Newcastle now. Lovely room she'd had at the Station Hotel and Jack had been so pleased to see her.

There wasn't much wrong with him, as far as she could see. A bit mutton jeff, as you would be, banged up in a tank that'd gone over a land mine. Other than that . . . He'd got his memory back and a lot more besides, he said. She supposed by that he meant his nurse, Susan. Nice little thing but you couldn't understand a word she was saying. If that was Geordie you could keep it. Still he was happy, that was the main thing.

He'd asked her to stay, meet Susan's mum and dad who was coming over from Sunderland but she'd had to come back. She'd missed two meetings; she couldn't miss another. Though she was looking forward to another tussle with the Sowness dark forces like a hole in the head. Why Marje had had to book her in here again, she couldn't think.

After the prayer they had *Lead, Kindly Light*. Taking the hint, somebody lit a couple of candles, though why, heaven knows; it was a bright day and the flames were almost invisible. When everyone sat down the flurry of dust in the sunbeams looked like spirits taking the quick route up. Nora struggled to her feet, trying to ignore the heaviness in her stomach, took a deep breath and waited for inspiration.

She thought she'd never seen a longer queue, except perhaps that day word got out the greengrocer had oranges under the counter. And they stood as patiently, as passively, with the same look of hopeless expectation on their faces, as them women with their poor thin shopping bags.

Uniforms outnumbered 'civvies' because that was how they wanted to be remembered, as fighting men. Fair enough. Not that she could tell one uniform from another when they was all together like that. Astral colours tended to swirl around, merging into dazzling white, with those pretty blues and greens and mauves round the edges. She was never sure what branch of the services the boys was in, not until she 'opened' to them.

Although she mostly spoke as she found, there was some things she kept to herself. Like it was only natural the spirits'd be feeling a bit sorry for themselves, having been cut

231

off in their prime, like. Well, you would. Feel like it wasn't fair, that you wasn't ready. There was all them things you could have done, you meant to do, and hadn't got round to, not to mention all the things you had done you shouldn't have. Things you was meaning to put right – after the war. All them hopes, all them plans . . .

No need for grieving women to know all that. They come here for a bit of cheering up, not to be made more bleeding miserable. And the boys did put a brave face on it, bless 'em:

Yes, Mother, I survived death; yeah, Sis, it's wonderful here, couldn't be better! No wounds, darling, no war, no hatred. Hallelujah!

*But* (ever so quietly), *I do miss you.*

Brave boys.

She thought of herself as a sort of telephone operator: *Putting you through now, dear!* connecting a caller to their spiritual party. Only difference was she knew exactly what they was going to say, give or take a sentiment or two. Men was the worst. Wind it up; play it again . . . that record of Vera Lynn's, *We'll Meet Again.* One more time . . . *Keep smiling through, just as you always do . . .* That was the message and it never varied.

And it could get you down a bit, night after night, month after month. So, as operator and switchboard both, she made it her business to add a bit of crackle and fizz to the proceedings. Messages wasn't enough. It had to be personal. Callers wanted proof. Name, age and distinguishing features. They wasn't satisfied until Nora had told them about their 'party's' natty taste in ties, how much he loved his game of football of a Saturday, his fickle temper, the way he played ukelele just like George Formby or his two left feet. And special things, special times was very important to the girls they left behind.

Like that little woman with the big bust, in the third row, waiting very patiently while Henry, a big bruiser of a bloke, scratched his head and ummed and aahed, and tried to think, at Nora's prompting, of something romantic that he could remind her of, to show he still cared. Poor boy, he couldn't remember, not off the top of his head. So Nora filled in with how well he was looking. What a gentle giant he was. How he was still playing rugby and scoring tries. Still nothing. So she thought she'd better give him a little nudge in the right direction.

'Any favourite places, duck?' she whispered. 'Somewhere you liked to drink?'

His eyes lit up.

'Oh, there *was* that little pub out at Woodleigh; what was the name of it, now? Dog and something?'

'Dog and Bone? Dog and Duck? Dog and Whistle?' Nora couldn't be more helpful.

'*Pig* and Whistle – that was it. And remember that church, Milly, St Mark's? We'd had such a skinful, we both tried to go through the kissing-gate together and got stuck! I had to ask you to set the date!'

The little woman had gone very pink. When she took her hand from her face you could see she didn't know whether to giggle or cry.

Then there was Clifford, who got his Vera laughing, when Nora asked him what they liked to do together.

'What about dancing?'

'Oh gosh, yes, my Vera loved to dance. Danced me off my feet, didn't you, dear? Wouldn't put me down! Oh gosh, yes!' Then he was off. 'Remember what we did, my last leave, Vera? Apart from the obvious! Planted that bed of leeks on top of the Anderson shelter, didn't we? O gosh, yes.'

'They all came up,' she said. 'Big fat white ones. Lovely. Reminded me of you, every time I pulled one!'

There were hoots of laughter both sides of the astral curtain.

With Nora's help, 'Orrie recalled Mavis knitting him those striped socks out of all the oddments in her wool-bag, and a scarf to match. He'd been wearing them on that last raid, when his plane came down in the North Sea.

There was an awful silence.

Until his widow said, 'Well, at least your feet were warm, Orrie!'

That was when Nora felt the 'dark forces' butting insistently against her defences. Enough hilarity, they had decided, time to make a move. When everyone was nice and relaxed.

233

They'd got it down to a Tee. They knew *exactly* what made you tick, and they'd keep on and on until you took some notice. Took you offguard and hopped over the breach.

And all they did was, they called your name. Someone calls your name you look to see what they want – if you don't know any better. It was the look that was fatal. But Whittaker had taught her well. She knew she had to keep her mind on the job, and trust that Marje and Eric and the rest had built a strong enough wall. A bit of prayer, a bellyful of positive thought and she'd be all right.

'Nora . . .' they were going, just like Mrs Next-door calling over the fence, or Aggie, opposite, when she rattled Nora's letterbox. And then they'd do her mother's voice, all sing-song, like she used to call her up the stairs: 'No-*rah*!' They even had Fred tickling her ear with his breath, 'Nora?' when he was trying to get round her. And she didn't look round.

She tried her very best to concentrate on the old man who'd had a 'funny turn', running for the bus, who was worried about his dog. Wanted to make sure that his daughter knew how much horsemeat to give him and when to take him to the vet's for his distemper inoculation . . . while the voices went on: 'Mrs Potter?' haughty, like Matron on a bad day, and 'Mrs *Po*tter . . .' all smarmy, like Mr Hawkins, the grocer, so pleased to see you, on pay day.

To add to the confusion, there was mad Auntie Maud, in the flesh, as it were, explaining that she couldn't stop in that house a minute longer, with all those noisy neighbours, all that banging and crashing, keeping you awake at night. She'd just called in to say 'Cheerio' and hoped that Nora wouldn't take it personally. She was off to pastures new.

'*No-ra. Nora! Mrs Potter!*' The weasling, wheedling, insistent voices of temptation, always there, at the back of her mind.

And in trooped the others, Uncle Harry and Auntie Vi.

'Just to say we're off now, Nora. Done all we can, can't do no more. Any time you want to get in touch, or the girl or her brother, just give us a call, won't you? Ta-ta, duck. Keep smiling!'

She'd forgotten how. Smile? How could she smile? She

234

supposed the house had been bombed good and proper to prompt this sudden exodus. On top of everything else.

She belched, but there was no relief. The pain went right through her, front to back. And what was all that about Lucy and her brother? Which brother, for Gawd's sake? Why oh why did ghosts always have to be so roundabout? They never give it to you straight.

'And tell Betty he likes a walk twice a day, along the front if you can manage it. Of course he'd prefer the beach, but wouldn't we all? And try and avoid that house at the top where the alsatian lives. Nasty brute. Nearly had his ear off!'

'Mrs Potter! Mrs P.' and 'Nora, love . . .' It *was* blooming Fred, wasn't it? Bli, what a one he was for picking his moments! But she never looked.

And how many ways was there of saying 'Ma'? In *all* the voices, from when they was tiny babies to schoolkids right through to grown-ups?

There's Siddy, she thought, wanting me to look what he's doing. There's little Mick wanting to be picked up. Arthur wanting a cuddle. Chas needing a bowl to be sick in. Then here's Lucy whining for something, 'cause all the other kids have got one, and Jack weasling to be let off his errands.

Kids were always saying 'Ma', even in their sleep. They wanted you to pay attention, or get them out of trouble, or just to stop being so bloody stupid. Ma, I'm hungry . . . Ma, I want a wee . . . Ma this and Ma that, got on your bleeding nerves. And this bleeding indigestion didn't let up for a minute. Nag, nag, nag!

She shut her eyes, took a breath and snapped.

'*What*?'

And they was on her. Whoosh! Knocking her flying. There was no way she could hold them, not on her own. They was slipping through, nasty, slimy things, sliding through her, all the way, using her.

She couldn't believe it. What was they doing, them pillars of the church in the front row? She turned to them, begging them to see her plight, rescue her, pleading with them, *do* something!

They nodded and smiled, snug as you like inside their own armour! Well done, Nora, keep up the good work! So wrapped

235

up in themselves they couldn't see what was happening.

Marje! Ted! Eric!

He did look up, give him that, but spread his hands helplessly.

What was she going to do? What a show-up! Nora Potter, a channel for evil! It'd been bad enough the other night at Whittleton, but this . . .

They was just pouring through now. Her spirit was running this way and that, trying to block them, send them back, but they just pushed past her into the congregation, a wagonload of monkeys, and poor Marje, in the front, was copping for most of them. Nora could see her eyes hardening, as her breastplate fell away, as her helmet toppled to the floor. All that rosy glow of hope and love for her dear dead mother faded to pale resentment, in thirty seconds flat. She was eyeing up some bloke across the aisle, running her hands up and down her skinny legs, like a common tart!

All round the hall there were curling lips, narrowing eyes, frowns, grimaces. Chairs began to squeak and scrape. Everyone was fidgeting. Feet tapping, fingers drumming. Handbags snapping open and shut. Men leaned back in their seats, their hands in their pockets, jingling money and anything else their itchy fingers encountered. They wanted to get out, away. They couldn't wait to get started on the path of corruption.

She didn't know what to do. It was out of control.

She must have cried out because, with bugles braying and side drums rolling, suddenly there was the cavalry! A force to be reckoned with. Stern and strong and tall and . . . *pretty*?

Someone else had spotted her, too. Seized his chance and squeezed through a crack in the door while Nora was gawping and rubbing her eyes. But Lucy's look of horror (for it was she) gave him away, and Nora turned to see an angel with a devil's smile, sidling past her skirts. If nothing else, Nora knew how to deal with naughty boys. Quick as a flash she got him by the ear.

Oh no, you don't, my lad!

As of one mind, Nora and her daughter took careful aim and booted Roy into Kingdom Come, and then shook hands on a job well done.

236

So her daughter had come to her rescue! The very last person Nora had expected. Miss Skeptic 1943! But there was no time for fond reunions. The meeting was in chaos and there was work to be done.

Lucy's spirit was even more formidable on this plane than in the physical world. She was always good at righteous indignation and now she seemed to know exactly what to do, sashaying around to some sort of violin music, herding the horde, rounding up the strays, slapping rumps, yelling 'Go-orn!' and 'Gercha!', heading them off, mending fences, closing gates, and when everything was tight and secure again, giving her mother a comforting psychic squeeze before leaving the field of battle.

Psychic or not, it had cured her indigestion. Wonderful. Nora scanned the hall, and came upon her brown-haired daughter in the press of bodies at the back of the hall, by the door, giving her V for Victory over the heads of other latecomers.

'I'll give you the V-sign, my girl,' muttered Nora. 'You been up to something, ain't you?'

'Don't be hard on her, Nora,' said Granny Farthing. 'She's been having a rough time.'

'She's been having something. Look at her. Miss Goody-goody, butter wouldn't melt . . . Well, she can't fool me.'

'What you on about, Nora?'

'Mum, I never see *one* ghost, not one, till me an' Fred . . . till our wedding night. Then five in a week. She's been and gone and done it, ain't she? Ooh, that Lucy! Give me boys every time. Not half the trouble. No, don't get me wrong, I love her dearly but if it's not one thing it's the other. No, I didn't meant that! Stop laughing, Mum! But it comes to something, don't it, when I can't trust her out of my sight for five minutes? I do my best, bring her up proper and look what she does, soon as my back's turned. It's that Joe, ain't it? Kept very quiet about him, didn't she? Tells her brother all about it, never a word to me, her own ma!'

'She would have, if you'd give her the chance. But you was off on your high horse, wasn't you? She said she was sorry but you had to make her sweat it out, didn't you?'

'Just as well, as it happened. Give her time to come to her senses, didn't it?'

'All six of 'em.'

'Best for her to do it on her own. Without me interfering, I mean.'

The old woman was chuckling. 'He's a nice bloke.'

'Not that nice, Mum. She ain't a virgin no more.'

'You've a lot to thank him for.'

'What? Ginger grandchildren? With her temper!'

'You could do worse. And she's barmy about him. Real cut up she was when his plane never came home.'

'What – is he dead, then? Oh, my poor Lucy! And there was I going on about ginger kids. Oh Luce!'

'Give over, Nora. He's only missing. Parachuted into the sea. Picked up and dried off. He'll be home by tea-time.'

'And she don't know?' Blimey, Mum, she'll be going up the wall with worry! I thought you was meant to be looking out for her. A fine guardian angel you turned out to be. Oh Mum. Oh Luce! You'll have to tell her . . .'

'Hold on, hold on, gel – where'd'you think I been all afternoon? Sunning meself on the prom?'

'Oh.'

Nora bustled about during the hymn, *Spirit of the Living God*, mopping up the worst ravages of the flood, flicking at the lust, sweeping up the crumbs of profanity, setting this psyche straight, polishing up that better nature. Only time for a cat's lick but it should see them all right.

'Shame, though,' she said, pulling Marje's spiritual skirt down. 'I had hopes of her palling up with Eric. Nice boy . . .'

Mabel had been like a woman possessed, chivvying Lucy from parsnip field to kitchen for her dinner, chasing her up to her room where hot water was steaming in an enamel jug, cold waiting in the ewer, soap and towel by the basin. She had shouted up the stairs to her until she was washed, dressed and combed, and then had frog-marched her over the fields to the village, to join the queue at the bus-stop.

'Not on your bike, today, Towngirl?' drawled Hettie Fitzell, opening the shop door at that precise moment, *ping* to

238

indicate that she was open for business after a prolonged dinner-hour. She missed the cold-weather bus queue warming round her oil-stove.

'Going to Sowness,' piped to Mabel. 'See Nora Potter talking to ghosts. *Her* mum!' she said, with proprietary pride.

At which the quietly stoical bus queue turned into a gaggle of honking geese. German pilots and stolen Fords and pea-pods and fortunes would have been pecked to shreds but happily the bus drew up and they all piled on, Eileen Cosgrove, who had steamed, flat-footed, across the green at the last minute, being heaved on board by the clippie and shoved from behind by her mother. Inquisitions were a little more difficult over noisy diesel and bumpy roads, and well-nigh impossible when a true obsessive decided to ask questions of her own.

'Where the green bus goin'?'

'Sowness, Eileen. We'm goin' to Sowness.'

'Where the green bus goin'?'

'Jus' told you, din' I? Sowness.'

'We nearly there?'

'Oh, Ei, we'm on'y jus' started, girl.'

'When us gettin' to Sowness?'

'Not long.'

'When?'

''Alf hour or so. Not long. Whyn't you look out the window? Look at the cows.'

'Where the green bus goin'?' Her hands were flapping, like a fledgeling's unfeathered wings.

'She'm a bit excited,' Mrs Cosgrove explained to Lucy, sitting in the seat across the aisle. 'Don' often get to go on the bus.'

'Where the green bus?'

'Ssshh. Sowness. Hands in your lap, Eileen, you'm workin' yourself up.'

'When? When we gettin' to Sowness?' Flap, flap. She was beginning to rock, now. Backwards and forwards. The clippie collected fares, from one side of the aisle and then the other, with never-say-die cheerfulness.

'Don' wanna talk about it no more, Eileen. Give it rest, girl.'

239

'Where the green bus?'

The conductress, her hair hidden in a turban-tied headscarf, took Mabel's three ha'pence and then Lucy's, clipped tickets in her machine and handed them over.

'Us goin' to Sowness, Eileen. Won't be long now. Goin' to a meetin'.'

'No! No meetin'. Eileen don' want no meetin' at Sowness.'

Good grief, thought Lucy, Nora was going to love this racket, all through her service. If Bella the dog could have spoken, she would have had a voice this deep and loud and insistent, though the words would have made more sense. Other conversations faltered and died, unable to compete. Poor Mrs Cosgrove, thought Lucy. A terrible punishment for a few moments' incest. Purgatory. No wonder she sat Eileen out on the green all day.

The engine growled at the hill and the driver changed down.

'Goin' to a meetin', talk to your dad.'

Because that was the pretence, thought Lucy – that Cosgrove was Eileen's father. That he had been killed in action.

He wasn't coming back, for sure. But Nora wouldn't find him on the astral plane. On leave in Diss, more like, with the new wife and baby son.

Mabel spoke across her prescience. 'You bain't takin' the girl in there, Annie? Frighten all they spirits away.'

'She be all right. Any old buck and she'm outside, strapped to the railings. Wanna get her in to that healer-man, see. Hettie says they do it, afore and after the service. Got to 'ave a go, Mabel. Try anything. She'm drivin' us barmy.'

'Can't do no 'arm, I s'pose. No worse'n the hospital, likely.'

'Bain't takin' her back up the hospital, Mabel. Don't do 'er a blind bit a good, all them electrics in her head. Just gets 'er upset.'

'Don't 'old wi' electrics meself.'

The driver changed to a lower gear as the hill fought back. The clippie was waiting to take Annie's money.

'Where the green bus goin' arter Sowness?'

240

'Arter Sowness, m'dear?' said the clippie kindly. ('*Don' ee tell 'er!' But Annie's warning came a fraction too late.*) 'Well,' the clippie was saying, 'arter Sowness 'tis Whittleton.'

'*No-o*!' That awful, piercing terror, the banging of the head on the window. 'Eileen don't wanna go to Whittleton. *No-o*!'

With cat craft, she turned and sprang at her tormentor but, with her mother as buffer, could only whisk off the headscarf and grab a couple of bobby pins and a snail of yellow hair. However, with that fingerhold she was able to pull the head closer, grab a second fistful of curls, wind her fat fingers to the roots and hang on tight. Thus pinioned and fighting blind, her victim could only beat about with the ticket board, clubbing the old man sitting in front. The leather money pouch tipped and shot a pile of coppers into Annie's lap, and the mechanical clipper swung forward and hit her on the nose. Buried between the assailants she was helpless to do anything about it.

In the screaming confusion, someone managed to tug out an SOS on the bell and the bus ground to a halt at the top of the hill. Lucy was on her feet, trying to prise open the fat fists.

'Go for the little finger,' someone advised her. It was Mrs Cosgrove, somewhere in there among the blood and tears and loose change. 'Right hand, right hand! Then give 'er to me.' Mrs Cosgrove's left hand came up through the muddle, like a periscope, bright rings catching the light as her fingers waggled, ready. 'And you stop pullin', silly cow, on'y make'n worse.' She poked the yellow head, which continued to yelp.

The grubby little finger gradually unlocked and, as Lucy bent it back, the other fingers sprang open, with a howl, releasing pins and tufts of torn hair. She took Eileen's empty hand and watched Annie's glittering fingers close over it, with interest. When the other hand was disentangled Lucy held it at bay while the clippie surfaced. Her mascara had streaked, her lipstick smudged, her nice white blouse was dishevelled and her curlers exposed. She was hurt and humiliated.

'Off!' she spat. 'Off!'

The driver, who had appeared briefly on the platform,

backed out and off to his cab again, as Annie Cosgrove led her daughter down the bus, struggling and screeching. But Lucy was behind, her arm linked and locked with the girl's and her knee nudging the big bottom. Mabel reluctantly brought up the rear.

The bus drove away, over the hill, with the faces of offended passengers pinned to the windows. A cane stick clattered into the road and split into spills.

Eileen screamed and kicked and pummelled out her temper, but she could do no more harm, face down in the grass with Lucy and Mabel sitting on her.

Annie Cosgrove was wincing and dabbing at a bite on her shoulder with a hanky. Lucy saw that her arms and legs were covered in bruises and abrasions.

'What's so awful about Whittleton?' asked Lucy.

'Ssshh!' Annie hissed despair as the mountain heaved and the afternoon was flavoured with the smell of ammonia and farts.

'Blow me,' muttered Mabel, sniffing the air. 'Summat's gettin' through. How that happen, I wonder? Fair given up on my nose, I had.'

'What's wrong with Whittleton?' Lucy repeated, catching the girl's wrists and pinning them to the ground so they could neither nip nor pinch nor gouge nor scratch.

'It's where her goes for her treatment. Whit . . . the W word, General Hospital.'

Lucy was breathing hard. It was like wrestling with a pig. She was cross and hot and her plans were going down the drain. She had hoped to contact Joe, at Sowness, with her mother's help.

Perversely she bent low and snapped at the girl's ear, 'Whittleton, Whittleton, Whittleton, Whittleton!' At which the pig let out a blood-curdling squeal and bucked and jiggled. The riders held on for dear life. 'Whittleton! Whittleton!'

The bronco ride lasted for five minutes, by which time everyone was exhausted and Eileen was giggling, her cheek on the grass, turning 'Whittleton!' over on her tongue like a tasty morsel, while Lucy stroked her straw hair and massaged her neck and shoulders.

'Want a lift, girls?'

A soldier leaned out of a lorry.

'Another time, thanks.'

They waved the wagonload of whistling, shouting men out of sight.

When they let her up she was still crooning, 'Whittleton.'

'Take my hat off to you, Towngirl. You done her good. Ain't never seed her like this afore, so happy. Her do seem to like you, Towngirl.'

'Lucy,' she informed her gently.

The woman's hand flew to her mouth and fluttered down. 'Never knowed that. Never knowed you was Lucy.' The diamonds glittered in the sun, the gold gleamed.

'Keep them,' said Lucy.

'Whassat?' she bristled.

'Keep them, the rings, they're more use to you.'

'What you on about?'

'Oh sorry, I thought you said . . .'

Somebody had. Told her the rings were the ones Roy had wanted to give her. In an envelope with *Lucy's rings* written in pencil. The German had stolen them along with Roy's uniform, had dropped them out of his pocket, out of the tree, and Eileen had found them and added them to her collection.

'Aren't they what he was hunting for in the pram that time?'

'Don't know what you'm on about. Cosgrove sent 'em from off his ship.'

Lucy nodded. Oh. Right. She understood. What did it matter? She leaned back on her elbows and looked down on Sowness, four miles distant, the sea, like spun sugar, the buildings shimmering, a mirage. A tiny aeroplane puttered out of the sky and landed on a pocket-sized airfield, bringing a flicker of hope to Lucy's heart.

'Can't see us getting there today,' said Mabel, thinking she was reading her thoughts.

'Eileen'm goin' to Sowness, Aunt Mabel,' the girl assured her.

'Fancy that!' said Mabel. 'Her en't called us that afore. Well, don't just stand there, Eileen, give us a hand up,' and she held out her arms.

243

The girl blinked, turned away, held out one hand behind her and, as Mabel caught hold, snatched it back.

'Nearly.'

'How are we going to get there, Eileen?'

Eileen turned to Lucy. Her eyes swivelled but then held steady. 'Green bus do go Sowness,' she said.

'But . . .?'

'Green bus heve gone . . .' Her voice faced into thought. And brightened. 'Us'll ride to Sowness in one o' they soldiers' lorries.'

'Good idea!'

'My Lord, she worked it out!' said Annie, gazing in awe at the prodigy. 'You'm really got the knack, Towngirl.'

'She'm her mother's daughter,' said Mabel, fondly.

'Too right,' said Lucy, and with Chopin tinkling promises in her head, she took Eileen's hands and waltzed her down the hill, while Granny Farthing counted, '*One*, two, three, *one*, two, three.'